PATTERNS

TOR BOOKS BY PAT CADIGAN

Tea from an Empty Cup

Patterns

PATTERNS

STORIES BY

PAT CADIGAN

TOR®

A Tom Doherty Associates Book
New York

PATTERNS

First published in the United States by Ursus Imprints

Copyright © 1989 by Pat Cadigan

Introduction copyright © 1989 by Bruce Sterling

This book is printed on acid-free paper.

A Tor Book
Published by Tom Doherty Associates, Inc.
175 Fifth Avenue
New York, NY 10010

Tor Books on the World Wide Web:
http://www.tor.com

Tor® is a registered trademark of Tom Doherty Associates, Inc.

Library of Congress Cataloging-in-Publication Data

Cadigan, Pat, 1953-
    Patterns / Pat Cadigan.— 1st ed.
        p.   cm.
    "A Tom Doherty Associates book."
    ISBN 0-312-86837-5
    1. Science fiction, American. I. Title.
PS3553.A3135P37   1999
813'.54—dc21

                                                        98-32220
                                                        CIP

First Tor Edition: March 1999

Printed in the United States of America

0   9   8   7   6   5   4   3   2   1

This is for my mother,
Helen Sapanara Kearney,
who knows these stories by heart
A N D
For my son,
Robert Michael Fenner,
Bobby Mike
Bobzilla
who is a different story altogether

...and always for Arnie

Many, many thanks to:
Gardner Dozois and Susan Casper, Ellen Datlow, Bruce and Nancy Sterling, Merrilee Heifetz, Sherry Gershon Gottlieb, Howard Waldrop, Michael Swanwick, Lisa Tallarico, Jeanne Hund, Kevin McKinney, Terry Matz and Ken Keller, Edward L. Ferman, Shawna McCarthy, Marta Randall, Mike and Rosa Banks, James Gunn, Terence M. Green, Kathye and David Griffin, Lew and Edie Shiner, Charles L. Grant, Michael Bishop, Tim Sullivan, Fred Duarte and Karen Meschke, Willie Siros, Spike Parsons, Laura Baker, Robert Haas, Vern Dufford, my husband Arnie Fenner, my mother Helen S. Kearney, my in-laws George and Marguerite Fenner, and Mr. and Mrs. Robert A. Heinlein. And to Sister Mary Laurita, wherever she is.

And of course to James P. Loehr, because we always promised each other this would happen one day.

CONTENTS

INTRODUCTION

BY BRUCE STERLING

Science fiction books are supposed to have red-hot pizzazz in the title, like *Rocket Thrust Galaxy Blast Trek!* Or maybe some bogus lyricism, with catchwords like "star," "song," "dream," or "dance." (*Star Song of the Dream Dancers* could be an SF bestseller, easy.)

But instead we've got this short story collection which is simply called *Patterns,* and when you look in here (as you will very soon, if you've got a lick of sense), you'll see that this is, well, pretty *unusual* science fiction. More like science fiction *fantasy,* actually. No, make that science fiction fantasy *horror* . . .

Or maybe it'd be best just to skip the usual labels, and put it this way. When you cut these Cadigan stories, they bleed real juice. It isn't *normal blood* exactly . . . kinda slick like high-grade silicone lubricant, and there's a whiff to it that makes you dizzy, maybe even (gulp) *thirsty* in a way you're not used to (and might not feel too cozy about).

These are *visionary* stories with . . . with a certain indefinable yet chilling insight into the *invisible infrastructure of the late twentieth century!* Yeah! This book, *Patterns,* is what contemporary "commercial science fiction" looks and sounds like when it's really *imaginative,* as opposed to just *cute.*

Cadigan's work *makes the invisible visible*. Certain aspects of contemporary reality emerge that you didn't used to see — *patterns,* really, that can only be called *Cadiganesque.* TV, God help us, is full of 'em. Like the pop-music program on BET cable—one of my personal favorites—called "Video Soul." The experienced Cadigan reader will sit bolt upright at a dead giveaway like that one.

And let's not forget the Postmodern Elvis, Michael Jackson. Michael Jackson is *flesh* and *blood,* right? I mean, he's a *person,* not a photographic negative. But Michael Jackson is so . . . well . . . *overexposed,* that people tend to just *absorb* his image, the way they soak up Chernobyl fallout.

Michael is a kind of ancestral Eohippus to the arch-hip quasi-naif antihero of Cadigan's "Pretty Boy Crossover." Read that story—it's in here and it's great—and you'll get a whole new slant on that record ad that sells (and I'm not kidding), "The Original Soul of Michael Jackson."

The world today is *sneaky.* There's so much going on that you can't *possibly* keep up with it. But if you have half a brain, you must be gnawingly aware that there are vast swarming activities going on behind the glossy surface of the fifteen-second video sound-bites. Global TV covers the Earth like Sherwin-Williams paint, but a lot of what you see in "the news" is exactly one phosphor dot thick.

And if you get up *really* close to TV—I mean, nose-pressing, touchy-feely close, so close that it's *scary*—you can see that there's really *nothing there at all,* nothing but these swarms of dots behind cold static-crackling glass. And suddenly you're in Cadiganland.

Pat Cadigan is sneaky, too. There's a lot going on inside her stories, a lot of depth and intelligence behind the page. Pat Cadigan always knows damn well what she's up to, long before we figure it out.

Her favorite weapon is the jolting one-liner, and one of her favorite images—watch for it—is the needle. These are needling stories, both in the sense that they can jab you wide awake, and in the sense that they can pump you full of mind-altering substances before you even know you're hit. In the typical Cadigan story (there's really no such thing, but bear with me) we're cruising along, fully informed, right on top of developments, when—yow!—what we thought was bedrock turns out to be Saran Wrap.

Things become revelatory—things become *unspeakably clear.* This sensation is what H.P. Lovecraft—one of the great SF/horror visionaries, who used to own the eldritch woods where Pat has built her condo and broadcast station—called "cosmic fear." It hasn't much to do with gore, or some guy with an axe jumping out *boo!* from the closet. No, this is a cool analysis of "sanity" and "the real world" unraveling at the seams.

Cadigan characters come in two basic patterns. The first is cool, collected, completely *together,* totally *with-it;* characters with a gloss on them like high-tech ceramic. The second pattern is *ontologically fractured:* people with insides like a bag of broken glass. (That much is easy—but now try to tell them apart!)

Characters like "Deadpan Allie," the wire-tough heroine of Cadigan's landmark SF novel *Mindplayers,* make an actual *career* of going from Pattern A to Pattern B and back again. When Allie makes it, she nets a bag of gleaming goodies from the public id. And she feels just great about it, too. At least until it's time for the next run, anyway.

But sometimes they don't make it. They find a trap, a sinkhole— maybe they explore too rashly, maybe they jump, maybe they're pushed; in the saddest cases they may even be *born there*. But it's a place, whether it's cold junkie streets or a high-tech altered state-of-mind, that they can never come out of again.

The common Cadigan voice is one of sardonic intelligence and crisp objectivity. But look at stories like "Angel" or "Eenie Meenie Ipsateenie," and it's clear that Pat Cadigan knows the deep recesses of the heart. Feelings are never cheap in Cadigan's fiction. She knows that tragedy exists, and she's willing to face it: even the grinding and unglamorous kind of tragedy that hurts a lot more than the swift dramatic variety. She will tackle situations that most other writers wouldn't touch with tongs. This gives her work a startling emotional dimension that—but don't mind me; just read the astonishing "My Brother's Keeper," with its killer last line, and you can see it shine for yourself, as clear as winter daylight.

Pat Cadigan writes "science fiction" (in its widest sense) for the best of reasons: because she can accomplish things in this mode of expression that are impossible elsewhere. She has the gift of a truly original vision, and the gift of expression with power and clarity. These gifts are rare enough in isolation, but when combined they burn with the proverbial hard gemlike flame.

Let me put it this way, in conclusion. In this, well, wonderful and frightening world of ours—our current milieu— this videocratic world of mirrors, lenses, scanners, public images, flashbacks, fast-forwards and freeze-frames, Russian dolls and Chinese boxes, the kind of thing the folks at Nanterre U. like to call *the precession of simulacra*—Pat Cadigan's patterns are the quote real unquote thing.

But don't take *my* word at face value. Better to look for yourself. Better to look much deeper.

Better to turn the page.

PATTERNS

Television will achieve its apotheosis when it is interactive.

Of course, some people think they have that now. For some people, TV reality is as much of a reality as what they move through most of the day. I remember listening to two people I used to work with discussing the horrible burden a character on a TV series would have to bear for causing someone's death in a fire. These were not uneducated or isolated people; they had simply been drawn in so far, they were projecting the characters well beyond the end of the show — indeed, beyond the life of the series itself. And we've all heard amusing stories about actors who play soap opera villains suddenly attacked by irate viewers who cannot separate *actor* and *character*. Maybe more people can't than can — the host of *Death Valley Days* was President of the United States for eight years.

Does TV encourage, or even induce, schizophrenia? Or does it create a separate reality in conjunction with our minds, something that is neither totally our inner life nor totally TV. The networks might call that *programming*. I call it . . .

PATTERNS

4

I have this continuing fantasy of assassinating the President. Any President.

To step forward within a crowd, raising my weapon and aiming it at the President's head. Sometimes in the movie unreeling in my mind, my hand comes up holding a Luger Parabellum P08 with the ridiculously long 190mm barrel. Other times I am holding a more likely Mauser Military Pistol. Twice I have found myself clutching an Uzi with the stock detached, three or four times I held a .357 Smith & Wesson Magnum. Once—only once—I stared down the length of a crossbow at the chief executive.

In the fantasy, I am not scared or angry. I don't think about the fact that I am taking a human life—the President, after all, is not so much human as manufactured, a product made flesh by the bipartisan system and the media in accidental conjugation. Is it wrong to fire at the dot pattern on a TV screen? I feel nothing beyond a mild nervousness, the slight (very slight) stage-fright I used to experience during my acting days. That my stage-fright was never acute enough to give me the cold sweats or send me vomiting into the handiest receptacle probably contributed to my lack of success in the theatre. In a one-person show, I could have been overlooked.

I know what you're thinking. I dream of assassination as a way to become visible at last. You are wrong. There is far more power in invisibility than in fame.

In fact, my fantasy movie has never proceeded beyond the point at which I raise my weapon and train it on the President. The action freezes when the President's gaze rests on the instrument of his/her destruction. But I know the rest of it:

I brace myself and fire. The President falls backwards, face a red ruin, body jerking in every direction. He/she is caught by aides and Secret Service agents and lowered to the ground. The crowd is completely silent. They are neither frightened nor in shock, just passive as the dot pattern rearranges itself. I lower the weapon to my side, then turn and walk away without hurry. Nobody looks at me. I walk some unmeasured distance to a car I recognize as mine, parked at an innocuous curb. I get in, twist the key waiting in the ignition and drive off.

In the days to come, there will be no mention of what happened to the President, ever, nor will there be any news about the government again. With one shot, I have obliterated not just the President but both Houses of Congress, the Supreme Court, Social Security, the National Endowment for the Arts, the Government Printing Office, the Gross National Product, the FTC, the CIA, the HEW and the Immigration and Naturalization Service, among others, as well as postponing forever the next election year. But life goes on anyway. I drive an endless highway across the United States and through the windshield I observe the permanent status quo I have visited on the American people. They don't know what has happened and they don't find it odd that they keep living in the same homes, working the same jobs, hearing the same music on the radio, watching the same dot patterns. Like me, they travel without destination. The days melt into each other with no distinguishing characteristics. The seasons come in and go out as they were meant to do in textbooks, but no one grows older. The treadmill has achieved a state of being both in motion and at rest simultaneously. Test pattern. Entropy.

All because I shot the President's dot pattern.

Seen in close-up, the dot pattern could almost be taken for a collection of organisms, very cooperative organisms which have discovered a choreography that will produce patterns pleasing to the eyes of much larger and much less cooperative organisms.

Quotation from Chairman Busby Berkeley and Miss Amy Lowell:
Christ! What are patterns for?
I'll tell you.

The screen crackles when I put my finger on it. Static electricity;
the dots warning me off their pattern. I pull my finger back and make
it a pistol barrel pointing at the President, who is giving the State of
the Union address. The President looks directly at "me" and hesitates.
The dots at work on his pattern burble and boil and show me the red
ruin that could be the result of my gun hand. Then the President's
head re-forms and he goes on with his speech. We are in great need
of re-form in this country, he says, but even so, the State of the Union
in general is most hope-inspiring.
Now. While there's still hope.
I cover the President's face with my finger. Loud crackling, followed
by a close-up which put my finger absurdly on the President's moving
mouth. He doesn't bite, but there is some mild electricity running up
my arm.

"It was all them cop shows," his mother said. "All that violence,
they oughta get it off the tube." She said it on television, at his tele-
vised trial. Christ! What are patterns for? First-degree murder.

"Always such a good kid," my mother would say. "Never a moment's
trouble. Helped around the house and never answered back, either.
Good-natured, you know. And when all the other kids were hanging
out on the streets or chasing each other around and getting into trouble,
my kid was studying. *My* kid always wanted to be somebody."
How true. I could have had my own show, in fact. If the technology
had been good enough in those days, I might have lived in a suburban
dot pattern, walked to school to my own theme music, mouthed dialog
to my own laugh track. And achieved endless childhood in syndication.
I could have been syndicated; I could have been a contender. Instead of
a COMMERCIAL INTERRUPT FOR STATION IDENTIFICATION. It is often
necessary to amputate a frame or two for the sake of format. So sorry,
apparently the program director spliced this one a little early. But
since it happened anyway, you have sixty seconds to contemplate your
mantra. *Now* how much would you pay?

Late at night, the patterns change and rearrange. I can't sleep. Two,
three, four in the morning, the dots perform before my dry eyes. Slices,
dices, juliennes. How much would you pay? Don't answer yet . . .

stainless steel never needs sharpening. Now how much would you pay? Don't answer yet . . . act now and we'll throw in the fabulous Kalashnikov rifle, the most successful automatic rifle ever made! Gas operated, simultaneous bolt action and cocking, with a handy selector lever for single shot or automatic at a rate of 100 rpm, that's 100 rpm! *Isn't that amazing?* A mere 8 pounds with a folding metal stock, perfect for the murder of the head of state of your choice! Call now, operators are standing by!

I blink. When you awake, you will remember everything.

I want to call friends to ask if they have just seen this, too. Then I remember, all my friends are electric.

In living color.

A Famous Actor has shot himself. When they found him, the television in his townhouse was still on, murmuring merrily to itself as it played one of his old movies. I see it on the six o'clock news. Dot pattern of a dot pattern.

Now how much would you pay?

I have taken to dreaming in dots. Reruns. I raise my arm. I am holding a Browning GP35. I know nothing about guns. Its rate of fire is 25 rpm with a muzzle velocity of 1110 feet per second and it is going to make cheap chuck of the President's face. I know nothing about guns. The dot pattern knows. Point-blank range is that distance at which the bullet achieves its highest velocity, the distance the President is from me now. And it's on every channel, even cable.

Cable?

When I awake, I remember everything, in dot patterns, in living color.

A soap opera actress reports being assaulted in a restaurant by an irate woman wielding a Totes umbrella, shouting, "You leave that nice lady's husband alone, you slut! Hasn't that poor woman had enough trouble without you trying to steal her man?" The actress's companions manage to pull the woman away. The rest of the people in the restaurant—diners, waiters, waitresses, busboys, maitre d'—all watch. They are neither frightened nor in shock.

And now, what will I do?

I consult the schedule. It is not time to run all the drug dealers out of Florida. Last night, the score was evened for the right-thinking on the mean streets of New York, it won't have to be done again for

7

another week. I think I will defend my heavyweight title against the challenger in Las Vegas. I double up my fists and inspect the knuckles. Yes, these can go fifteen rounds, piece of Duncan Hines cake.

I press my knuckles against the screen. Wild crackling. The dots swarm in liquid patterns around each point of contact. Electricity is flowing up both arms, dancing through the nerve endings which sizzle into life and join the pattern.

My hands are being taped as I hold them out. I got to keep my fuckin hands up, do I hear, just keep my fuckin hands up and let him dance himself out and then jab his motherfuckin head off. The dots pulse, live from Caesar's Palace, more live than life. Fitted out with this dot pattern to wear, I could strike sparks in the moving, living air.

Now I know it can be done. The fight goes by in a swirl of dot pattern light. I keep my fuckin hands up and let him dance himself out and then jab his motherfuckin head off. The fight is not important. Now I know it can be done.

But I have to wait until the swelling goes down and the black eye fades. Never mind. You should see the other dot pattern.

More on that story from our correspondent in Washington.

Dot-pattern Washington snaps under the scanning line. The White House looks a little fuzzy. So does our correspondent. I touch her microphone; the dots leap in frenzy as I reshape their pattern into a 127mm barrel version of the Gyrojet pistol and then back into a microphone. Not yet. Tonight there is a press conference.

Brought to you by, sponsored in part. The whole world is waiting and watching. Ladies and gentlemen on every channel, the President of the United States. The reception has never been so good, it must be me. The dots dance for me now and we know each other; tropism. Whenever they appear, I turn to look and my looking excites the patterns.

What are patterns for?

I'll show you. I'll . . . *show* . . . you. As I show myself.

The dots sparkle around my hands in the continuing fantasy shown live on every channel. I run my fingers through them like a helping of stardust and reshape the pattern. They know what I need here. The Colt Commando with telescopic butt fully extended for shoulder firing, as used by the Green Berets, who have also been on this channel. The dots remember the pattern and here it is.

I step forward in the crowd of reporters demanding to be called on. The President's dot pattern scans the room, looking for a likely questioner. Then he sees "me" and hesitates. I have raised the Colt to my shoulder. Everyone is watching.

I touch my finger to the screen. The President's head disappears in a red mist, dot patterns gone insane. The room is completely silent, neither frightened nor shocked. Behind the podium, the Great Seal, the curtains, the President's aides, and Secret Service agents begin to unravel from the hole where the President's head was.

Embarrassed, puzzled anchorman. We are sorry for the interruption in transmission. Apparently we are having technical difficulties. We'll have more information for you after this.

No, we won't. That is all the information we are ever going to have, ever.

Fade to commercial. Dogs pounce on bowls of food. I sit on the couch, nodding. It's all over now. It wasn't quite how I expected it to go but it was, after all, adapted for television.

The commercial is followed by another commercial and then the embarrassed, puzzled anchorman. Apparently we are permanently cut off from our hook-up in the nation's capital. We will try to have some news on the rest of the press conference as soon as possible.

A fast recap of the statements and questions up until the moment I murdered the President's dot pattern, when things unraveled like celluloid melting away, a promise of an update soon. They patch the foreshortened evening schedule with a made-for-TV movie. Time to go.

I leave my apartment, go down to my car parked at an innocuous curb. The key is not waiting in the ignition but in my pocket. Such a good kid, never a moment's trouble. We can live in the same homes, work at the same jobs, hear the same music on the radio, watch the same dot patterns. We travel without destination. What are patterns for?

Nothing, any more.

There used to be too much violence on TV. But not now.

9

INTRODUCTION TO
EENIE, MEENIE, IPSATEENIE

If you're over the age of sixteen, you can relax now. The worst is over. You're never going to be as terrified again as you were in childhood. Not that nothing bad will happen, or that you won't have anything to fear. But if you really think that nothing could scare you as much as, say, the IRS, you're just not remembering it right. The monster under the bed should have been something as innocuous as an IRS agent with an audit request—then it would only have been after money, and the grown-ups handled that stuff.

Take my word for it, childhood is a time of unrelenting terror. That many of us don't remember it that way lets us recover and go on with our lives. But if you carry with you a certain fear you are helpless in the face of, that you live with but will never overcome, you probably acquired it in childhood. You may deal with it like a champ, but inside you're cold water and you truly understand the phrase, "Fate worse than death."

This story is a love letter to my old neighborhood in Fitchburg, Massachusetts, now gone forever. They even tore down the tenement I grew up in. It's also the best way I could think of to preserve that old chant we used to use, better than "eenie, meenie, miney, mo" or "one potato, two potato." Most of our families could ill-afford much besides potatoes.

And it's a big Bronx cheer to the game of hide-and-seek. Some sadist must have thought up that one.

EENIE, MEENIE, IPSATEENIE

*I*n the long, late summer afternoons in the alley behind the tenement where Milo Sinclair had lived, the pavement smelled baked and children's voices carried all over the neighborhood. The sky, cracked by TV aerials, was *blue,* the way it never is after you're nine years old and in the parking lot of La Conco D'Oro Restaurant, the garlic-rich aroma of Siciliano cooking was always heavy in the air.

It had never been that way for the boy walking down the alley beside Milo. La Conco D'Oro didn't exist any more; the cool, coral-tinted interior now held a country-western bar, ludicrous in a small industrial New England town. He smiled down at the boy a little sadly. The boy grinned back. He was much smaller than Milo remembered being at the same age. Milo also remembered the world being bigger. The fence around Mr. Parillo's garden had been several inches higher than his head. He paused at the spot where the garden had been, picturing it in front of the brown and tan Parillo house where the irascible old gardener had been landlord to eleven other families. The Parillo house was worse than just gone — the city was erecting a smacking new apartment house on the spot. The new building was huge, its half-finished shell spreading over to the old parking lot where the bigger boys had sometimes played football. He looked at the new building with distaste. It had a nice clean brick facade and would probably hold a hundred families in plasterboard box rooms. Several yards back up the alley, his old tenement stood empty now, awaiting the wrecking ball. No doubt another erstwhile hundred-family dwelling would rise there, too.

Beside Milo, the boy was fidgeting in an innocent, patient way. Some things never changed. Kids never held still, never had, never would. They'd always fumble in their pants pockets and shift their weight from one foot to the other, just the way the boy was doing. Milo gazed thoughtfully at the top of the white-blond head. His own sandy hair had darkened a good deal, though new grey was starting to lighten it again.

Carelessly, the boy kicked at a pebble. His sneaker laces flailed the air. "Hey," said Milo. "Your shoelaces came untied."

The boy was unconcerned. "Yeah, they always do."

"You could trip on 'em, knock your front teeth out. That wouldn't thrill your mom too much. Here." Milo crouched on one knee in front of the boy. "I'll tie 'em for you so they'll stay tied."

The boy put one sneaker forward obligingly, almost touching Milo's shoe. It was a white sneaker with a thick rubber toe. And Milo remembered again how it had been that last long late summer afternoon before he and his mother had moved away.

There in the alley behind Water Street, in Water St. Lane, when the sun hung low and the shadows stretched long, they had all put their feet in, making a dirty canvas rosette, Milo and Sammy and Stevie, Angie, Kathy, Flora and Bonnie, for Rhonda to count out. Rhonda always did the counting because she was the oldest. She tapped each foot with a strong index finger, chanting the formula that would determine who would be IT for a game of hide'n'seek.

> *Eenie, meenie, ipsateenie*
> *Goo, gah, gahgoleenie*
> *Ahchee, pahchee, Liberaci*
> *Out goes Y-O-U!*

Stevie pulled his foot back. He was thin like Milo but taller and freckled all over. Protestant. His mother was living with someone who wasn't his father. The Sicilian tongues wagged and wagged. Stevie didn't care. At least he didn't have an oddball name like Milo and he never had to get up for church on Sunday. His black high-top sneakers were P.F. Flyers for running faster and jumping higher.

> *Eenie, meenie, ipsateenie . . .*

Nobody said anything while Rhonda chanted. When she counted you, you stayed counted and you kept quiet. Had Rhonda been the first to say *Let's play hide'n'seek?* Milo didn't know. Suddenly all of them had been clamoring to play, all except him. He hated hide'n'seek, especially just before dark, which was when they all wanted to play most. It was the only time for hide'n'seek, Rhonda always said. It was more fun if it was getting dark. He hated it, but if you didn't play you might as well go home, and it was too early for that. Besides, the moving van was coming tomorrow. Aunt Syl would be driving him and his mother to the airport. He might not play anything again for months. But why did they have to play hide'n'seek?

Out goes Y-O-U!

Kathy slid her foot out of the circle. She was never IT. She was Rhonda's sister, almost too young to play. She always cried if she lost a game. Everyone let her tag the goal so she wouldn't cry and go home to complain Rhonda's friends were picking on her, bringing the wrath of her mother down on them. Her mother would bust up the game. Milo wished she'd do that now, appear on the street drunk in her house-dress and slippers, the way she did sometimes, and scream Rhonda and Kathy home. Then they'd have to play something else. He didn't like any of them when they were playing hide'n'seek. Something happened to them when they were hiding, something not very nice. Just by hiding, they became *different,* in a way Milo could never understand or duplicate. All of them hid better than he could, so he always ended up being found last, which meant that he had to be IT. He had to go look for them, then; he was the hunter. But not really. Searching for them in all the dark places, the deep places where they crouched breathing like animals, waiting to jump out at him, he knew they were all the hunters and he was the prey. It was just another way for them to hunt him. And when he found them, when they exploded from their hiding places lunging at him, all pretense of his being the hunter dropped away and he ran, ran like hell and hoped it was fast enough, back to the goal to tag it ahead of them. Otherwise he'd have to be IT all over again and the things he found squatting under stairs and behind fences became a little worse than before, a little more powerful.

Out goes Y-O-U!

Sammy's sneaker scraped the pavement as he dragged it out of the circle. Sammy was plump around the edges, the baby fat he had carried all his life melting away. He wore Keds, at war with Stevie's P.F. Flyers to see who could *really* run faster and jump higher. Sammy could break your arm. Milo didn't want to have to look for him. He'd never be able to outrun Sammy. He stared at Rhonda's fuzzy brown head bent over their feet with the intentness of a jeweler counting diamonds. He tried to will her to count him out next. If he could just make it through one game without having to be IT, then it might be

13

too late to play another. They would all have to go home when the streetlights came on. Tomorrow he would leave and never have to find any of them again.

Out goes Y-O-U!

Bonnie. Then Flora. They came and went together in white sneakers and blue Bermuda shorts, Bonnie the follower and Flora the leader. You could tell that right away by Flora's blue cat's-eye glasses. Bonnie was chubby, ate a lot of pasta, smelled like sauce. Flora was wiry from fighting with her five brothers. She was the one who was always saying you could hear Milo coming a mile away because of his housekeys. They were pinned inside his pocket on a Good Luck key chain from Pleasure Island, and they jingled when he ran. He put his hand down deep in his pocket and clutched the keys in his sweaty fist.

Out goes Y-O-Me!

Rhonda was safe. Now it was just Milo and Angie, like a duel between them with Rhonda's finger pulling the trigger. Angie's dark eyes stared out of her pointy little face. She was a thin girl, all sharp angles and sharp teeth. Her dark brown hair was caught up in a confident ponytail. If he were IT, she would be waiting for him more than any of the others, small but never frightened. Milo gripped his keys tighter. None of them was ever frightened. It wasn't fair.

Out goes Y-O-U!

Milo backed away, his breath exploding out of him in relief. Angie pushed her face against the wall of the tenement, closing her eyes and throwing her arms around her head to show she wasn't peeking. She began counting toward one hundred by fives, loud, so everyone could hear. You couldn't stop it now. Milo turned and fled, pounding down the alley until he caught up with Stevie and Sammy.

"Don't follow us!" "Your keys are jingling!" "Milo, you always get caught, bug off!" Stevie and Sammy ran faster, but he kept up with them all the way across the parking lot down to Middle Street, where they ducked into a narrow space between two buildings. Milo slipped past them so Stevie was closest to the outside. They stood with their backs to the wall like little urban guerrillas, listening to the tanky echoes of their panting.

"She coming?" Milo whispered after a minute.

"How the hell should we know, think we got X-ray vision?"

"Why'd you have to come with us, go hide by yourself, sissy-piss!"

Milo didn't move. If he stayed with them, maybe they wouldn't change into the nasty things. Maybe they'd just want to hurry back and tag the goal fast so they could get rid of him.

Far away Angie shouted, "Ready or not, here I come, last one found is IT!" Milo pressed himself hard against the wall, wishing he could melt into it like Casper the Friendly Ghost. They'd never find him if he could walk through walls. But he'd always be able to see them, no matter where they hid. They wouldn't make fun of him then. He wouldn't need his housekeys anymore, either, so they'd never know when he was coming up behind them. They'd be scared instead of him.

"My goal one-two-three!" Kathy's voice was loud and mocking. She'd just stuck near the goal again so she could tag it the minute Angie turned her back. Angie wouldn't care. She was looking for everyone else and saving Milo for last.

"She coming?" Milo asked again.

Sammy's eyes flickered under half-closed lids. Suddenly his hand clamped onto Milo's arm, yanking him around to Stevie, who shoved him out onto the sidewalk. Milo stumbled, doing a horrified little dance as he tried to scramble back into hiding. Sammy and Stevie blocked his way.

"Guess she isn't. Coming." Sammy smiled. Milo retreated, bumping into a car parked at the curb as they came out and walked past him. He followed, keeping a careful distance. They went up the street past the back of Mr. Parillo's to the yard behind the rented cottage with the grapevine. Sammy and Stevie stopped at the driveway. Milo waited behind them.

The sunlight was redder, hot over the cool wind springing up from the east. The day was dying. Sammy nodded. He and Stevie headed silently up the driveway to a set of cool stone steps by the side door of the cottage. The steps led to a skinny passage between the cottage and Bonnie's father's garage, and ended at the alley directly across from the goal. They squatted at the foot of the steps, listening. Up ahead, two pairs of sneakers pattered on asphalt.

"My goal one-two-three!" "My goal one-two-three!" Flora and Bonnie together. Where was Angie? Sammy crawled halfway up the steps and peeked over the top.

"See her?" Milo asked.

Sammy reached down and hauled him up by his shirt collar, holding him so the top step jammed into his stomach.

"*You* see her, Milo? Huh? She there? Sammy snickered as Milo struggled out of his grasp and slid down the steps, landing on Stevie, who pushed him away.

"Rhonda's goal one-two-three!" Angie's voice made Sammy duck down quickly.

"Shit!" Rhonda yelled.

"Don't swear! I'm tellin'!"

15

"Oh, shut up, you say it, too, who're you gonna tell anyway?"

"Your mother!"

"She says it, too, tattletale!"

"Swearer!"

Milo crept closer to Stevie again. If he could just avoid Angie till the streetlights came on, everything would be all right. "She still there?" he asked.

Stevie crawled up the steps and had a look. After a few seconds, he beckoned to Sammy. "Let's go."

Sammy gave Stevie a few moments headstart and then followed. Milo stood up. "Sammy?"

Sammy paused to turn, plant one of his Keds on Milo's chest, and shove. Milo jumped backward, lost his balance, and sat down hard in the dirt. Sammy grinned at him as though this were part of a prank they were playing on everyone else. When he was sure Milo wouldn't try to get up, he turned and went down the passage. Milo heard him and Stevie tag their goals together. He closed his eyes.

The air was becoming deeper, cooler, clearer. Sounds carried better now. Someone wished on the first star.

"That's an airplane, stupid!"

"Is not, it's the first star!"

And then Angie's voice, not sounding the least bit out of breath, as though she'd been waiting quietly for Milo to appear after Sammy: "Where's Milo?"

He sprang up and ran. Sammy would tell where they'd been hiding and she'd come right for him. He sprinted across Middle Street, cut between the nurse's house and the two-family place where the crazy man beat his wife every Thursday to Middle St. Lane. Then down to Fourth Street and up to the corner where it met Middle a block away from the Fifth Street bridge.

They were calling him. He could hear them shouting his name, trying to fool him into thinking the game was over, and he kept out of sight behind the house on the corner. Two boys went by on bikes, coasting leisurely. Milo waited until they were well up the street before dashing across to the unpaved parking area in front of the apartment where the fattest woman in town sat on her porch and drank a quart of Coke straight from the bottle every afternoon. There was a garbage shed next to the house. The Board of Health had found rats there once, come up from the polluted river running under the bridge. Milo crouched behind the shed and looked cautiously up the alley.

They were running back and forth, looking, listening for the jingle of his keys. "He *was* back there with us!" "Spread out, we'll find him!"

"Maybe he sneaked home." "Nah, he couldn't." "Everybody look for him!" They all scattered except for Kathy, bored and playing a lazy game of hopscotch under a streetlight that hadn't come on yet.

Impulsively, Milo snatched open the door of the shed and squeezed in between two overflowing trash barrels. The door flapped shut by itself, closing him in with a ripe garbagey smell and the keening of flies. He stood very still, eyes clenched tightly and his arms crossed over his chest. They'd never think he was in here. Not after the rats.

Thick footsteps approached and stopped. Milo felt the presence almost directly in front of the shed. Lighter steps came from another direction and there was the scrape of sand against rubber as someone turned around and around, searching.

"He's gotta be somewhere." Sammy. "I didn't think the little bastard could run *that* fast." Milo could sense the movement of Sammy's head disturb the air. The flies sang louder. "We'll get him. He's gonna be IT."

"Call 'Olly, olly, out-free.'" Stevie.

"Nah. Then he won't have to be IT."

"Call it and then say we had our fingers crossed so it doesn't count."

"Let's look some more. If we still can't find him, then we'll call it."

"He's a sissy-piss."

They went away. When the footsteps faded, Milo came out cautiously, choking from the smell in the shed. He stood listening to the sound of the neighborhood growing quieter. Darkness flowed up from the east more quickly now, reaching for the zenith, eager to spill itself down into the west and blot out the last bit of sunlight. Above the houses a star sparkled and winked, brightening. Milo gazed up at it, wishing as hard as he could.

> *Star light, star bright*
> *First star I see tonight*
> *I wish I may, I wish I might*
> *Have this wish . . .*
> *Eenie, meenie, ipsateenie . . .*
> *Don't let me be IT.*

He stood straining up at the star. Just this once. If he wouldn't have to be IT. Just this once—

"Angie! Angie! Down here, quick!"

He whirled and found Flora pointing at him, jumping up and down as she shouted. *No!* he wanted to scream. But Flora kept yelling for Angie to hurry, *hurry,* she could still get him before the streetlights came on. He fled to Middle Street, across Fourth to the next block, going toward the playground. There was nowhere to hide there among the swings and seesaws, but there was an empty house next to it.

Without much hope, Milo ran up the back steps and pushed at the door.

He found himself sprawling belly-down on the cracking kitchen linoleum. Blinking, he got to his feet. There was no furniture, no curtains in the windows. He tried to remember who had lived there last, the woman with the funny-looking dogs or the two queer guys? He went to one of the windows and then ducked back. Angie was coming down the sidewalk alone, smiling to herself. She passed the house, her ponytail bobbing along behind her. Milo tiptoed into the living room, keeping close to the wall. Shadows spread from the corners, unpenetrated by the last of the daylight coming through the windows and the three tiny panes over the front door. He ran to the door and pulled at it desperately, yanking himself back and forth like a yo-yo going sideways.

"Milo?"

He clung to the door, holding his breath. He had left the back door open and she was in the kitchen. The floor groaned as she took one step and then another. "I know you're hiding in here, Milo." She laughed.

Behind him were stairs leading to the second floor. He moved to them silently and began to crawl upward, feeling years of grit in the carpet runner scraping his hands and knees.

"You're gonna be IT now, Milo." He heard her walk as far as the entrance to the living room and then stop.

Milo kept crawling. If the streetlights went on now, it wouldn't make any difference. You couldn't see them in here. But maybe she'd give up and go away, if he could stay in the dark where she couldn't see him. She had to see him, actually lay eyes on him, before she could run back and tag his goal.

"Come on, Milo. Come on out. I know you're here. We're not supposed to be in here. If you come out now, I'll race you to the goal. You might even win."

He knew he wouldn't. She'd have Sammy waiting for him, ready to tackle him and hold him down so she could get to the goal first. Sammy would tackle him and Stevie would sit on him while everyone else stood and laughed and laughed and laughed. Because then he'd have to be IT forever. No matter where he went, they'd always be hiding, waiting to jump out at him, forcing him to find them again and again and again and he'd never get away from them. Every time he turned a corner, one of them would be there yelling, *You're IT, you're IT!*

"What are you afraid of, Milo? Are you afraid of a girl? Milo's a fraidycat! 'Fraid of girl, 'fraid of a girl!" She giggled. He realized she was in the middle of the living room now. All she had to do was look up to see him between the bars of the staircase railing. He put his hand on the top step and pulled himself up very slowly, praying the stairs wouldn't creak. His pants rubbed the dirty runner with a sandpapery sound.

"Wait till I tell everyone you're scared of a *girl*. And you'll still be IT, and everyone will know." Milo drew back into the deep shadows on the second-floor landing. He heard her move to the bottom of the stairs and put her foot on the first step. "No matter where you go, everyone will know," she singsonged. "No matter where you go, everyone will know. Milo's IT, Milo's IT."

He wrapped his arms around his knees, pulling himself into a tight ball. In his pocket the housekeys dug into the fold between his hip and thigh.

"You'll have to take your turn sometime, Milo. Even if you move away, everyone will know you're IT. They'll all hide from you. No one will play with you. You'll always be IT. Always and always."

He dug in his heels and pushed himself around to the doorway of one of the bedrooms. Maybe she wouldn't be able to see him in the darkness and she'd go away. Then he could go home.

"I heard you. I heard you move. Now I know where you are. I'm gonna find you, Milo." She came up the last steps, groping in the murky shadows. He could just make out the shape of her head and her ponytail.

"Got you!" She sprang at him like a trap. "You're IT!"

"No!"

Milo kicked out. The darkness spun around him. For several seconds he felt her grabbing his arms and legs, trying to pull him out of hiding before her clutching hands fell away and her laughter was replaced by a series of thudding, crashing noises.

On hands and knees, panting like a dog, he crept to the edge of the top step and looked down. Angie's small form was just visible where it lay at the foot of the stairs. Her legs were still on the steps. The rest of her was spread on the floor with her head tilted at a questioning angle. Milo waited for her to get up crying, *You pushed me, I'm telling!* but she never moved. Slowly he went halfway down the stairs, clinging to the rickety bannister.

"Angie?"

She didn't answer. He descended the rest of the way, careful to avoid her legs in case she suddenly came to life and tried to kick him.

"Angie?"

He knelt beside her. Her eyes were open, staring through him at nothing. He waited for her to blink or twitch, but she remained perfectly still. Milo didn't touch her. *She'd have done it to me,* he thought. She would have, too. She'd have pushed him down the stairs to get to the goal first. After all, Sammy had kicked him off the other stairs so he couldn't touch goal with him and Stevie. Now they were even. Sort of. Sammy had been on her side, after all. Milo stood up. She wouldn't chase him any more and she'd never touch his goal on him.

He found his way to the back door, remembering to close it as he left. For a few moments he stood in the yard, trying to find the star he had wished on. Others were beginning to come out now. But the streetlights—something must be wrong with them, he thought. The city had forgotten about them. Or maybe there was a power failure. He should have wished for them to come on. That would have sent everyone home.

While he stood there, the streetlights did come on, like eyes opening everywhere all over the neighborhood. Milo's shoulders slumped with relief. Now he really had won. Everyone had to go home now. The game was over. It was over and he wouldn't have to be IT.

He ran through the playground, across Water St. Lane and up Water, getting home just as the final pink glow in the west died.

20

"There." Milo finished tying a double bow in the boy's shoelaces. "Now they won't come undone."

The boy frowned at his feet critically. "How'm I gonna get 'em off?"

"Like this." Milo demonstrated for him. "See?" He retied the bow. "It's easy when you get the hang of it."

"Maybe I'll just leave 'em on when I go to bed."

"And when you take a bath, too?" Milo laughed. "Sneakers in the tub'll go over real well with your mom."

"I won't take baths. Just wipe off with a washcloth."

Milo restrained himself from looking behind the kid's ears. Instead, he stood up and began walking again. The boy stayed beside him, trying to whistle between his teeth and only making a rhythmic hissing noise. Milo could have sympathized. He'd never learned to whistle very well himself. Even today his whistle had more air than tune in it. Sammy had been a pretty good whistler. He'd even been able to whistle between his fingers like the bigger boys. Stevie hadn't been able to, but Sammy hadn't made fun of him the way he'd made fun of Milo.

Milo half-expected to see Sammy and Stevie as he and the boy approached the spot where the garbage shed had been. Now there was a modern dumpster there, but Milo imagined that the rats could get into that easily enough if any cared to leave the river. Aunt Syl had written his mother that environmentalists had forced the city to clean up the pollution, making it more livable for the rats under the bridge.

But the dumpster was big enough for someone Sammy's size to hide behind. Or in. Milo shook his head. Sammy's size? Sammy was all grown up now, just like he was. All of them were all grown up now. Except Angie. Angie was still the same age she'd been on that last day, he knew that for a fact. Because she'd never stopped chasing him.

It took her a long, long time to find him because he had broken the rule about leaving the neighborhood. You weren't supposed to leave the neighborhood to hide. You weren't supposed to go home, either, and he had done that, too.

But then he'd thought the game was really over. He'd thought it had ended at the bottom of the stairs in the vacant house with the day-light's going and the streetlights' coming on. Rhonda had been the last one found, the *only* one found, so she should have been IT, not Milo. The next game should have gone on without him. Without him and Angie, of course. He thought it had. All through the long, dull ride to the airport and the longer, duller flight from New England to the Midwest, through the settling in at the first of the new apartments and the settling down to passable if lackluster years in the new school, he thought the game had continued without him and Angie.

But the night came when he found himself back in that darkening empty house, halfway up the stairs to the second floor. He froze in the act of reaching for the next step, feeling the dirt and fear and approach of IT.

When the floor creaked, he screamed and woke himself up before he could hear the sound of her childish, taunting voice. He was flat on his back in bed, gripping the covers in a stranglehold. After a few moments he sat up and wiped his hands over his face.

The room was quiet and dark, much darker than the house had been that last day. He got up without turning on the light and went to the only window. This was the fourth apartment they'd had since coming to the Midwest, but they'd all been the same. Small, much smaller than the one in the tenement, done in plaster ticky-tacky with too few windows. Modern housing in old buildings remodeled for modern living with the woodwork painted white. At least the apartment was on the eighth floor. Milo preferred living high up. You could see everything from high up. Almost.

The street that ran past the building gleamed wetly under the street-lights. It had rained. He boosted the window up and knelt before the sill, listening to the moist sighing of occasional passing cars. A damp breeze puffed through the screen.

Across the street something moved just out of the bright circle the streetlight threw on the sidewalk.

When the streetlights came on, it was time to go home.

A stray dog. It was probably just a stray dog over there. In the distance, a police siren wailed and then cut off sharply. Milo's mouth was dry as he squinted through the screen. It was too late for kids to be out.

But if you didn't get home after the streetlights came on, did that mean you never had to go home, ever?

The movement came again, but he still couldn't see it clearly. A shadow was skirting the patch of light on the pavement, dipping and weaving, but awkwardly, stiffly. It wanted to play, but there was no one awake to play with, except for Milo.

He spread his fingers on the windowsill and lowered his head. It was too late for kids to be out. Any kids. The streetlights—

Something flashed briefly in the light and then retreated into the darkness. Milo's sweaty fingers slipped on the sill. The game was *over.* He wasn't IT. He *wasn't.* She'd found him but she hadn't tagged his goal and all the streetlights had come on. The game was over, had been over for years. It wasn't *fair.*

The figure made another jerky movement. He didn't have to see it clearly now to know about the funny position of its head, its neck still crooked in that questioning angle, the lopsided but still confident bobbing of the ponytail, the dirty-white sneakers. Another police siren was howling through the streets a few blocks away, but it didn't quite cover up the sound of a little girl's voice, singing softly because it was so late.

> *Eenie, meenie, ipsateenie*
> *Goo, gah, gahgoleenie*
> *Ahchee, pahchee, Liberaci*
> *Out goes Y-O-U!*
> *Eenie, meenie, ipsateenie*
> *Goo gah gahgoleenie . . .*

He covered his ears against it, but he could still hear it mocking him. No one was being counted out, no one would ever be counted out again because he was IT and he had missed his turn.

Come out, Milo. Come out, come out, come out. You're IT.

He pressed his hands tighter against his ears, but it only shut the sound of her voice up in his head and made it louder. Then he was clawing at the screen, yelling, "I'm not! I'm not! I'm not IT, the game's over and *I'm not IT!*"

His words hung in the air, spiraling down around him. There was a soft pounding on the wall behind the bed. "Milo!" came his mother's muffled, sleepy voice. "It's four in the morning, what are you screaming for?"

He sank down onto the floor, leaning his head hopelessly against the windowsill. "A, a dream, Mom," he said, his voice hoarse and thick in his tight throat. "Just a bad dream."

The wind poured through his hair, chilling the sweat that dripped down to his neck. Laughter came in with the wind, light, careless, jeering laughter. He knew Angie was looking up at his window, her sharp little teeth bared in a grin.

"'Fraid of a girl," the laughter said. "'Fraid of a girl . . ."

The boy was staring at his pants pocket and Milo realized he'd been jingling his loose change without thinking as they walked. He thought about giving the kid a quarter, but his mother had probably warned him not to take candy or money from strangers. Most likely he wasn't even supposed to talk to strangers. But most kids were too curious not to. They were programmed to answer questions from adults anyway, so all you had to do was ask them something and pretty soon you were carrying on a regular conversation. As long as you didn't make the mistake of offering them any money or candy, the kids figured they were safe.

"Housekeys," Milo lied, jingling the change some more. "When I was your age, my mother pinned them inside my pocket and they jingled whenever I ran."

"How come she did that?"

"She worked. My father was dead. I had to let myself in and out when she wasn't home and she didn't want me to lose my keys."

The boy accepted that without comment. Absent fathers were more common now anyway. The boy probably knew a lot of kids who carried housekeys, if he wasn't carrying any himself.

"She pin 'em in there today?"

"What?" Milo blinked at him.

"Your housekeys." The boy grinned insolently.

Milo gave him half a smile. Some things never changed. Kids still thought a joke at someone else's expense was funny. He glanced down at the double bows he'd tied in the boy's laces. Yeah, he could picture one of those sneakers on some other kid's chest, kicking him off some steps. The boy looked more like Stevie than Sammy, but that didn't matter. Stevie would have done it if he'd had the chance. Milo was sure this boy would have been great friends with Angie.

They were past the dumpster, almost to the corner where Water St. Lane crossed Fourth. The house where the fattest woman in town had consumed her daily quart of Coke straight from the bottle was still inhabited. Somewhere inside, a radio was boasting that it had the hits, all the hits and nothing but the hits. Milo didn't think it would be long before this house stood as empty as his old tenement, condemned and waiting to fall. It wasn't about to collapse by itself. These old houses had been built to stay up, no matter how tired and shabby they became. Endurance, that was what it was. But anything could reach the end of its endurance eventually—a neighborhood, a building, a person. Neighborhoods and buildings had to be taken care of, but people could take things into their own hands. You didn't have to endure something past the point when it should have ended. Not if you knew what to do.

Milo hadn't known what to do at first, though. He found himself helpless again, as helpless as he'd been on those old stairs so many years ago. In the dream or wide-awake, crouched at his bedroom window while the little-girl thing that hadn't made it home before dark played on the sidewalk and called him, he was helpless. Angie didn't care that Rhonda should have been IT. Rhonda and the others had gone home after the streetlights had come on, but Angie hadn't. The game wasn't done even though it was just the two of them now.

Slowly he began to realize it was the other kids. One of the bigger boys with the bikes must have seen him climb into the car with his mother and Aunt Syl the next day and passed it on to another kid who passed it on to another kid in a long, long game of Gossip that stretched over hundreds and hundreds of miles, with Angie following, free to leave the neighborhood because he had, free to stay out late because she had never gone home. Angie, following him all the way to the Midwest, to the new neighborhood, to the new apartment because of the new kids at the new school who had been happy to tell her where he was because everyone loved a good hunt. The new kids, they were all just Sammys and Stevies and Floras and Bonnies with different names and faces anyway. They all knew he was IT and had missed his turn. Even his mother knew something; she looked at him strangely sometimes when she thought he didn't know, and he could feel her waiting for him to tell her, explain. But he couldn't possibly. She had taken her turn a long time ago, just like all the adults, and when you took your turn, you forgot. She couldn't have understood if he had explained until the day he died.

So he'd held out for a long, long time and they moved to new apartments, but Angie always found him. Kids were everywhere and they always told on him. And then one day he looked at himself and found Milo staring out at him from a grown-up face, a new hiding place for the little boy with the same old fear. And he thought, *Okay; okay. We'll end it now, for you and for Angie.* He was big now, and he hadn't forgotten. He would help little Milo still helpless inside of him, still hiding from Angie.

He went back. Back to the old neighborhood, taking Angie up on her offer of a race to the goal at last.

Deep summer. The feel of it had hit him the moment he'd walked down to the alley from the bus stop at Third and Water, where most of the old buildings were still standing all the way down to St. Bernard's Church. In the alley, things had changed, but he wouldn't look until he had walked deliberately down to the tenement.

He knew then she must have won. He put his face close to the wall and closed his eyes. The smell of hot baked stone was there, three-quarters of a century of hot summer afternoons and children's faces pressed against the wall, leaving a faint scent of bubble gum and candy and kid sweat. The building had stood through the exodus of middle-class white families and the influx of poor white families and minorities and the onslaught of urban renewal, waiting for Angie to come back and touch it one more time, touch it and make him really and truly IT. And now he was here, too, Milo was here, but grown big and not very afraid anymore, now that it was done. If he had to be IT, if he had no choice — and he'd never had, really — he would be a real IT, the biggest, the scariest, and no one would know until it was too late.

Counting to one hundred by fives hadn't taken very long at all — not nearly as long as he had remembered. When he'd opened his eyes, he'd found the boy hanging around in front of the rented cottage.

"Hi," he'd said to the boy. "Know what I'm doing?"

"No, what?" the boy had asked.

"I'm looking for some friends." Milo had smiled. "I used to live here."

Now they stood at the end of the alley together and Milo smiled again to see that the house was still there. But then, he'd known that it would be. He walked slowly down Fourth to stand directly across the street from it, staring at the stubborn front door. It probably still wouldn't open. The red paint had long flaked away and been replaced by something colorless. What grass had surrounded the place had died off. Overhead the sky, almost as blue as it had been that day, was beginning to deepen. He listened for children's voices and the sound of the bigger boys' English bikes ticking by on the street. If he strained, he could almost hear them. It was awfully quiet today, but some days were like that, he remembered.

25

"Who lives there?" he asked the boy. "Who lives in that house now?"
"Nobody."

"Nobody? Nobody at all?"

"It's a dump." The boy bounced the heel of his right sneaker against the toe of his left. "I been in there," he added, with only a little bit of pride.

"Have you."

"Yeah. It's real stinky and dirty. Joey says it's haunted, but *I* never seen nothin'."

Milo pressed his index finger along his mouth, stifling the laugh that wanted to burst out of him. *Haunted? Of course it's haunted, you little monster—I've been haunting it myself!* "Must be fun to play in, huh?"

The boy looked up at him as though he were trying to decide whether he could trust Milo with that information. "Well, nobody's supposed to go in there anymore, but you can still get in."

Milo nodded. "I know. Say, did you ever play a game where you have to put your feet in and somebody counts everybody out and the last one left is IT?"

The boy shrugged. "Like 'eenie, meenie, miney, mo?'"

"Something like that. Only we used to say it differently. I'll show you." Milo knelt again, putting the toe of his shoe opposite the boy's sneaker, ignoring the boy's bored sigh. Oh, yes, he'd show the boy. It wouldn't be nearly as boring as the boy thought, either. The boy was a Stevie. That meant pretty soon there'd be a Sammy coming along and then maybe a Flora and a Bonnie and all the rest of the ones who had helped look for him and who had told Angie where to find him. But he'd give all of them a better chance than they'd given him. He'd do the chant for them, the way he was doing now for the boy, starting with the boy's foot first.

> *Eenie, meenie, ipsateenie*
> *Goo, gah, gahgoleenie*
> *Ahchee, pahchee, Liberaci*
> *Out goes Y-O-U!*

Milo grinned. "Looks like I'm IT." He stood up. Still IT, he should have said. They hadn't let him quit; they hadn't let him miss his turn. All right. He would take it and keep taking it, because he was IT and it was his game now.

"C'mon," he said to the boy as he stepped off the curb to cross the street. "Let's see if that old house is still fun to play in."

VENGEANCE IS YOURS

I think of this as a watershed story. It was my sixth professional sale and my first to Ellen Datlow at *Omni*. Working with Ellen on the revisions for this story taught me a great deal about writing. Up until then, I'd been stumbling around, sometimes selling a story, sometimes not—it was all very hit-and-miss. After working with Ellen, I never failed to place a story again (though not everything sells the first time out, and I still have to do revisions now and then, even for Ellen). It gives me great pleasure to acknowledge her help, and it takes nothing away from the other fine editors I've worked with.

As for the story itself, I would not presume to say that Ellen has a mean streak. But *I* do.

VENGEANCE IS YOURS

I told the bartender I'd give him a fat tip if he'd make me something that looked deadly and smelled more so. On the spot he invented the Silver Bombe—tonic water with a pearl onion, a pimiento speared on a giant, curved upholstery needle, and a spoonful of those little silver balls you sprinkle on cupcakes. The finishing touch was the leftover Christmas tinsel tied around the stem of the glass. You didn't look at it, you beheld it. Behold, the Silver Bombe. It smelled like a bender. I pushed the glass back toward the bartender. "I said, no booze."

"That's just a little grain alcohol I wiped around the outside of the glass here, miz," the bartender said, pushing the Bombe back at me. "You said you wanted aroma."

"I can smell it inside the glass, too."

"Just a kiss. For *aroma*. I swear to God a baby wouldn't feel it."

God being unavailable for comment, I decided to believe the bartender. He was a skinny blond kid who didn't look as though he'd learned how to lie yet. I had a sip of the Bombe while he bright-eyed me. As a drink it was a real bomb, but I wasn't about to complain. It was just a prop, after all. "Good work."

He glowed. "I swear I'm a genius, miz, I really am. Every part of that drink means something, you know? See, there's the drink itself, and the onion represents the bomb, the pimiento's the fuse—lit, as it were—the needle means you'll really feel it, and the silver balls stand for little explosions."

The metaphysics of drinking—I hadn't known there were any. Maybe they were teaching that at bartending school now along with mixology. Ever since the turn of the century, people seem a little crazier to me. "What about this?" I flipped a strand of tinsel with my index finger. "What does this mean?"

"That's Happy New Year."

I didn't comment on the fact that it had been Happy New Year for something over three weeks now. He reached for the bill I was sliding to him across the bar, but I didn't take my hand from it. His smile vanished. "I just got married. I'm not going home with you or anyone else."

I grinned. This was the glorious liberated future humanity had been striving for, where everyone's a sex object or in training to be one. "All I want is for you to keep our little arrangement confidential. Even from the other bartender. If anyone asks you, this is a vodka drink."

"How about gin?" he suggested, brightening perceptibly.

"Whatever." I couldn't stand gin, myself, but the drink was his invention, not mine. I took my hand off the bill and he made it disappear into his perky red paper vest.

"Thanks, miz. Flag me when you're ready for another." He began puttering around, arranging glasses and checking drink programs on the console under the espresso machine. Down at the other end of the long bar, the other bartender had most of the action, which at the bare beginning of Attitude Adjustment Hour wasn't much. But things were going to pick up soon and Jeremy Currin would be in for his regular Wednesday night hit in about fifteen minutes if he was lucky enough to make all the lights coming down VanBendt. He usually was. He was that kind of man.

I leaned against the barstool backrest (mandatory for all bars in the city since the infamous, if comic, Hund vertebrae lawsuit of 1998) and looked around. It was easy to see why Currin liked this place. It was a dark-wood-and-brass lounge with an abundance of antique accents, including a mirror behind the bar—just the sort of place where a data analyst with lumberjack fantasies could sip whiskey and pretend he had calluses. What the hell—if a button-pusher thousands of miles from a sequoia wanted to affect the look of the Great Northwest of yesteryear, nobody really cared much.

It wasn't my night to be critical anyway. I was just supposed to pick him up, which wasn't going to be very difficult.

I'd been hanging in with the man for close to three months, firsthand and by proxy. He had regular habits with a spontaneity factor of under ten percent—set in his ways but open to suggestion if the timing was right. Single, never married, and never would be. Definitely not my type, which was why I was drinking an unloaded Bombe. I'd have to be sober to take him, and I never could hold my booze. But after Currin smelled the Bombe, he'd probably think I was the baddest-drinking woman in the place.

'Way back in the corner, two big guys were dwarfing a silly little table piled with hors d'oeuvres and watching me while they stuffed up on shrimp. I swiveled around and gave them a deadly glare, which put an end to that. When I'm on a job, I don't need people screwing me around by staking me out or just looking like they are.

A chill gust sent my cocktail napkin flapping away as a group of young up-and-comers came in. Currin wasn't among them. In another three minutes he'd be officially late. I wouldn't have to get edgy for a quarter of an hour. If he didn't show by then it would mean he'd decided to break his pattern for some reason. *Stay in your rut, Currin,* I begged silently. *Don't make me have to set this up again.*

The people at the other end of the bar began to spread out as the music came up a little louder. A couple of them gave me a glance, but I knew they didn't recognize me. I'd kept a low profile before, never coming in alone or sitting at the bar. I turned sideways, indicating I was not annexable. None of them were Currin's friends.

My bartender was coming back to me when the front door opened again and I saw a familiar blond head gleaming in the overhead light of the crowded vestibule.

"One second," I said to the bartender and craned my neck to see where Currin would go. The bartender followed my gaze, standing on tiptoe to see who I was looking at. Currin began walking toward my end of the bar and I turned away quickly.

"Oh," said the bartender.

"Oh, yourself. Freshen this. If you can find a bigger needle, put it in."

Currin passed behind me, with another man and three women in tow. The five of them clustered against the wall around the curve of the bar so Currin could watch the talent easily. From the corner of my eye I tried to see him just as Karen Kitterman had seen him.

He was one of those variegated blonds—pale hair overlaying darker hair—and his beard had come in fuzzy and brown. His shoulders stretched the plaid flannel of his shirt as he hung his fleece-lined jacket on the back of his stool. One of the women said something to him and he burst into hearty laughter. He had a surprisingly good laugh. His eyes were very blue and his teeth, splitting the beard into a wide smile, were perfect.

A new Silver Bombe, with a needle large enough to qualify as a spear, appeared in front of me. I looked up to tell my bartender to run me a tab, but he was already over at Currin's party taking orders. I stirred my Bombe with the needle and thought about Karen.

It was like a story from thirty or forty years ago. Woman meets man, woman loves man, woman loses man, woman loses mind, woman cuts throat. You'd have thought women would have stopped agonizing over men, but people never really change. Revenge, for example, is still sweet, something Karen had realized before she'd selected a serrated carving knife for herself. In spite of her rather fatal foible, she'd been an extraordinary person in a lot of ways, and tonight Currin was going to find out just how extraordinary.

A man squeezed behind me, shouting "Jeremy!" over the music, which got louder every time more people came in. I leaned toward the bar, catching Currin's eye as he looked up to greet the newcomer. His gaze snagged on me briefly and when he sat down again, he was facing me directly.

I was contemplating my next move when someone slid onto the stool next to me; I was immediately sorry I hadn't brought another woman or two. Well, I couldn't think of everything. To my relief, the man beside me seemed more interested in one of the women competing for Currin, probably any one that Currin didn't want. My hope that he'd ignore me completely was dashed when he tapped me on the arm.

"What kind of drink is that?" he bellowed over the music.

"Silver Bombe!" I bellowed back, trying to look bored, which is hard to do when you have to shout. "If you want one, he's your man!" I pointed at my bartender, who was busily sorting out drinks for Currin's entourage and having a hard time of it.

Currin smiled at me as he picked up his two fingers of Jack Daniels. With a very subtle motion he toasted me and I nodded once in acknowledgment.

It wasn't lost on the man beside me, even while my bartender was explaining the loaded version of the Silver Bombe, which he decided didn't appeal to him.

"If you're here to get lucky," he shouted, "you just hit the mother-lode—or at least the mother. A regular bar star, that one. Can have anyone he wants!"

"No offense, but who asked you?" I swiveled around and faced Currin again. People were accumulating around him like old magazines.

The alcohol and atmosphere were really working on him now. He wasn't the cheap drunk I was, but it didn't take him long to adjust *his* attitude. His face was glowing and snatches of his conversation came to me as his voice and spirits rose together.

He caught my eye again while someone was shouting something into his right ear; we exchanged grins. I began feeling slightly trashy.

I managed to grab my bartender as he was on his way back from delivering a round to the gigglers on my left. "The whiskey-sipping gentleman is ready for another. Put it on my tab and tell him about it." I figured it was safe to do that by now.

"*He* already told me to bring you another when you're ready!"

"Okay." I chugged the tonic water, almost choking on some of the silver balls. "I'm ready!" He sighed, took my glass, held up a hand to someone who was shouting at him, and backed into the other bartender. Currin grinned at me, shaking his head. I laughed at nothing.

"You've made a conquest," the man beside me said, his lips brushing my ear.

I drew away showily. "Back off, will you?"

He stared at me for a moment and then turned away to move into the crowd. I made sure Currin was watching as I took my purse and put it on the now-empty stool. Understanding crossed his face, then my bartender arrived with the drink I'd bought him. The timing couldn't have been better. I dropped my gaze innocently, fishing a large bill out of my sleeve for the bartender; I wanted to make up for the way I'd been tying him up with dummy Silver Bombes during the the rush. Slipping it under the base of my glass, I looked up to smile at Currin again. He was gone.

"This yours?"

I turned around. Currin was holding my purse out to me as he sat down. He had his coat with him.

"Thanks." I put the purse back on the bar without looking at it.

"No, thank *you*. It isn't often a lady buys me a drink." A third Silver Bombe appeared and the old one was swept away, money and all, without comment. "That's on me."

"I appreciate it."

"Mind telling me what it is?"

"Silver Bombe." I quickly gulped down half of it to discourage him from asking for a taste.

"Silver Bombe." He shook his head. "I never did go in for mixed drinks. I like my whiskey unadorned. What's your name?"

"Lissa," I lied. Lissa sounded like someone who'd hang out in a bar to make friends.

"I'm Jeremy." He laughed a little. "I know, I don't look much like a Jeremy but I'm stuck with it. You, on the other hand, look exactly like your name."

Thanks. "I do?"

"Sure. Lissa. That's your whole name, right? Not short for Melissa or anything?"

Why not. I nodded.

"I knew it. I'm not an expert on names — I'm in data, actually — but some people you can just tell certain things about." He looked around. "Be nice if we could continue this discussion at one of the tables, but they all seem to be taken."

I stood up abruptly and pretended to survey the room. "In the corner." I pointed with my drink. "Those two look like they're ready to leave."

"Where?"

"Follow me." I grabbed my purse and his sleeve in one movement and headed for the table I'd pointed at. The two guys sitting there finished their beer and rose just as we reached them. I grinned up at Currin while they vacated and then let him seat me.

He wasn't really a bad sort. A little shallow maybe, but nobody goes to bars to find philosophers — philosophers buy their booze in bottles and drink it at home. Currin was glib enough, and under other circumstances I might have found it easy to believe he was sincere. That had been Karen's mistake. I smiled as he made a joke I couldn't quite hear and he waved at the overworked waitress for this section. The former occupants of our table were explaining something to her as they stood near my old spot at the bar.

By the time she got to us, Currin's arm had fallen off the back of the chair onto me. He was friendly when he was high, but he was even friendlier drunk. He remained coherent, but I could tell that everything was looking better to him with each swallow, especially me. His smile got broader, he laughed louder, and he seemed to be unaware of how drunk he was getting, which suited me just fine. If he didn't know how drunk he was, then he wouldn't know how drunk I wasn't.

About the time he hit what I had gauged was his saturation point, he suggested we get something to eat. I had to boost him up out of his chair without seeming to, and we did a little tango while I helped him on with his coat. He was happy to let me lead him between the tables, one hand on my shoulder to steady himself.

People were calling to him, but I kept moving so he had to stay with me or fall down. We had to wait at the front door to let in a crowd that had had its attitude adjusted elsewhere and was coming in to try its new outlook on the positive drinkers in here. I slipped us out before Currin had a chance to recognize any of them.

"Whoa!" He staggered a bit as the cold air hit him. "Talk about an eye-opener!" He looked down at me and yanked me close, enfolding me in his open coat. "You must be freezing."

We stood there snuggling for a few moments and I began to feel a little regret for what was about to happen. Currin wasn't totally incapable of being a nice guy in his own simple way. *Might as well get this over with,* I thought, and pulled loose.

"I'd better drive," I said and herded him down the sidewalk. "My car's right here at the corner."

"Yours?" He stood back to admire the low, fast lines of the Electra-Charger. His own car, I remembered, drank a lot of house current. I unlocked the passenger-side door and raised it for him. He sort of poured into the front seat. "Always wanted an ElectraCharger," he muttered enviously. I tucked his legs in and then ran around to the driver's side. In spite of the thermal skins under my clothes, the chill was biting into me.

"Hey," Currin said, putting a hand on my arm as I inserted the wire into the ignition. I turned toward him and got a faceful of fuzzy brown beard. I managed to get one arm free and reached into my purse without disturbing him. "I can't remember when I've had more fun getting acquainted with someone," he said after a while.

"Me, too." I got my right arm up around his shoulders and played with his hair. "And you know what?" I asked, drawing my head back a little.

"What?"

There wasn't even time for him to be surprised. He was still trying to raise his eyebrows when he pitched forward on top of me, pinning me against the door.

I tried shoving him back with my left hand while I held the right clear. I didn't want to give him another jolt with the joybuzzer and I didn't want to zap myself, either. My fingers were tingling painfully. No matter how they try to insulate those things, you always get a little punch yourself. I twisted around to no effect at all, struggling with him, cursing the tight quarters of the ElectraCharger's front seat. Then, through the windshield, I saw two large shapes coming down the street toward the car—the same ones who had been staring at me earlier. One of them came around to my side of the car and raised the door. I fell backward and hung there with my hair dragging the pavement. The guy stood over me and tried hard not to laugh.

"About time," I said as he helped me sit up. "Get him off me, will you? Watch it, I've still got the buzzer in my palm."

Currin slept peacefully as we loaded him into the van and he was still sleeping when Coll and Phinny unloaded him in the cemetery. We had his hands and feet cuffed by then, not tight enough to hurt him, but too tight to let him move around much when he woke up.

They wanted to put him right on top of the grave, but I wasn't too sure about that. Eventually, we compromised—half on, half off. He had to be positioned just right.

"You coming back to the van?" Phinny asked as he finished arranging Currin.

I shook my head. "I'm going to watch right here."

"You'll have to move back some. Otherwise the camera'll pick you up."

"Fine. I'll call you."

Phinny and Coll headed back to the van, which was parked up the hill on one of the cemetery's narrow roads. I waited until I heard the door slam and then got the adrenaline patch out of my purse.

Currin was snoring when I opened his shirt and jammed the patch onto his chest. For a moment nothing happened. Then his eyelids fluttered and he made a small noise. I put my hand over his heart. It was just starting to race. Good. I'd put exactly the right amount of adrenaline in the patch. He was going to wake up jitterbugging.

"Jeremy?" His eyes and opened and I moved away before he could focus on me. There was more than enough light to see by from the cemetery lamps, and I watched him discover that he couldn't get his hands out from behind his back or pull his feet apart. He tried to sit up and flopped over onto his stomach with a moan of pain. Now he was finding out about his head—I understand being joybuzzed is a lot like being kicked by a mule with steel hooves. He looked up, blinking, and then saw the gravestone. It took him over a minute to read the words on it. I was too far away to read it myself, but I knew what it said: KAREN KITTERMAN.

HE WENT *ah-ah-ah* and tried to squirm away, but the adrenaline was jerking him in ten directions at once, so all he did was twitch around. Then a clod of dirt hit him in the face and he stopped, trembling.

The soil on the grave was moving, and as Currin watched, a hand broke the surface, fingers flexing and clutching at nothing. I heard him suck wind with a whooping sound. Then there were two hands, small, feminine, and pasty white. A dank, rotten smell was in the air, making him choke on the breath he'd just taken.

The hands reached up, pulling free of the grave, and the arms that appeared were mottled, as though the flesh had fallen away in spots. The fingers groped, just missing Currin by inches. He howled and tried to stand up again, forgetting about the cuffs, and rolled himself into the gravestone instead. His whole body was shaking as he watched the thing wrench itself from the ground, dirt flying and the smell getting even stronger. It wasn't very big—it had only managed to free its upper body. Most of its hair was gone and its sunken face was silvery in spots. Lying on his side, looking up at it, Currin lost his voice altogether. The rotted arms opened to embrace him.

"Jeremy," said a high, female voice. "I've missed you so."

I hugged myself against the chill.

"It's me. Karen," said the thing, bending forward. One hand found his coat and dragged him, kicking and squirming, to itself. "You haven't forgotten me, have you? I haven't forgotten you." The voice was sticky with yearning. "So glad to see you." Currin managed one more scream before the thing bent its head to kiss him and bashed him squarely in the face. "So glad to see you." The thing's left arm jerked back and forth, the hand opening and closing in spasms. There was blood on Currin's face. "So glad to see you. So glad to see you," the thing repeated, its head slamming into his each time.

"Oh, *shit*." I ran forward, intending to pull Currin away from it when it suddenly collapsed on top of him with a ragged little moan. Currin was out again, blood pouring from his broken nose. I dragged him onto the grass, turning him on his side so the blood wouldn't go down his windpipe. Coll and Phinny were running down to the grave from the van.

"What the hell happened?" I demanded. "It was supposed to kiss him with its rotting, grave-fresh lips, press him to its deathly cold bosom. And that's a direct quote."

Coll and Phinny pulled the mecho gently out of the dirt and examined it by flashlight. "Dirt in the mechanism," Coll said. "it's all in the circuits and everything."

"Oh, that's wonderful!" I leaned on the gravestone. "I had to bribe the general manager at Sartaine's Department Store so I could borrow it from their display. It's supposed to be back tomorrow afternoon and if there's anything wrong with it, I'm out five grand."

Coll looked up at me. "That much?"

"It's an anti-shoplifting device besides being a mobile display unit."

"Better not tell them you buried it, then." Coll chuckled. "There's no permanent damage done. A little forced air'll take care of the dirt and she'll be good as new." He picked it up, slung it over his shoulder, and went back to the van with it. Phinny and I began replacing the dirt on the grave, stamping it down with our feet until it looked normal again.

"This is gonna give me nightmares," Phinny complained.

"Help me get the facade off this headstone and don't think about it." The two of us pulled at the front of the marker until the panel we'd pasted on earlier popped off.

"Easy for you to say. This isn't *your* grandmother's grave."

"No, and it won't be hers much longer, either. After the spring thaw the city's going to reclaim this land and all the bodies'll be cremated. What's left of them." I patted Phinny's shoulder sympathetically. "But we'll order a few months of perpetual care to make it up to her."

"How can a few months be perpetual?"

"Don't quibble, Phinny. I'd like to get the hell out of here. Desecrating a grave is still illegal, even if cemeteries are going the way of the dodo." I checked to see that Currin was still breathing. The blood on his face was icing over now. He would be okay, but he was going to have nightmares worse than Phinny's. Eventually he'd realize what had happened to him, but it wouldn't do him much good. There wasn't anyone to blame for it but Karen, and she was dead. He'd never find out about her will.

I took the cuffs off his wrists and ankles, rubbing them a little to make the marks disappear.

"I've got the camera," Phinny called to me. "Let's go, if you're so anxious to get out of here."

I glanced skeptically at the minicam in his hand as we trudged up the hill toward the van. I'd never worked with a videocamera that small before and I was afraid the picture was going to be kind of muddy. But I was surprised when I replayed the tape on the way home. The picture was as clear as anything I'd ever seen. Phinny had mounted the camera on the headstone next to his grandmother's and it had picked up every detail right down to the flying dirt and blood on Currin's face. That was going to need a little judicious editing. The executor of Karen's will wouldn't care, but I thought it looked sloppy.

After we'd put several blocks between us and the cemetery, I had Phinny make an anonymous call to the police to report someone asleep or dead near one of the graves. They'd take their time investigating it, but Currin would probably be at a hospital within half an hour or so. I felt bad about his nose, but they'd give him a new one.

I had intended to wait until morning to call the executor of Karen's estate, but I decided I didn't have to be the only one losing sleep over this. As it turned out he wasn't at all upset that I'd gotten him out of bed — just the opposite.

"I'm so pleased you were able to bring it off," he gushed through a yawn. "Frankly, I wasn't sure you'd be able to do it."

"It wasn't that hard. I'll get the videotape to you tomorrow."

"Good. The terms of Ms. Kitterman's will are quite specific on that point."

The terms of Ms. Kitterman's will were quite specific on all points. She'd videotaped it and ended it graphically with her suicide, but I didn't mention that.

"I wouldn't have gone along with this," he continued, "except there is a great deal of money involved and—"

"Speaking of money," I said.

"Ah. Yes, of course. How, ah—"

"Just the way we discussed. Get a money order and make it out to Vengeance Is Yours, Inc. You have the address."

He started to say something else but I hung up on him. My father had begun this business and he'd told me always to deal in money orders, none of this computer-transfer stuff.

That had been back in the days when V.I.Y., Inc. would just throw a pie in somebody's face for twenty bucks. We're more sophisticated now, but I get a certain amount of satisfaction from making clients go to the trouble of getting an old-fashioned money order. Revenge, after all, is kind of an old-fashioned thing anyway.

I left the videotape in the machine so I could get right to it the next day. After I cleaned it up a little, I'd send it to Karen's executor so he could play it for her brothers and sisters, who couldn't have cared less. All it was to them was a freaky little show they had to sit through before they could inherit her money. Her humiliation by Currin had been nothing to them, and her revenge wouldn't be much more.

That's the funny thing about vengeance. Half the time people hire me, they're getting back at the wrong persons for all the wrong reasons. I should know. I'm an authority.

But then again, the vengeance isn't mine.

THE DAY THE MARTELS GOT THE CABLE

Are you cable-ready? Before you answer, you might want to consider all the possible meanings of that phrase. *Cable-ready. Interactive TV.* So many aspects there.

And did you ever wait at home for some kind of service people— repairers, installers, deliverers—and then when they arrived, they were kind of . . . well, *weird?*

My friend Kathye McAndrew Griffin pointed out that the Martels are a Boston-based rock band. This isn't about them. It's about being cable-ready. When this story appeared in *The Magazine of Fantasy and Science Fiction* in 1982, cable TV was still relatively new in our area. I had to update some of the wording a bit, but the cable hardware itself is now outdated. I only point this out because you'll notice. I've let the story stand mostly as is, as a reminder of how quickly the technology can change. Back when I wrote this story, someone said "Betamax," and I said, "Huh?"

It's embarrassing to admit that. And if you don't keep up with the new developments, you could end up worse than embarrassed.

THE DAY THE MARTELS GOT THE CABLE

*L*ydia had stayed home from work to take delivery on the washer and dryer. So this time David would have Lydia call him in sick and he would wait for the cable TV people to come. Sitting at the kitchen table enjoying the luxury of a second cup of coffee, he skimmed the front page of the newspaper as Lydia hurriedly made herself up in the tiny downstairs bathroom.

"You sure you don't want me to drive you in?" he called over his shoulder.

Lydia poked her head out of the bathroom, holding a mascara brush between two fingers. "Not unless you want the car for some reason. Do you?"

"Nah. I was just thinking though, I always do the driving and you're not really used to the rush-hour traffic. Awake, anyway."

She stuck her tongue out at him. "*That* to you. I was driving in rush hour long before I hooked up with you and I'll be driving in it long after you run off and leave me for a younger woman." She disappeared back into the bathroom.

"*That* will be the day." He got up and went to the doorway of the bathroom. "When I go, I'm taking the car with me."

"Men," Lydia said, staring down at the hand mirror as she worked on her eyelashes. "You're all alike."

"We attend a special school for it when we're young." David looked at her admiringly. She had on what she called her dress-for-success get-up, tailored navy-blue jacket and skirt with a soft white blouse. What the well-dressed board chairperson was wearing this year. David had asked her once if it wasn't a bit overwhelming for an office manager. All in fun, of course. Truth to tell, her career was outstripping his own.

He reached out and stopped her as she was about to apply her lipstick. "Sure you don't want me to call you in sick, too? We could wait for the cable people together and then afterwards not watch the movie channel."

"That would look good, wouldn't it?" She gave him a quick but thorough kiss before she put on her lipstick. "I mean, the both of us working at the same company and we both happen to come down with stomach flu—ho, ho—on the same day. They'd buy that, for sure."

David shrugged. "So? We've got two bathrooms. Two toilets, no waiting. They can send the corporate secret police out to check if they want."

"David."

"I know, I know." He sighed. "It was worth a try."

"Don't think I don't appreciate it." She grinned redly, looking him up and down. "And don't think I'm not tempted. Say, poppa, did anyone ever tell you you do things for a bathrobe and pajamas that no other man can do?"

"Plenty of women, all the time." He stepped in and posed behind her in the mirror over the sink. They made a perfect portrait of the odd married couple, one with her blonde, chin-length hair carefully combed and the other with his tangled hair standing on end and morning stubble shading his cheeks. "Hey, if this were 1956, you'd be the one in the bathrobe, you know."

Lydia looked pained. "Promise me that after we get the cable, you won't tune in Channel 87 in Dry Rot, Egypt, for old *Leave It To Beaver* reruns."

"How about *Ozzie and Harriet?*"

"I *never* liked them." She gave him a push. "Let me out. I gotta go set the world on fire."

David backed up and blocked the doorway. "Last chance, woman. Eight hours of work or sixteen hours of ecstasy—the choice is yours." He made a thrusting motion with his hips.

"Sixteen hours of ecstasy or twenty-six weeks of paid unemployment. Outta my way, hot pajamas." She honked him as she slipped past and he chased her into the living room.

"Anything I should know about this cable thing?" he asked as she rummaged through her shoulder bag for her car keys.

"Like what?"

"I dunno. You're the one who filled out all the forms and made the arrangements. Am I supposed to do anything with the TV before they get here?"

"Not that I know of." Lydia hooked the keyring around her little finger and pushed several papers back into her purse. "Just stand back and don't get in anybody's way."

David put his hands on his hips. "Well, if they come during *Donahue,* they're just going to have to *wait!*" He tossed his head.

"I never liked him either. He's insincere." Lydia offered her cheek for a kiss. Instead, he bit her on the neck and gave her an impertinent squeeze.

"Don't you love permanent press?" he whispered in her ear. "You can do all sorts of things and your clothes never wrinkle."

She poked his ticklish spot and squirmed away. "Try not to eat too many chocolate-covered cherries while you're watching the soaps this afternoon, dear. And be dressed for when the cable people come, will you?"

"Yes, dear," he said nasally. "Honestly, work, work, work—that's all I ever *do* around this place."

Lydia's smile was only half amused. "And take the chicken out to thaw for supper tonight."

"I will."

"I mean it. Don't forget."

"All right, already. I'll take the chicken out to thaw. I was taking chicken out to thaw long before I hooked up with you and I'll be taking it out to thaw long after you run off and leave me to find yourself."

"Just make sure that you do it *today.*"

"I will. I *promise.* Now go to work before I rip all your clothes off." He did another bump and grind and she escaped out the door, laughing.

He watched from the living room window as she maneuvered the car out of the cramped parking lot in front of the townhouse. Then he went upstairs to take a quick shower, keeping one ear cocked for the sound of the doorbell in case the cable people came early. Why was it cable installers and delivery people could never give you a definite time when they would arrive at your home? They'd just tell you the date and you had to be there. Of course, they didn't come on a Saturday. They worked a straight Monday-to-Friday week, God *forbid* they should arrange their time to accommodate customers with like schedules.

42

Decadently, he decided not to shave after dressing and went back downstairs to pour himself a fresh cup of coffee and finish the newspaper. At ten o'clock he was fresh out of lazy things to do and just beginning to feel hungry. Well, what the hell—this was a free day. If he wanted to eat lunch early, he could.

The house seemed so quiet, he thought, as he flopped down on the couch with a magazine and a sandwich. As he ate, he turned pages without really looking at them. Playing hooky from work wasn't much fun when there was no one else to share it with.

He laughed at himself. *You sound like an old married man, fella.* An old married man. That wasn't such a bad description, considering whom he was married to. How did that old song go? *Lydia, ho, Lydia . . .* something, something. The Marx Brothers had done it in one of their movies, hadn't they?

Lydia. He'd had some kind of industrial-strength good luck going for him when he'd met her. Everything had just fallen into place— their relationship had progressed to marriage without missing a beat, and their marriage hadn't had anything missing in three and a half years. Companionship, love, sex, and everything in between—it was all there, just the way he might have imagined it. He *had* imagined it a few times, but in an abstract sort of way. There had been no one he would have filled in the woman's part with until Lydia had come into his life.

Not that he was living some kind of fairy tale, though. They had their problems, they argued, and Lydia had the ability to play the bitch just as well as he could be the bastard. But there was nothing seriously wrong, nothing that threatened them. Hell, he didn't even feel funny about her making more money than he did. They were beyond that kind of macho silliness.

David got up and looked out the window at the parking lot. No sign of the cable truck yet. He supposed they would come in a truck with all kinds of equipment, ready to plug him into the wonderful world of pay-TV. He'd had a few misgivings about it when Lydia first suggested they subscribe to the cable. The image of himself and Lydia sitting in front of the TV, slaves of the tube and its programming hadn't been terribly appetizing. As a rule, they weren't much for TV watching. But there was the movie channel, and the idea of being able to watch uncut films at home appealed to him. It would probably make them lazy about getting out to the theaters, but that wouldn't be so bad. During the week they were both tired, and on the weekends they had to fight the crowds—the terminal acne couples, the families with the restless kids and/or squalling babies, and let's not forget the inveterate

43

chatterboxes who seemed to think they were in their living rooms and couldn't refrain from adding their stupid comments at the tops of their lungs. Yeah, cable TV would be worth it if it would spare them that.

At 11 o'clock, when he was already giving thought to having another sandwich, the doorbell rang. "Hallelujah," he muttered and went to answer it.

The small woman smiling up at him on the doorstep had a wildly growing-out permanent and a broad, plain face. There was a length of black cable coiled around one shoulder and she held a bag of tools in her hand. "You Mr. Martel?"

He blinked. "Can I help you?"

"Cable-Rama. I'm here to put in your cable."

David looked past her, saw the truck sitting in their usual parking place. "Oh. Sure. C'mon in."

The woman gave him a big grin, the skin around her eyes crinkling into a thousand deep lines. "Every time." She walked in, looked around, and went immediately to the television. David hesitated.

"Just you?" he asked. "I mean, did they send you out all by yourself?"

"Every time," she said again and dropped her tool bag on the carpet.

"Every time what?" David asked, closing the door.

The woman never stopped grinning, even as she rolled the television on its cart out from the wall and knelt behind it. "Every time they open the door and see the cable guy's a woman, their mouth falls open. Or they blink a lot." She showed her teeth cheerily. "Like you. They can't believe I can do it all alone."

David felt his face grow slightly warm. "That's not it at all. I just— well, these days you know, sending a woman by herself to people's houses is a risky kind of thing. I mean, times being what they are."

The woman detached the rabbit ears and UHF antenna and set them aside. "Yeah? You mean, like if somebody tries something funny or like that?" She picked up a tool David couldn't imagine a use for, a thing that seemed to be a cross between a wrench and a pair of pliers. "Anybody tries something, I adjust their fine tuning. See?" She wiggled her eyebrows. "They said you guys seemed to be okay."

"Oh, we are. but I thought they'd have to send three, four g— people out to do this."

"Oh, yeah. Back in the early days." She kept working on the back of the television set as she spoke, occasionally reaching for a different tool or gadget from her bag. "Now it's easy. Someday the technology's gonna get so good, you'll be able to install this stuff yourself. Just click it onto the back of your set or something." She grimaced at the tip of a Phillip's-head screwdriver and wiped it on her workshirt. "You guys into video games?"

David shook his head.

"Ah. That's good. Video games are shit. Burn your goddam tube out quicker. So do those videotape recorders. But you got a good cable-ready set here, you know that?"

"No."

"Yeah, you do. So you don't have to go unhooking this and hooking it back up again if you get a VCR. Better if you just leave it, unless the set has to go in for servicing."

"I wouldn't know how to remove it anyway."

"S'easy. But best not to fool with it. Play around back here, don't know what you're doing, next thing you know—*zzzzt!* Fried poppa." She raised one eyebrow. "Kids. You got any?"

"Nope."

"Good. I mean, well, you want 'em, you have 'em, I don't care. But if you have any in visiting or anything sometime, don't let them fool with this."

45

"*Zzzzt,*" said David, smiling.

"You got it." She picked up one end of the cable which she had let slide off her shoulder onto the floor and began connecting it to the back of the television. The other end she screwed into a silvery outlet in the wall. Then she got to her feet. "Gonna play outside for a few minutes now. Don't touch anything. Don't turn the set on, okay? I'll try to get this finished up by the time *Donahue* comes on."

"We don't like him," David said. "We think he's insincere."

"Suit yourself. Half the women in this town get cable just so they can see him better. It's all the same to me." Still grinning, she stepped over the tools and let herself out.

All delivery and service people, David decided, had to go to some kind of training camp for vocational-quirkiness lessons. Then again, maybe if he made a living connecting people to *Donahue,* he'd be a character himself. He couldn't wait to tell Lydia about this one. Lydia had thought the two guys who had delivered the washer and dryer had been lunatics.

When the woman hadn't returned for several minutes, he went to the window to check on her. She was standing at the open back of the truck with some kind of meter in her hand. It was attached to a cable that ran out of the truck over the sidewalk and around the side of the house. She seemed to be muttering to herself as she twisted a button or dial on the meter. David raised the window.

"Are you sure you don't need me to turn on the set?" he called.

She looked up at him, startled. "Don't touch it! You *didn't* touch it, did you? Well, don't! Can't take any power right now; you'll blow up all my equipment!"

"Okay. He left the window up and wandered into the kitchen. Was it considered improper to fix yourself something to eat while a service person who was probably dying for lunch herself was still on the premises? Almost certainly. His stomach growled. He snagged a piece of cheese out of the refrigerator and then crammed the whole thing into his mouth as he heard her come back into the house.

"Almost done," she sang. "Few more adjustments, you're ready for the glory of Living Room Cinema. Trademarked."

He went back to the living room, trying to chew inconspicuously. The woman glanced up at him as she connected wires from a small brown box to the back of the set.

"Ah. Lunch. I'm dyin' for lunch. That's what I'm goin' for next, you bet." She pushed her frizz back from her forehead. "Okay. C'mere. I'm gonna show you."

David swallowed the cheese and wiped his hand across his mouth.

"This here on top of the cable selector. S'got two buttons, A and B. One group of stations is on A, the other's on B. A is simple, mostly the local stations. B is complex—satellite stations and movie channel, sports and news networks, that stuff."

"How do I know what channels to turn to?"

"I'll give you a card before I leave, it's got all that stuff on it. And there's a free program guide. Right now, we wanna see how good it comes in, okay? Great. Go for it and turn her on."

David laughed a little and turned on the television. A game show sprang into life on the screen, looking a bit purple.

"Okay. You're on A right now, see? The A button is pushed in. Flip around the dial and let's see everything else."

More game shows, some soap operas and a flurry of commercials flashed on the screen before David returned to the original game show.

"Great picture, huh?" said the woman, tapping his arm lightly with a screwdriver.

"*Purple* picture."

"You can fix that yourself later. Right now we're just interested in your reception. No snow, no rolling. Great. Isn't that great?"

"It's great," David said. Strange how service people always seemed to crave praise for whatever company they represented. "Do *you* have the cable?"

46

The woman's eyes widened as though he had asked her about her sex life. "Do I look like someone who would need the cable? Try the B channels. No, keep your hand on the dial, in case you've got to fine tune."

David opened his mouth to tell her there was no fine tuning connected with the channel selector and decided to humor her. Then perhaps she'd take her quirky little self out of his living room faster. He was beginning to tire of her and her jackrabbity conversational style.

He reached up with his left hand and touched the box on top of the TV set. It was warm and tingly on his fingertips, and he almost snatched his hand back. The woman shifted her weight impatiently, and he thumbed down the B button.

Something hot and sizzling jumped into his left hand and shot up his arm. To his horror, he couldn't let go of the box. The hot, sizzling feeling hit his chest and streaked down his other arm before it began to burn through his torso. His last thought, as he turned his head toward the woman, was that she was reacting awfully nonchalantly to the electrocution of one of her customers.

The woman stood staring at David with her arms folded. The fading expression on his face was typical—shock, panic, maybe a little betrayal. Probably thought he was being electrocuted. She'd heard the final connection was something like that, getting fried. *Zzzzt!* She grinned.

When the last bit of emotion had drained from David's face and his eyes had gone opaque, she produced something that might have been a lecturer's metal pointer form her back pocket and stepped around behind the television again. She did something else to the connections she had made, and the TV screen went dark. David's arms dropped abruptly. The woman punched the A button. "Straighten up," she ordered.

David did so, his head still facing where she had been standing previously. She moved back in front of the TV and twisted the channel selector. David took three steps backwards and bumped into the coffee table.

"Easy there, poppa." She patted her pockets and found the small white card she needed. "Okay. Here we go. Channel 4, right. Channel 5." David held his arms out to his sides as if waiting either to catch someone up in a hug or be crucified. She changed the channel again and he bent forward at the waist.

"Lotta talent there." The woman flipped through the channels, watching closely as David bent forward at the waist, bobbed up again, combed his hair with his fingers, pinched his nose and opened his

47

mouth. "Siddown on the couch. Stand up. Stand on your left foot." David obeyed, his movements smooth and almost graceful. "Okay. Now the B channels. Do your stuff, poppa."

David walked around the room, turned on a lamp and shut it off again, mimed opening a drawer and searching through some files and danced a few shuffling steps.

"Great reception," the woman said. "One more and you're set." She consulted the card and turned to Channel 9. David did a bump and grind, slow and then fast. "Relax. This is only a test." She laughed and switched back to the A button. He stood motionless again, awaiting instructions. "You're doin' great. Siddown."

David collapsed to the floor cross-legged. "Oops. Shoulda told you to sit on the couch. Hell. Just stay there. Gonna take care of momma next. After lunch." She went into the kitchen and found the cheese in the refrigerator. She nibbled at it while she got the peanut butter and a loaf of bread out of the cupboard. As an afterthought, she opened a can of black olives.

48

Lydia Martel was having a carton of strawberry yogurt for lunch at her desk when the phone rang. She dabbed at her lips with a napkin before picking up the receiver.

"Lydia Martel." She paused, sitting back. "Oh, good. Any problems? How's the reception, any static?" She paused again, listening. "Good. Good. Now, how much did you say the installation fee would be? Uh-huh. And the regular monthly charge is what?" She scribbled the figures on a memo pad. "Yes, it *is* reasonable. That includes everything, right?" Lydia laughed a little indulgently. "I *can't* get away before 4:30. — Yes, there *is* something. Put him on vacuum before you leave. He knows where it is, even if he's never touched it. *All* the rooms. After that he can clean up the kitchen, I'm sure he left a mess from lunch. Have him take the chicken out to thaw, I'm positive he forgot.

"And, oh, yes—have him shave, will you? Thanks."

ROADSIDE RESCUE

Michael Swanwick told me he felt used after reading this story. Gardner Dozois calls it "genuinely mean." If I tell my friends I've written a nasty story, they usually ask me if it's as nasty as this one. You'd think I wasn't a nice person or something, mentioning my mean streak, and now this. It's not really a very big mean streak. I wouldn't really hurt anybody. Under normal circumstances.

I was about seven months pregnant when I wrote this, and constantly hungry. But it was too early for lunch, so I was thinking about . . . well, other things. One of the things that crossed my mind was Robert Sheckley's fine and funny "Untouched By Human Hands," which postulates that if one person's meat is another's poison, but you're on an alien planet where both meat and poison are your poison, you have to eat . . . well, other things. And I was thinking at the time that it must work in reverse. For other things, too.

ROADSIDE RESCUE

*B*arely fifteen minutes after he'd called Area Traffic Surveillance, Etan Carrera saw the big limousine transport coming toward him. He watched it with mild interest from his smaller and temporarily disabled vehicle. Some media celebrity or alien—more likely an alien. All aliens seemed enamored with things like limos and private SSTs, even after all these years. In any case, Etan fully expected to see the transport pass without even slowing, the navigator (not driver—limos drove themselves) hardly glancing his way, leaving him alone again in the rolling, green, empty countryside.

But the transport did slow and then stopped, cramming itself into the breakdown lane across the road. The door slid up, and the navigator jumped out, smiling as he came over to Etan. Etan blinked at the dark, full-dress uniform. People who worked for aliens had to do some odd things, he thought, and for some reason put his hand on the window control as though he were going to roll it up.

"Afternoon, sir," said the navigator, bending a little from the waist.

"Hi," Etan said.

"Trouble with your vehicle?"

"Nothing too serious, I hope. I've called Surveillance, and they say they'll be out to pick me up in two hours at most."

"That's a long time to wait." The navigator's smile widened. He was very attractive, holo-star kind of handsome. *People who work for aliens,* Etan thought. "Perhaps you'd care to wait in my employer's transport. For that matter, I can probably repair your vehicle, which will save you time and money. Roadside rescue fees are exorbitant."

"That's very kind," Etan said, "but I *have* called, and I don't want to impose—"

"It was my employer's idea to stop, sir. I agreed, of course. My employer is quite fond of people. In fact, my employer loves people. And I'm sure you would be rewarded in some way."

"Hey, now, I'm not asking for anything—"

"My employer is a most generous entity," said the navigator, looking down briefly. "I'll get my tool kit." He was on his way back across the road before Etan could object.

Ten minutes later, the navigator closed the power plant housing of Etan's vehicle and came around to the window again, still looking formal and unruffled. "Try it now, sir."

Etan inserted his key card into the dash console and shifted the control near the steering module. The vehicle hummed to life. "Well, now," he said. "You fixed it."

That smile again. "Occasionally the connections to the motherboard are improperly fitted. Contaminants get in, throw off the fuel mixing, and the whole plant shuts down."

"Oh," Etan said, feeling stupid, incompetent, and worst of all, obligated.

"You won't be needing rescue now, sir."

"Well. I should call and tell them." Etan reached reluctantly for the console phone.

"You could call from the limo, sir. And if you'd care for a little refreshment—" The navigator opened his door for him.

Etan gave up. "Oh, sure, sure. This is all very nice of you and your, uh, employer." What the hell, he thought, getting out and following the navigator across the road. If it meant that much to the alien, he'd give the alien a thrill.

"We both appreciate this. My employer and I."

Etan smiled, bracing himself as the door to the passenger compartment of the limo slid back. Whatever awkward greeting he might have made died in his throat. There was no one inside, no one and nothing.

"Just go ahead and get in, sir."

"But, uh—"

"My employer is in there. Somewhere." Smile. "You'll find the phone by the refrigerator. Or shall I call Surveillance for you?"

"No, I'll do it. Uh, thanks." Etan climbed in and sat down on the silvery grey cushion. The door slid partially shut, and a moment later Etan heard the navigator moving around up front. Somewhere a blower went on, puffing cool, humid air at his face. He sat back tentatively. Luxury surroundings—refrigerator, bar, video, sound system. God knew what use the alien found for any of it. Hospitality. It probably wouldn't help. He and the alien would no doubt end up staring at each other with nothing to say, feeling freakish.

He was on the verge of getting up and leaving when the navigator slipped through the door. It shut silently as he sat down across from Etan and unbuttoned his uniform tunic.

"Cold drink, sir?"

Etan shook his head.

"Hope you don't mind if I do." There was a different quality to the smile now. He took an amber bottle from the refrigerator and flipped the cap off, aiming it at a disposal in the door. Etan could smell alcohol and heavy spicing. "Possibly the best spiced ale in the world, if not the known universe," the navigator said. "Sure you won't have any?"

"Yes, I—" Etan sat forward a little. "I really think I ought to say thank you and get on. I don't want to hold you up—"

"My employer chooses where he wants to be when he wants to be there." The navigator took another drink from the bottle. "At least, I'm calling it a he. Hard to tell with a lot of these species." He ran his fingers through his dark hair; one long strand fell and brushed his temple. Etan caught a glimpse of a shaved spot. Implant; so the navigator would be mentally attuned to his employer, making speech or translation unnecessary. "With some, gender's irrelevant. Some have more than one gender. Some have more than *two*. Imagine taking *that* trip, if you can." He tilted the bottle up again. "But my present employer, here, asking him what gender he is, it's like asking you what flavor you are."

Etan took a breath. One more minute; then he'd ask this goof to let him out. "Not much you can do, I guess, except to arbitrarily assign them sex and—"

"Didn't say *that*."

"Pardon?"

The navigator killed the bottle. "Didn't say anything about sex."

"Oh." Etan paused, wondering exactly how crazy the navigator might be and how he'd managed to hide it well enough to be hired for an alien. "Sorry. I thought you said that some of them lacked sex—"

"Never said anything about sex. Gender, I said. Nothing about sex."

"But the terms can be interchangeable."

"Certainly *not*." The navigator tossed the bottle into the disposal and took another from the refrigerator. "Maybe on this planet but not out there."

Etan shrugged. "I assumed you'd need gender for sex, so if a species lacked gender, they'd uh . . ." He trailed off, making a firm resolution to shut up until he could escape. Suddenly he was very glad he hadn't canceled his rescue after all.

"Our nature isn't universal law," said the navigator. "Out there—" He broke off, staring at something to Etan's left. "Ah. My employer has decided to come out at last."

The small creature at the end of the seat might have coalesced out of the humid semidark, an off-white mound of what seemed to be fur as close and dense as a seal's. It would have repelled or disconcerted him except that it smelled so *good,* like a cross between fresh-baked bread and wildflowers. The aroma filled Etan with a sudden, intense feeling of well-being. Without thinking, he reached out to touch it, realized, and pulled his hand back.

53

"Going to pet it, were you? Stroke it?"

"Sorry," Etan said, half to the navigator and half to the creature.

"I forgive you," said the navigator, amused. "He'd forgive you, too, except he doesn't feel you've done anything wrong. It's the smell. Very compelling." He sniffed. "Go ahead. You won't hurt him."

Etan leaned over and gingerly touched the top of the creature. The contact made him jump. It didn't feel solid. It was like touching gelatin with a fur covering.

"Likes to stuff itself into the cushions and feel the vibrations from the ride," said the navigator. "But what it *really* loves is talk. Conversation. Sound waves created by the human voice are especially pleasing to it. And in *person,* not by holo or phone." The navigator gave a short, mirthless laugh and killed the second bottle. "So. Come on. Talk it up. That's what you're here for."

"Sorry," Etan said defensively. "I don't know exactly what to say."

"Express your goddamn *gratitude* for it having me fix your vehicle."

Etan opened his mouth to make an angry response and decided not to. For all he knew, both alien and human were insane and dangerous besides. "Yes. Of course I do appreciate your help. It was so kind of you, and I'm saving a lot of money since I don't need a roadside rescue now—"

"Never called it off, did you?"

"What?"

"The rescue. You never called to tell Surveillance you didn't need help."

Etan swallowed. "Yes. I did."

"Liar."

All right, Etan thought. *Enough is too much.* "I don't know what transport services you work for, but I'll find out. They ought to know about you."

"Yeah? What should they know—that I make free repairs at the bidding of an alien hairball?" The navigator grinned bitterly.

"No." Etan's voice was quiet. "They should know that maybe you've been working too long and too hard for aliens." His eyes swiveled apologetically to the creature. "Not that I mean to offend—"

"Forget it. It doesn't understand a goddamn word."

"Then why did you want me to talk to it?"

"Because *I* understand. We're attuned. On several frequencies, mind you, one for every glorious mood it might have. Not that it's any of your business."

Etan shook his head. "You need help."

"Fuck if I do. Now finish your thanks and start thinking up some more things to say."

The bread-and-flowers aroma intensified until Etan's nerves were standing on end. His heart pounded ferociously, and he wondered if a smell could induce cardiac arrest.

"I think I've finished thanking your employer." He looked directly at the creature. "And that's all I have to say. Under more pleasant circumstances, I might have talked my head off. Sorry." He started to get up.

The navigator moved quickly for someone who was supposed to be drunk. Etan found himself pinned against the back of the seat before he realized that the man wasn't jumping up to open the door. For a moment, he stared into the navigator's flushed face, not quite believing.

"Talk," the navigator said softly, almost gently. "Just talk. That's all you've got to do."

Etan tried heaving himself upward to throw them both off the seat and onto the floor, but the navigator had him too securely. "Help!" he bellowed. "Somebody help me!"

"Okay, yell for help. That's good, too," said the navigator, smiling. They began to slide down on the seat together with Etan on the bottom. "Go ahead. Yell all you want."

"Let me up and I won't report you."

"I'm sure I can believe *that.*" The navigator laughed. "Tell us a whole fairy story now."

"Let me go or I swear to Christ I'll kill you and that furry shit you work for."

"What?" the navigator asked, leaning on him a little harder. "What was that, *sir?*"

"Let me go or I'll *fucking kill you!*"

Something in the air seemed to break, as though a circuit had been completed or some sort of energy discharged. Etan sniffed. The bread-and-flowers aroma had changed, more flowers, less bread, and much weaker, dissipating in the ventilation before he could get more than a whiff.

The navigator pushed himself off Etan and plumped down heavily on the seat across from him again. Etan held still, looking first at the man rubbing his face with both hands and then turning his head so he could see the creature sliding down behind the cushion. *We scared it,* he thought, horrified. *Bad enough to make it hide under the seat.*

"Sir."

Etan jumped. The navigator was holding a fistful of currency out to him. The denominations made him blink.

"It's yours, sir. Take it. You can go now."

Etan pulled himself up. "What the hell do you mean, it's mine?"

"Please, sir." The navigator pressed one hand over his left eye. "If you're going to talk anymore, please step outside."

"Step outs—" Etan slapped the man's hand away and lunged for the door.

"Wait!" called the navigator, and in spite of everything, Etan obeyed. The navigator climbed out of the transport clumsily, still covering his eye, the other hand offering the currency. "Please, sir. You haven't been hurt. You have a repaired vehicle, more than a little pocket money here—you've come out ahead if you think about it."

Etan laughed weakly. "I can't believe this."

"Just take the money, sir. My employer wants you to have it." The navigator winced and massaged his eye some more. "Purely psychosomatic," he said, as though Etan had asked. "The implant is painless and causes no damage, no matter how intense the exchange between species. But please lower your voice, sir. My employer can still feel your sound, and he's quite done with you."

"What is that supposed to mean?"

"The money is yours from my employer," the navigator said patiently. "My employer loves people. We discussed that earlier. *Loves* them. Especially their voices."

"So?" Etan crossed his arms. The navigator leaned over and stuffed the money between Etan's forearms.

"Perhaps you remember what else we were discussing. I really have no wish to remind you, sir."

"So? What's all that stuff about gender—what's that got to do with . . ." Etan's voice died away.

"Human voices," the navigator said. "No speech where they come from. And we're so new and different to them. This one's been here only a few weeks. Its preference happens to be that of a man speaking from fear and anger, something you can't fake."

Etan took a step back from the man, unfolding his arms and letting the money fall to the ground, thinking of the implant, the man feeling whatever the creature felt.

"I don't know if you could call it perversion or not," said the navigator. "Maybe there's no such thing." He looked down at the bills. "Might as well keep it. You earned it. You even did well." He pulled himself erect and made a small, formal bow. "Good day, sir," he said, with no mockery at all and climbed into the transport's front seat. Etan watched the limo roll out of the breakdown lane and lumber away from him.

56   After a while, he looked down. The money was still there at his feet, so he picked it up.

Just as he was getting back into his own vehicle, the console phone chimed. "We've got an early opening in our patrol pattern," Surveillance told him, "so we can swing by and get you in ten minutes."

"Don't bother," Etan said.

"Repeat?"

"I said, you're too late."

"Repeat again, please."

Etan sighed. "There isn't anything to rescue me from anymore."

There was a brief silence on the other end. "Did you get your vehicle overhauled?"

"Yeah," Etan said. "That, too."

INTRODUCTION TO
ROCK ON

Sometimes when I've got nothing better to do, or even when I have, I wonder why it took us so long to come up with MTV. We were ready for it by 1967, but it didn't go on the air for something like fourteen years.

Of course, 1967 was part of the Psychedelic Era. A lot of us ingested certain things, put on the headphones, and watched abstract video on the ceiling. Later on, a lot of us took to discos, where the atmosphere was conducive to acting out dance fantasies—i.e., video. By 1981, the party was over—it was time for Just Say No and thirtysomething angst about being grown-up, and we consigned the video to TV, where it can't get loose and get into any trouble.

Yet.

I'm waiting for the circle to close, myself.

ROCK ON

*R*ain woke me. I thought, shit, here I am, Lady Rain-in-the-Face, because that's where it was hitting, right in the old face. Sat up and saw I was still on Newbury Street. See beautiful downtown Boston. Was Newbury Street downtown? In the middle of the night, did it matter? No, it did not. And not a soul in sight. Like everybody said, let's get Gina drunk and while she's passed out, we'll all move to Vermont. Do I love New England? A great place to live, but you wouldn't want to visit here.

I smeared my hair out of my eyes and wondered if anyone was looking for me now. Hey, anybody shy a forty-year-old rock'n'roll sinner?

I scuttled into the doorway of one of those quaint old buildings where there was a shop with the entrance below ground level. A little awning kept the rain off but pissed water down in a maddening beat. Wrung the water out of my wrap pants and my hair and just sat being damp. Cold, too, I guess, but didn't feel that so much.

Sat a long time with my chin on my knees; you know, it made me feel like a kid again. When I started nodding my head, I began to pick up on something. Just primal but I tap into that amazing well. Man-O-War, if you could see me now. By the time the blueboys found me, I was rocking pretty good.

And that was the punchline. I'd never tried to get up and leave, but if I had, I'd have found I was locked into place in a sticky field. Made to catch the b&e kids in the act until the blueboys could get around to coming out and getting them. I'd been sitting in a trap and digging it. The story of my life.

They were nice to me. Led me, read me, dried me out. Fined me a hundred, sent me on my way in time for breakfast.

Awful time to see and be seen, righteous awful. For the first three hours after you get up, people can tell whether you've got a broken heart or not. The solution is, either you get up *real* early so your camouflage is in place by the time everybody else is out, or you don't go to bed. Don't go to bed ought to work all the time, but it doesn't. Sometimes when you don't go to bed, people can see whether you've got a broken heart all day long. I schlepped it, searching for an un-crowded breakfast bar and not looking at anyone who was looking at me. But I had this urge to stop random pedestrians and say, Yeah, yeah, it's true, but it was rock'n'roll broke my poor old heart, not a person, don't cry for me or I'll pop your chocks.

I went around and up and down and all over until I found Tremont Street. It had been the pounder with that group from the Detroit Crater — the name was gone but the malady lingered on — anyway, him, he'd been the one told me Tremont had the best breakfast bars in the world, especially when you were coming off a bottle drunk you couldn't remember.

When the c'muters cleared out some, I found a space at a Greek hole-in-the-wall. We shut down 10:30 A.M. sharp, get the hell out when you're done, counter service only, take it or shake it. I like a place with Attitude. I folded a seat down and asked for coffee and a feta cheese omelet. Came with home fries from the home fries mountain in a corner of the grill (no microwave *gar-bazhe,* hoo-ray). They shot my retinas before they even brought my coffee, and while I was pour-ing the cream, they checked my credit. Was that badass? It was badass. Did I care? I did not. No waste, no machines when a human could do it, and real food, none of this edible polyester that slips clear through you so you can stay looking like a famine victim, my deah.

They came in when I was half finished with the omelet. Went all night by the look and sound of them, but I didn't check their faces for broken hearts. Made me nervous but I thought, well, they're tired; who's going to notice this old lady? Nobody.

Wrong again. I became visible to them right after they got their retinas shot. Seventeen-year-old boy with tattooed cheeks and a forked tongue leaned forward and hissed like a snake.

"Ssssssssinner."

The other four with him perked right up. "Where?" "Whose?" "In here?"

"Rock'n'roll sssssssinner."

The lady identified me. She bore much resemblance to nobody at all, and if she had a heart it wasn't even sprained a little. With a sinner, she was probably Madame Magnifica. "Gina," she said, with all confidence.

My left eye tic'ed. Oh, please. Feta cheese on my knees. What the hell, I thought, I'll nod, they'll nod, I'll eat, I'll go. And then somebody whispered the word, *reward.*

I dropped my fork and ran.

Safe enough, I figured. Were they all going to chase me before they got their Greek breakfasts? No, they were not. They sent the lady after me.

She was much the younger, and she tackled me in the middle of a crosswalk when the light changed. A car hopped over us, its undercarriage just ruffling the top of her hard copper hair.

"Just come back and finish your omelet. Or we'll buy you another."

"No."

She yanked me up and pulled me out of the street. "Come on." People were staring but Tremont's full of theaters. You see that here, live theater; you can still get it. She put a bring-along on my wrist and brought me along, back to the breakfast bar, where they'd sold the rest of my omelet at a discount to a bum. The lady and her group made room for me among themselves and brought me another cup of coffee.

"How can you eat and drink with a forked tongue?" I asked Tattooed Cheeks. He showed me. A little appliance underneath, like a *zipper.* The Featherweight to the left of the big boy on the lady's other side leaned over and frowned at me.

"Give us one good reason why we shouldn't turn you in for Man-O-War's reward."

I shook my head. "I'm through. This sinner's been absolved."

"You're legally bound by contract," said the lady. "But we could c'noodle something. Buy Man-O-War out, sue on your behalf for nonfulfillment. We're Misbegotten. Oley." She pointed at herself. "Pidge." That was the silent type next to her. "Percy." The big boy. "Krait." Mr. Tongue. "Gus." Featherweight. "We'll take care of you."

I shook my head again. "If you're going to turn me in, turn me in and collect. The credit ought to buy you the best sinner ever there was."

"We can be good to you."

"I don't have it anymore. It's gone. All my rock'n'roll sins have been forgiven."

"Untrue," said the big boy. Automatically, I started to picture on him and shut it down hard. "Man-O-War would have thrown you out if it were gone. You wouldn't have to run."

"I didn't want to tell him. Leave me alone. I just want to go and sin no more, see? Play with yourselves, I'm not helping." I grabbed the counter with both hands and held on. So what were they going to do, pop me one and carry me off?

As a matter of fact, they did.

In the beginning, I thought, and the echo effect was stupendous. *In the beginning . . . the beginning . . . the beginning . . .*

In the beginning, the sinner was not human. I know because I'm old enough to remember.

They were all there, little more than phantoms. Misbegotten. Where do they get those names? I'm old enough to remember. Oingo-Boingo and Bow-Wow-Wow. Forty, did I say? Oooh, just a little past, a little close to a lot. Old rockers never die, they just keep rocking on. I never saw The Who; Moon was dead before I was born. But I remember, barely old enough to stand, rocking in my mother's arms while thousands screamed and clapped and danced in their seats. *Start me up . . . if you start me up, I'll never stop . . .* 763 Strings did a rendition for elevator and dentist's office, I remember that, too. And that wasn't the worst of it.

They hung on the memories, pulling more from me, turning me inside out. *Are you experienced?* Only a record of my father's, because he'd died too, before my parents even met, and nobody else ever dared ask that question. *Are you experienced? . . . Well, I am.*

(Well, *I* am.)

Five against one and I couldn't push them away. Only, can you call it rape when you know you're going to like it? Well, if I couldn't get away, then I'd give them the ride of their lives. *Jerkin' Crocus didn't kill me but she sure came near . . .*

The big boy faded in first, big and wild and too much badass to him. I reached out, held him tight, showing him. The beat from the night in the rain, I gave it to him, fed it to his heart and made him

61

live it. Then came the lady, putting down the bass theme. She jittered, but mostly in the right places.

Now the Krait, and he was slithering around the sound, in and out. Never mind the tattooed cheeks, he wasn't just flash for the fools. He knew; you wouldn't have thought it, but he knew.

Featherweight and the silent type, melody and first harmony. Bad. Featherweight was a disaster, didn't know where to go or what to do when he got there, but he was pitching ahead like the *S.S. Suicide*.

Christ. If they had to rape me, couldn't they have provided someone upright? The other four kept on, refusing to lose it, and I would have to make the best of it for all of us. Derivative, unoriginal— Featherweight did not rock. It was a crime, but all I could do was take them and shake them. Rock gods in the hands of an angry sinner.

They were never better. Small change getting a glimpse of what it was like to be big bucks. Hadn't been for Featherweight, they might have gotten all the way there. More groups now than ever there was, all of them sure that if they just got the right sinner with them, they'd rock the moon down out of the sky.

We maybe vibrated it a little before we were done. Poor old Featherweight.

I gave them better than they deserved, and they knew that, too. So when I begged out, they showed me respect at last and went. Their techies were gentle with me, taking the plugs from my head, my poor old throbbing abused brokenhearted sinning head, and covered up the sockets. I had to sleep and they let me. I heard the man say, "That's a take, righteously. We'll rush it into distribution. Where in *hell* did you find that sinner?"

"Synthesizer," I muttered, already alseep. "The actual word, my boy, is synthesizer."

Crazy old dreams. I was back with Man-O-War in the big CA, leaving him again, and it was mostly as it happened, but you know dreams. His living room was half outdoors, half indoors, the walls all busted out. You know dreams; I didn't think it was strange.

Man-O-War was mostly undressed, like he'd forgotten to finish. Oh, that *never* happened. Man-O-War forget a sequin or a bead? He loved to act it out, just like the Krait.

"No more," I was saying, and he was saying, "But you don't know anything else, you shitting?" Nobody in the big CA kids, they all shit; loose juice.

"Your contract goes another two and I get the option, I always get the option. And you love it, Gina, you know that, you're no good without it."

And then it was flashback time and I was in the pod with all my sockets plugged, rocking Man-O-War through the wires, giving him the meat and bone that made him Man-O-War and the machines picking it up, sound and vision, so all the tube babies all around the world could play it on their screens whenever they wanted. Forget the road, forget the shows, too much trouble, and it wasn't like the tapes, not as exciting, even with the biggest FX, lasers, spaceships, explosions, no good. And the tapes weren't as good as the stuff in the head, rock'n'roll visions straight from the brain. No hours of setup and hours more doctoring in the lab. But you had to get everyone in the group dreaming the same way. You needed a synthesis, and for that you got a synthesizer, not the old kind, the musical instrument, but something— somebody—to channel your group through, to bump up their tube-fed little souls, to rock them and roll them the way they couldn't do themselves. And anyone could be a rock'n'roll hero then. Anyone!

In the end, they didn't have to play instruments unless they really wanted to, and why bother? Let the synthesizer take their imaginings and boost them up to Mount Olympus.

Synthesizer. Synner. Sinner.

Not just anyone can do that, sin for rock'n'roll. I can.

But it's not the same as jumping all night to some bar band nobody knows yet. . . . Man-O-War and his blown-out living room came back and he said, "You rocked the walls right out of my house. I'll never let you go."

And I said, "I'm gone."

Then I was out, going fast at first because I thought he'd be hot behind me. But I must have lost him and then somebody grabbed my ankle.

Featherweight had a tray, he was Mr. Nursie-Angel-of-Mercy. Nudged the foot of the bed with his knee, and it sat me up slow. She rises from the grave, you can't keep a good sinner down.

"Here." He set the tray over my lap, pulled up a chair. Some kind of thick soup in a bowl he'd given me, with veg wafers to break up and put in. "Thought you'd want something soft and easy." He put his left foot up on his right leg and had a good look at it. "I *never* been rocked like that before."

"You don't have it, no matter who rocks you ever in this world. Cut and run, go into management. The *big* Big Money's in management."

He snacked on his thumbnail. "Can you always tell?"

"If the Stones came back tomorrow, you couldn't even tap your toes."

"What if you took my place?"

"I'm a sinner, not a clown. You can't sin and do the dance. It's been tried."

"*You* could do it. If anyone could."

"No."

His stringy cornsilk fell over his face and he tossed it back. "Eat your soup. They want to go again shortly."

"No." I touched my lower lip, thickened to sausage-size. "I won't sin for Man-O-War and I won't sin for you. You want to pop me one again, go to. Shake a socket loose, most likely, give me aphasia."

So he left and came back with a whole bunch of them, techies and do-kids, and they poured the soup down my throat and gave me a poke and carried me out to the pod so I could make Misbegotten this year's firestorm.

I knew as soon as the first tape got out, Man-O-War would pick up the scent. They were already starting the machine to get me away from him. And they kept me good in the room—where their old sinner had done penance, the lady told me. Their sinner came to see me, too. I thought, poison dripping from his fangs, death threats. But he was just a guy about my age with a lot of hair to hide his sockets (I never bothered, didn't care if they showed). Just came to pay his respects, how'd I ever learn to rock the way I did?

Fool.

They kept me good in the room. Drunks when I wanted them and a poke to get sober again, a poke for vitamins, a poke to lose the bad dreams. Poke, poke, pig in a poke. I had tracks like the old B&O, and they didn't even know what I meant by that. They lost Featherweight, got themselves someone a little more righteous, sixteen-year-old snipe girl with a face like a praying mantis. But she rocked and they rocked and we all rocked until Man-O-War came to take me home.

Strutted into my room in full plumage with his hair all fanned out (hiding the sockets) and said, "Did you want to press charges, Gina, darling?"

Well, they fought it out over my bed. Misbegotten said I was theirs now; Man-O-War smiled and said, "Yeah, and I bought *you*. You're *all* mine now, you *and* your sinner. *My* sinner." That was truth. Man-O-War had his conglomerate start to buy Misbegotten right after the first tape came out. Deal all done by the time we'd finished the third one, and they never knew. Conglomerates buy and sell all the time. Everybody was in trouble but Man-O-War. And me, he said. He made them all leave and sat down on my bed to re-lay claim to me.

"Gina." Ever see honey poured over the edge of a sawtooth blade? Ever hear it? He couldn't sing without hurting someone bad and he couldn't dance, but inside, he rocked. If I rocked him.

"I don't want to be a sinner, not for you or anyone."

"It'll all look different when I get you back to Cee-Ay."

"I want to go to a cheesy bar and boogie my brains till they leak out the sockets."

"No more, darling. That was why you came here, wasn't it? But all the bars are gone and all the bands. Last call was years ago; it's all up here now. All up here." He tapped his temple. "You're an old lady, no matter how much I spend keeping your bod young. And don't I give you everything? And didn't you say I had it?"

"It's not the same. It wasn't meant to be put on a tube for people to *watch*."

"But it's not as though rock'n'roll is dead, lover."

"You're killing it."

"Not me. You're trying to bury it alive. But I'll keep you going for a long, long time."

"I'll get away again. You'll either rock'n'roll on your own or you'll give it up, but you won't be taking it out of me any more. This ain't my way, it ain't my time. Like the man said, 'I don't live today.'"

Man-O-War grinned. "And like the other man said, 'Rock'n'roll never forgets.'"

He called in his do-kids and took me home.

65

INTRODUCTION TO
HEAL

Before Jim and Tammy fell, before Jimmy S. cried on TV, Ellen Datlow was pulling together one of the *Omni* fiction features she has become famous for, five or six short-shorts commissioned around a theme. Fictionettes, as it were. The theme I wrote "Heal" for was *A Handful Of Horror.*

Around our house, if we want someone to get up and do something, we yell, "I *know* you can *walk without that chair!*" That's not mean. You know what's mean? Yelling that at someone who can't, especially when the person doing the yelling claims to have the power to . . .

HEAL

"*I*N THE NAME OF JESUS!" the Reverend Jesse Rapture screamed and slapped his open palm down on the woman's forehead. The crowd in the tent roared as she spasmed in her wheelchair.

Rapture began running both hands over the woman's pathetic, twisted body. "God-Jesus-Jesus-oh-Christ, help me, help me rebuke this vile sickness, Jesus, Jesus, I cast it out, CAST IT OUT!"

The uniformed nurse who had come to the platform with the woman turned away, obviously repelled, as he straightened the clawed fingers, the arms, the shoulders, working his way down the rest of her body. "Jesus-Jesus-Jesus-GOD-LORD-CHRIST-ALMIGHTY!" he finished and stepped back to the other end of the platform.

"Now, daughter, I KNOW you can WALK without THAT CHAIR!"

The woman looked at her hands incredulously. "Praise Jesus!"

The crowd took it up as a chant. "Praise Jesus! Praise *Jesus!*"

"I COMMAND you to GET UP and WALK WITHOUT THAT CHAIR!"

"Praise Jesus and *walk without that chair!*" the crowd roared over and over, until it seemed as though the combined force of their voices lifted the woman out of the wheelchair and sent her hobbling across the platform to collapse, sobbing, in Rapture's arms.

* * *

Counting the take back at the motel was Rapture's favorite part, but, as usual, a quarrel broke out between Kitty and Sylvia as to who should play the cripple at their next gig. Kitty was the better contortionist, there was no doubt about that, but Sylvia looked the part, thin as a stick no matter how much she ate.

Tonight he was too tired to go through any of that again and he directed his assistant Martin to get them out of his sight. "Buy them something to eat. Go to a drive-in and stay in the car. And bring me back something, while you're at it." He knew Martin didn't really like the idea of leaving him to count the take alone, but Martin could lump it. They were all expendable, even Martin, and they all knew it.

Ten minutes after they'd left, there was a light tapping at the motel room door. Rapture folded the coverlet around the cash he'd been sorting on the bed and strode across the room to jerk the door open. "Dammit, I thought I *told* you—"

"Reverend Rapture?" The woman standing outside was tall and well-built, especially in the places that counted. Plain in the face, but Rapture wasn't too fussy about faces. "I was in the tent tonight and I saw what you did. I've been traveling all over the state to every tent revival I could find and now I know you're the man I've been looking for."

"I remember you, daughter," he lied. "What is it that you need my spiritual help with?"

She stepped inside and looked around. "Are you alone?"

"I was just making my devotions to Jesus, yes." He glanced at the bed a little nervously. He'd have to get her good and worked up so she wouldn't hear the coins clink when he took the coverlet off. Or maybe she'd settle for the floor. Plenty of them did.

"My husband has need of your healing powers."

A small warning bell went off in Rapture's mind. Husbands could be problems. "Daughter, I'm awfully tired this night—"

"I have great faith. And two hundred dollars."

"That *is* great faith," Rapture said, thinking of how the others would never have to know. "But we will have to pray an almighty prayer together—"

"I'll do anything." Her breathing quickened with desperation and Rapture realized that in spite of her composure, she was having a hard time containing herself.

"I don't know what Jesus may ask of you, daughter—"

"Whatever he wants, he can have. Just heal my husband."

"*If* your faith is great enough, it will be done."

"I'll get him. He's in the truck." She darted out. Rapture hurried to move the coverlet from the bed to the small round table near the window. He should have asked what was wrong with the man, he thought, so he would know what lies to tell and how to maneuver them. Oh, well, if nothing else, he'd end up with two hundred extra dollars and that was nothing to sneer at.

"Reverend!" She was standing in the doorway again with a wheel-chair in front of her. "My husband. Jim. Heal him."

Rapture never heard her. The plastic-wrapped thing in the wheel-chair was past healing by—well, there was no telling. Weeks, maybe even months. She had done something to the body, coated it with something to slow the deterioration so that the bullethole over the left eye socket was still fairly obvious. There were strange round things stuck all over the plastic which Rapture realized, to his horror, were deodorizers.

"It was an accident," the woman said. "I didn't mean to shoot him. Just that painted-up whore he was with." She kicked the door shut behind her and rolled the chair into the room near the foot of the bed. "Just heal him. You don't have to worry about *her.*"

"Oh, Jesus—" he moaned, backing away.

"Yes. Jesus. Go on. He was a son-of-a-bitchin', no-good lyin' tom-cat, but I know you'll heal him of that, too." She knelt down next to the wheelchair.

"God-Jesus-Jesus-oh-*Christ!*" Rapture yelled and the woman repeated it, word for word, lifting her arms to heaven.

"Yes? Yes?" she said to Rapture. "Pray more! Oh, Jim!" She embraced the corpse, jerking a fresh howl from Rapture. "Jim, I know you'll rise, I know it! And we'll make a new start, I forgive you for what you did with that bitch." The corpse's head, protruding from the plastic wrapping, dropped bonelessly to one side, tearing the rotted flesh. The ghastly odor hit Rapture full in the face for the first time, making him gag.

"Noooo! *Noooo!*" he howled. "Get him out, *get him out!*"

The woman got up and ran to him, seizing his arms. "Lay your hands on him now, make him rise!"

"Oh, Jesus, help me, HELP ME, no, DON'T!" he screamed. The woman was amazingly strong, far stronger than he was in his hysteria. She actually managed to drag him, struggling and twisting, over to the corpse. The cocked head stared at him eyelessly.

"Say it now!" She gave him a mighty shove and he landed on the dead man with a hopeless scream, feeling the rot under the plastic squash at the contact. "Say, 'I know you can walk without that chair,' say it!"

Rapture scrambled onto the bed, wiping desperately at himself. "Get him out, *get him out of here, Jesus, help, God, police, SOME-BODY!"*

The woman stared hard at him as he pushed himself against the wall, babbling.

"Hey, wait a minute, here. You're not laying your hands on him!"

"You're goddam right I'm not!" Rapture panted hoarsely. "I'm not touching that thing, now you get out, get-out-GET-OUT!"

The woman's eyes narrowed. "You can't heal?"

"No, no, I can't heal, I can't, I can't—"

She reached under the plastic and came up with a gun. A bit of something rotten was stuck to the barrel.

"No, wait, what are you *doing?"* Rapture screamed.

"You son-of-a-bitchin', no-good—" She climbed onto the bed and came at him. "Drive all over this state with him in the back of the truck, I came two hundred miles from the last one, *two hundred miles,* and what do I find," she said angrily, shoving the pistol under his chin. *"Another* fucking fake."

And she pulled the trigger.

70

ANOTHER ONE HITS THE ROAD

I don't run, trot, jog, or anything like it. This is what I told Ed Ferman when I sold him this story for *The Magazine of Fantasy and Science Fiction.* It's not quite true any more—I've since acquired a bundle of self-winding energy known as my son, whom I have to chase around after frequently. But run a marathon? Forget about it.

Well, this doesn't deal with exercise, but with obsession and contagion, a two-headed concept that happened to connect up with a painting I saw by the marvelous Don Ivan Punchatz, of a runner being pursued by his double—except the double is obviously satanic. My description does this visual experience no justice; you have to be there. Thanks, Don.

A few years after this story appeared, Jerry Pournelle took me aside at a party and said, "You know that story you wrote about all those people running? That's the dumbest, silliest premise for a story I've ever heard of—but I can't get that damned story out of my head."

High praise from a writer I respect, and my point exactly.

ANOTHER ONE HITS THE ROAD

"*L*emmings would be the obvious comparison," said my father, looking down his nose at his coffee cup. "But it's not true about them drowning themselves. They don't make a suicide march to the sea. I think it's closer to medieval dancing mania."

"Bushwa," said my mother without lowering her newspaper. "And what do you know about medieval dancing mania, anyway?"

"Not much, really, except that bands of people would come dancing through villages in Europe and somehow the dancing was contagious. The villagers would join in and dance themselves to exhaustion. Sometimes even death."

Behind the newspaper, my mother sniffed. "Well, there's only one thing wrong with that theory, Zeke." Zeke was not my father's name. It was what my mother called anyone she thought was trying to swim in the shallow end. "Nobody's dying. And nobody seems to be exhausted, either. So how about that?"

My father shrugged. "A miracle."

They didn't ask me for my opinion. As a divorced woman temporarily returned to the nest, I was relegated to seen-and-not heard status during their conversations at table. My parents had never given a fig for Dr. Spock or Montessori. I ate my waffle slowly, listening with my mind in neutral.

"Miracles don't grow on trees," said my mother. "And only God can make a miracle."

"It's all a miracle." My father sat back and stared into space. Sunlight coming in through the window over the sink sliced across the top of his bald head, giving him a bright, slightly lopsided skullcap. "Breathing. Living. Black holes. All creation. It's all one miracle after another. So why not this miracle, too?"

"Because all the other miracles ought to be enough for anyone."

"And it's funny that this time it's Running and not dancing. I don't find that reassuring at all." He looked at me, just to show he knew I was still there. I was going to have to be out by the end of the week.

My mother deigned to lower her newspaper a few inches. "I don't think they're Running to reassure you or anyone else. Damned selfish of them, carrying this fitness thing to such an extreme. You know, they're already talking shortages in the East."

"Shortages?" My father sat up, leaning his arms on the table. "What kind of shortages?"

"Food. And clothing. Especially running shoes. Electricity. And services like trash removal."

"There's an electricity shortage?" My father's voice was sour with skepticism.

"Well, power outages, blackouts and brownouts in some areas."

My father frowned deeply. "This is going to get bad."

I wanted to laugh at the idea of an Adidas shortage. Instead, I dragged the last fragment of my waffle through the maple syrup, put my plate in the sink, and went out for a ride on my bike.

"They'll be here in a couple of days," my mother was saying as I was going out the back door.

I never thought of riding a bike just for the sake of exercise. I rode whenever I felt the need of motion. In the six weeks before I'd left Marv, I must have done over two hundred miles. Of course, I reasoned; I'd been traveling away from him symbolically and I'd been riding around in circles, also symbolically. I must have finally tired of living symbolically. I had certainly tired of living with Marv.

The streets of Colburn Springs were empty, as they always were on a weekday morning. Everyone was at work thirty miles down the turnpike in the same city where I'd left Marv to his fate. I'd come up the turnpike driving against the current. Like swimming upstream so as not to spawn.

The day was almost warm, almost cool, as clear and tart as natural crystal. A good day to ride a bike or run a long distance. Some amount of miles to the east, it was the same day. A classic marathon day. It was my father's opinion that they were Running east to west because of a tendency to follow the sun. Considering the earth's rotation, he'd added, this would make the planet a giant treadmill, except that since the Runners were not up to rotational speed, they were losing ground, even though they were clocked as going just a bit faster every day.

On television, they had shown the film of the bridge collapse in Pennsylvania, where five hundred had died. The thousands behind them had Run in place at the edge of the abyss until a few thought to lead them on a detour. The five hundred were replaced and then exceeded, stretching the mass out and out and out, until the gap between the group that had gotten across the bridge and the group left behind after the collapse had been filled.

I thought about it as I rode, mostly in a westerly direction. I stopped at the city limits and was home long before lunch.

It seemed to strike only if you were on foot.

". . . mayor had sharply criticized the Colburn Springs Running Club," the radio said solemnly, "stating that the raising of a banner welcoming the Runners encourages and abets victims of mass hysteria in need of psychiatric help.

"In Ohio, an attempt by a family to remove their twenty-year-old son from the mass of Runners and have him deprogrammed failed when the would-be deprogrammers were apparently infected by the crowd and simply kept Running."

My father shut off the radio. "Listen, Pamela," he said. I moved my legs so he could sit down on the couch with me. "I've been making a list of expressions that have to do with running."

I put down the magazine I'd been reading, since he had decided to confer the status of adulthood on me, at least for the time being.

"Letting your emotions run away with you, running out, running on empty, on the run, run-on, run down, run over, hit-and-run, runaway, run like sixty. *Rat race.*" He raised his eyebrows in a significant way.

I winced inwardly. He was being a bore again, but I couldn't tell him so.

"Can you think of any others?"

"No, Dad." I went back to my magazine, but he wasn't through with me.

"How about synonyms for running?"

"I don't know. Jogging. Trotting. Sprinting. I don't know."

"Did you notice the way they said it on the radio just now? Runners, with a capital *R* that you can actually hear." He put the list on the coffee table and stared at it. "It's medieval dancing mania all over again. It would be better if it were dancing. You dance to music. There's nothing so bad about music. Running implies fright from— excuse me, *flight from* something." He looked about the living room. "Where's your mother?"

I couldn't resist. "I think she ran down to the store for something."

He gave me a look. "You think that's funny. Well, it's not. She could catch it and want to Run with them." He slipped a ball-point pen out of his shirt pocket. "There's another. Run with the pack." He added it to the list.

"I can't picture Mother jogging. She's more the weight-lifter type than she is track and field."

"This isn't jogging, it's mania." My father plunked his chin on his folded hands.

"Maybe it isn't flight from something," I said after a bit. "Maybe they're all Running *to* something and we just don't know what it is."

My father exhaled noisily. "People only run *from*. They walk *to*, but they run *from*. When you get to be my age, you'll realize that. Run *from*, walk *to*." He sat tensely on the edge of the sofa cushion until we heard my mother come in.

Colburn Springs had a bar for every church. Both kinds of establishments had been built to hold very small congregations. I took in an afternoon service at Edith's Tap Room. The drink of the day was The Runner—vodka and prune juice. The cocktail waitress was wearing track shoes. So was the bartender and one of the half a dozen other customers. The television over the bar was on for anyone who wanted to keep up with the soaps.

I wasn't in the habit of drinking in the afternoon, but it was something else to do besides sit around my parents' house just being divorced.

"Sure you don't want a Runner?" said the bartender when he brought me my second beer.

"If I wanted to Run, it wouldn't be to the bathroom."

"That's what they all say." He stroked his moustache absently. "One of my best jokes and it fell flat as old beer."

"Not many prune juice drinkers around."

"When they get here, are you gonna Run?" he asked me.

"Hadn't thought about it. You?"

He shrugged. "I don't know. I was sorta thinking I might see how long I could go along with them. I do two miles every morning. That's my limit, two miles. Been running every day for the last year and I can't get past two miles. I just don't understand it."

75

The man sitting three stools away from me turned to look at the bartender in disbelief. "You kiddin'? You could get infected."

"Infected?" The bartender laughed. "What do you think they got, measles?"

"That's what they call it on the news, gettin' infected. Buncha fitness freaks in West Virginia did just what you're talkin' about doin'. Most of 'em are still goin'."

"Yeah. That must be something." The bartender stared into space and smiled. "Like some kind of afterburner kicking in. I've heard runners talk about it. How they'd be going along, fighting for every step, about to collapse, and then suddenly they get their second wind. They say it's like a power switch cuts in somewhere in their bodies and the pain disappears. They feel light, like there was less gravity holding them down and they were being carried along on the air. Body becomes a machine. A running machine. It could go on forever. The mind becomes clear, like it went up to a higher place, like being way up on top of a mountain where there's no smog or traffic or noise or anything, just pure, clean world, and you could take one more step beyond that, right into the sky itself."

The man stared at him and then finished the last third of his drink in one gulp. "Jesus. You're infected already."

The bartender shook his head. "I wish I were. But I'm not."

"You wait," said the man. "They'll come through here and take you right along with them." He held up his glass. "You wanna hit me again before you go? Like one for the road, only my one and your road."

The bartender made him another drink. On the television, the soap opera ended and was replaced by a title card, big white letters on a blue background. *Update — Day 22: The Runners.* A moment later, a deep male voice intoned the same words for the benefit of the illiterate in the audience. Edith's Tap Room went quiet. The picture switched to a woman sitting behind a news desk.

"This is Glenda Blaylock with an update on the progress of the compulsive marathon that began twenty-two days ago in New England. Thus far, the Runners' circuitous route has taken them down along the Eastern seaboard, then back up—"

"Nuts," said the man who'd been talking to the bartender. "Crazy, all of them. People are like sheep. All you got to do is tell them to do something and they'll do it. Follow the leader. Nobody's got their own mind anymore. If you went on TV said it was chic—" he pronounced it *chick* "—to jump off the top of a high building, they'd be lining up at the nearest skyscraper in two seconds."

The cocktail waitress swatted him with a Handi-Wipe as she went by carrying a tray of empty glasses. "Fasten it, Bill, I want to hear this."

He looked scornfully at her running shoes. They were bright blue and didn't go with her straight black skirt at all. "Yeah, you'll probably take off, too. Like to see you Running in that skirt."

"I've got a pair of shorts in my locker just in case. Now will you button up?"

The man hunched lower over the bar, muttering something.

"—where they immobilized the city for three days just by sheer numbers, Thus far, four main groups of Runners have been distinguished, but there is no accounting as yet for various smaller groups that may be en route to join one of the larger ones.

"Efforts to stop one of the Runners and conduct an examination have met with no success, and medical authorities are still at a loss to explain the phenomena—"

"Phenomenon," said the man at the bar. "It's phenomenon, singular. One phenomenon, two phenomena."

"You're a phenomenon, Bill," the cocktail waitress said. "You drink while they Run. I'm sending my kids to college just on what I make on you."

"Then you better hope I keep comin' in here," Bill said evenly. Instead of telling him to be quiet, the bartender reached up and turned the volume control on the television.

"—interview taped with a Rhode Island woman three days ago."

The newswoman was replaced by a thirtyish woman in T-shirt and shorts, filmed from a slow-moving truck that had managed to find an uncrowded spot on a highway filled with Runners.

"How long have you been Running, Jeannie?" asked an unseen interviewer.

"Almost a week," she answered, puffing only a little. Her fists moved up and down out of the picture like pistons.

"And how do you feel?"

"Great!" She flashed a smile as she brushed her frizzy blonde hair back so it wouldn't flop in her eyes.

"What happened to your shoes?"

"The laces broke so I just Ran out of them." The camera panned down her body to her bare feet and back up again.

"Doesn't it hurt to Run barefoot?"

"Uh-uh. Feels great." Another quick smile.

"Do you think it's because the skin on your soles has thickened or calloused because of all the miles you've gone?"

"I don't know, I'm not a doctor."

77

"Bounce, bounce," jeered Bill. "This must be the world's longest-running jiggle show. The next thing she's going to Run out of is her bra."

"And you're not tired at all?" said the interviewer. The back of his head and one hand holding a microphone appeared briefly at the bottom left of the picture.

"Nope. I feel wonderful. The more I Run, the more I can Run."

The truck accelerated a little too much and the woman was suddenly several feet behind. There was a glimpse of dozens of other people around her before the truck slowed down to let her catch up.

"So how long are you going to keep on Running, Jeannie?"

"I dunno."

"What about your family?"

"My husband's around here somewhere."

"Do you have any kids?"

"Yeah, two boys, seven and five. They're about five miles back, I think. Their little legs can't keep up as well."

"Aren't you worried about them?"

"Uh-uh."

"Do you have any idea where you're going?"

"Bye," she said and veered off into a thick pack of Runners. In another moment she was gone, obscured by the pack. The truck came to a stop so the camera could show us all the Runners passing by. Then it panned down the road. There were people as far as the eye could see, all bobbing up and down the way people do when they run.

"And they're coming this way," said Bill disgustedly. "Buncha fruit-cakes."

"Supermen," said the bartender, adding, "and superwomen," with a glance at the waitress. "They can Run forever, never getting tired, never getting hurt. Did you see that woman's feet? They weren't bleeding or anything. She looked beautiful. And happy."

"—through the blockade, injuring several guardsmen." The news-woman was back on the screen. "Five guardsmen abandoned their posts and took off after the Runners, shedding their helmets and weapons. Other attempts to halt the Runners have met with similar results. One man was almost killed when he was trampled by—"

I looked away from the TV, pretending I was a camera panning the room. Two men at a dinky little table were watching the report expressionlessly, their hands feeding nuts to their mouths in a mindless, automatic way. Another man sitting by himself stirred a drink that was slightly amber, pushing the ice cubes down with a swizzle stick and watching them pop up again. The woman sitting two tables away from him looked as though she were about to pass out. Her eyelids kept fluttering closed.

"—sixteen, including ten men and six women before state police shot him. He was identified as Malcolm Corby, thirty-four, of Seattle. He had apparently traveled across the country specifically to shoot at the Runners. The sixteen dead people have not yet been reliably identified. The bodies are currently undergoing autopsy, but results so far have not been disclosed.

"Twenty-five miles south, on the same highway, the National Guard released tear gas in an unsuccessful attempt to halt the Run. Runners simply Ran through the gas without stopping. Protests from various groups around the country, including the American Civil Liberties Union and the Red Cross, have caused the President to issue a ban on any further action of this nature. In a statement to the press—"

I finished my beer and put the mug down on the bar with a thump. The bartender didn't look away from the television.

"They're not supermen," Bill said with acid satisfaction. "They can be killed."

"Killed but not stopped," the bartender said dreamily. "They're still Running and there are more of them than ever."

Bill snorted like a horse.

"—from Ann Arbor this morning, proclaiming themselves the Runners for Jesus. Ten miles out, most of them had already collapsed and had to be taken to hospitals. The last Runner for Jesus gave up three miles later. Elsewhere—"

"Shut it off," said Bill suddenly, with a begging note in his voice. "This is depressing. Things are bad enough without—"

"This isn't necessarily bad," said the bartender, losing only a fraction of his dreaminess. "And if you don't like it, you don't have to drink here."

"—deny rumors that a woman Runner thrust her six-month-old son into the arms of a bystander and Ran on. A spokesperson for the mayor's office stated that this was, quote, indicative of the mythology already springing up around this thing, unquote.

"So far, only half a dozen towns have found it necessary to declare martial law. Police and National Guardsmen are still traveling with the Runners in makeshift escort, which authorities believe has kept the number of civil disturbances to a minimum.

"Meanwhile, mental health clinics and hospitals are reporting a large influx of people who are troubled because they do *not* have Running Fever. Here with an in-depth report on this phenomena—"

I put a ten-dollar bill on the bar and walked out. No one noticed me leave.

He flagged me down three blocks from my parents' house. Not much more than a kid, twenty-one or twenty-two, with a tape recorder swinging from one shoulder and a camera hanging off the other. One of the advance guard of reporters following the Runners. There'd be a lot more of them soon, as well as police and National Guard. I hadn't thought of that. In spite of the news reports, I'd actually just expected to see the Runners come down the highway as though they were in a normal marathon, only larger.

"Ma'am, you got a few minutes to talk?" the reporter asked as I pulled my bike over to the curb.

"You want to ask me about the Runners."

"Right. I'm doing a series of articles on the small towns along the Runners' route, and I'd like to interview you, get your reactions to what's been happening over the last three weeks."

I shrugged and pulled my bike up onto the sidewalk. "Don't know if I can really help you. I've been busy getting divorced."

"Oh. I'm sorry."

"Don't be. It's not your fault." I paused. "Is it?"

He laughed. "I'm Jim Andros."

"Pamela."

My leaving off a surname caught him by surprise briefly. Then he was all business and professional journalism. I wondered if the ink on his diploma was still wet. His red hair was thick, growing out from a hairstyle that had been meant for blow-drying. "Have you been following the Runners on the news?"

"I just saw a report on a TV in Edith's Tap Room, but I haven't been following them deliberately. You don't really have to. They follow you, as it were. They're all over the news."

"How do you think Colburn Springs is taking the imminent on-slaught of Runners?"

I frowned at him.

"What I mean is, have you noticed a change in the tenor of the town. As it were."

I shook my head. "I guess you're talking to the wrong person. Up until three weeks ago, I was living in the city for the last six years. I don't know anything about the tenor of Colburn Springs, as it were or as it weren't."

"Oh. Well—" he gave me a helpless grin and held up his tape recorder gamely. "What do *you* think about it personally? About the Run."

Unconsciously, I'd begun to walk toward my parents' house. He walked with me; the bicycle ticked between us. He was almost a head shorter than I was. "It doesn't seem real yet. Just a thing on the news. 'Day 22, America on the Run.'" I shrugged again.

"Why do you think so many people are 'on the Run,' as you put it?"

"Maybe they think something's chasing them. Maybe they're all going somewhere they haven't told us about yet." Really, I thought, it was amazing what you'd say to a reporter. As though he were an artificial person, a mechanism not meant to engage your feelings or judge them, or you. I smiled at the tape recorder.

"How do you think you'll feel when they finally hit Colburn Springs?"

"What do you mean?"

"Do you think you'll catch Running mania?"

"Me?" I hadn't considered that at all. "I can't imagine it." Then the words he had used registered on me. "You should come home with me and talk to my parents. My father calls it mania, too. He has an interesting theory you might want to hear."

Jim Andros's eyes lit up. "Do you think your parents would let me interview them?"

"They might." Or they might throw you out, I added silently, and didn't know why.

"I left my car parked back there."

"That's all right. We're only a block and a half away from my parents' house. Your car will be safe."

"Mania," my father said.

"Fitness," said my mother. "It's this fitness thing, it's gotten out of hand. Mass hysteria or hypnosis or something like that."

I almost felt guilty for the way I had arranged for them to double-team Jim Andros, ace cub reporter for a magazine he'd never named. Perhaps there wasn't one and he was just out to win the Pulitzer Prize on spec. I left them in the living room and puttered around in the kitchen, thinking I might have a snack to take the edge off my beer high. I could hear them quite clearly.

". . . miracle," my father was saying. "It *is* miraculous when people can Run for days without eating or sleeping or going to the bathroom."

"Bushwa. A yogi could do it, you know, one of those men who sleeps on a bed of nails and pokes spikes through his cheeks. Mind over matter. It happens every day."

"But the body would eventually break down under so much punishment. Because the concentration would eventually break down, they couldn't maintain it. Stress fractures, shin splints, torn feet, sprains, muscle spasms—"

Jim Andros said nothing. He must have been very small on the couch, serving as a conduit for their argument. There was a radio on the counter, but I didn't turn it on.

I was surprised when the reporter agreed to stay for supper. The argument was still picking up momentum, but I thought he'd have run out of tape by then. Perhaps he was just recording over previous, slower portions of the argument. I didn't pay much attention.

They paused to watch the evening news together, all three of them. They sat in a row on the couch. What a sight. The news said the northern group was veering south little by little, but the southern group was still hugging the Gulf of Mexico. There were the usual films, including a clip of children from about kindergarten age through early teens amid a phalanx of adults. Day care on the hoof. The oldest Runner that anyone knew of was a sixty-nine-year-old woman named Emma Kent, who had Run away from a retirement community.

My parents resumed talking to the reporter during the meager sports segment (it seemed major league baseball teams as well as fans had been depleted by the Run). I went out for another ride on my bike.

Neither the National Guard nor the police had shown up in Colburn Springs as yet, but there were plenty of cars with out-of-state license plates parked in the slanted spaces on the main drag. Not much of a main drag, bearing the grandiose name of Broadway. More reporters, I figured, finally coming in. A good majority of them had probably gone straight to the city, where the disturbances and the news to report about disturbances would be much showier. Running Mania had begotten Pulitzer Mania.

I rode in circles around Colburn Springs, making each one wider in a lopsided way. I rode faster sometimes and slower other times, but always I kept the curve of the circle going inward. I had no desire not to.

Edith's Tap Room was much too crowded for me. I could hear the voices inside from the street. It was starting to get dark, anyway, and I doubted my ability to operate a bicycle on two or three beers at night. On my way home, I saw him again in almost the same spot as before. He looked worn thin, eroded by my parents. His limpness seemed to extend to his equipment. I pulled over to the curb without waiting for him to wave at me.

"Did you get what you wanted?" I asked.

He patted the tape recorder with a tired smile. "Your parents spoke very freely and at great length. I had to record over some of the earlier stuff they said before they really got going."

"Take any notes?"

"No." The smile turned sheepish. "I'm not a reporter." He stared down at the front wheel of my bike for several seconds. "I'm just following the Runners."

I was surprised and not surprised all at once. "Is it your girlfriend or a relative? Or just a close friend?"

"What?" He squinted at me. The streetlight overhead buzzed as it went on.

"The Runner you're following. Is it your wife or—"

He shook his head. "I don't know any of the Runners. I'm following them because I'm following them. I want to."

"How long have you been at it?" I should have been a reporter, I thought.

"Ten, eleven days, I guess. I want to understand about them. I want to know. But I can't Run. I've tried, I just can't. I tried to build up my endurance so I could be with them—*in* them—but I couldn't even go half a mile. None of them would Run with me, anyway. They all ignored me, like I wasn't there. So now I go where they go and talk to people. Maybe something someone says will help me understand. They're all so—they're just—they're—"

"Supermen. And superwomen."

He nodded reluctantly. "Oh, yes. There's that. They are. I guess I'm jealous. I don't know why I can't be one of them. Why do they all get to Run and not me? Why can't I, even though I want to?" He tilted his head back and looked at me as though from a great distance. "Have you ever in your whole life been taken by something?"

"Taken?"

"Yeah. You know, taken. *Taken.* Found something and had it come to life inside you so that you were wrapped in it and wrapped around it at the same time, and there was nothing you did that was not for its sake and no place that you could go where it wasn't?" He could have been about to smile or cry, but he did neither. "I've never had that, ever. And it feels like I've never had anything." He fidgeted with the tape recorder absently. "Nothing has ever consumed me. I'd like to feel like that someday. Just once. Like the Runners. I'd like to have some kind of power in me. I think that must make you—I don't know— bigger, somehow."

I came close to telling him I knew a bartender he could talk to. Anything that anyone did apparently had the potential for groupies.

83

At last I said, "Well, at least you've got all the material for a series of articles. You could do them, anyway, even if you're not a reporter."

He frowned, vaguely annoyed. "I'm not a Runner and I can't Run, anyway. You know, if you put your ear to the ground, you can hear them coming. If they're close enough. I've done it. Like in the movies, when you'd see an Indian listening for horses or buffalo approaching."

"Look—" But I didn't know what I wanted him to look at, and he wasn't interested; abruptly, he wandered past me, moving eastward where night and the Runners were coming on together.

I got on my bike.

"Like waiting for a storm, a big one. A bad hurricane, or a tornado," my father said. We were staring at the television, which was temporarily devoid of any reports on the Runners.

"Bush and wa," said my mother firmly. "If people had the good sense not to pay attention to them, not go out and watch them like a damned parade, you'd see it come to an end pretty quick. They'd all take trains and planes and buses home just as soon as they saw they wouldn't be getting any more publicity."

"What'll they do when they get to California?" my father said, giving my mother no attention. "I mean, when they get to the ocean? They won't be able to just Run across *that*."

"Good question," I said. "Of course, by then they'll be backed up to Salt Lake City."

"Maybe it will be like those ants. Soldier ants or whatever they're called, where they make living bridges of their bodies, some of them sacrificing themselves so that others can cross a water barrier. A bridge of people from California to Hawaii, from Hawaii to Asia. They could Run all the way around the world like that."

"And if they do, *then* what happens?" asked my mother. "Do they just start over?"

"You *persist* in misunderstanding, don't you?" my father bellowed.

"What's there to understand?" my mother shrieked back.

"You don't *want* to understand! *Fitness* craze? *Fitness* craze, when people can Run for three weeks without—"

"Craze as in crazy!"

Then they were both shouting at each other simultaneously, their words colliding and splintering unintelligibly. Underneath, the TV hummed in faulty transmission, drowning out the bubbly sitcom, adding an edge. My teeth seemed to be vibrating in my head.

The humming rose and parents' voices rose with it. I got up from the easy chair and shut off the television. The screen went dark, but the humming remained. It was in my ears. My parents kept hollering. I put my hands over my ears, and the humming became a roar trapped in my head. The room dimmed, brown fog suddenly obscuring everything. I'd gotten up too fast.

I moved unsteadily to the glass patio door and shoved it open. The backyard was dark and unexpectedly cool, but I couldn't feel that very well through the humming.

You know, if you put your ear to the ground, you can hear them coming. If they're close enough.

I knelt and pressed one ear, then the other, into the sparse, scrubby grass that refused to become a lawn. The humming receded, but I couldn't hear them. They weren't close enough. How close did they have to be? Jim Andros had never said.

The news had said we could expect the first Runner to arrive in Colburn Springs at about noon. That wasn't right. The first Runner went through the main drag at 10:32 A.M., Running all alone down the center of Broadway while most of Colburn Springs's population gaped from behind long barricades on the sidewalks. I watched it on television. The Runner was a youngish man in unremarkable running clothes; he also wore running shoes, which was remarkable. That meant he was a fairly new Runner. There was some speculation on the part of the reporter with the live minicam team that the man was perhaps not a real Runner but an athletic attention-seeker. She was wrong. He was a Runner. Anyone could see it, the way his body moved in a long-established rhythm. I wondered how many days he'd been going. The camera zoomed in awkwardly on his face. There was no perspiration on his skin, no fatigue pulling his features down. The camera watched him go and then searched the crowd for reaction. There was little among all the faces, young, old, middle-aged, ageless. No use trying to go to work today. The Runners would still be tying up the turnpike by quitting time, thousands and thousands of bodies. I felt guilty looking at all those familiar and almost-familiar faces. There was something indecent about watching something happen less than a mile away on television.

Twenty minutes later the next Runners showed up, perhaps four dozen men and women of varying ages, all more ragged than the first Runner had been. Over half of them were barefoot.

"They Run out of their shoes," explained the reporter, as though no one had ever heard that before. "The laces break due to the constant friction. And their socks, of course, those wear out—"

I turned down the sound and watched the Runners in silence. There was a heavy man with a moustache; his stringy dark hair flapped up and down and his belly jiggled slightly. To his left was a boy of seventeen or eighteen with a winestain birthmark splayed over one cheek like the mark of a strange slap. Just behind them was a secretaryish-looking woman with smooth mahogany skin and determined set to her mouth. She was wearing a skirt and blouse, no shoes. The blouse had pulled out of the waistband of the skirt, the underarm seams had ripped out, and most of the buttons had come off. Her slip peeked through the open blouse. The man and woman beside her were obviously Running together, at least for the time being. They seemed to be chatting.

My mother leaned over me to turn up the sound and I jumped. I hadn't heard her come up behind me. "Bunch of fools," she said. "There's a network report on Channel 7." She tapped a spot on the screen. "There's their camera crew. They're in a better position. Looks like they've got people prepared to run alongside Runners for interviews, too."

Obediently I changed the channel and saw the Runners from the other side of the street, and closer to the corner they were coming around from the road leading off the turnpike exit. Or entrance, depending on your point of view.

"They could have bypassed Colburn Springs completely," my mother said, throwing in a disapproving *tch*. "They could have stayed on the turnpike and gone straight to the city. But no, they have to come through here and make spectacles of themselves. Showing off."

"Picking up more Runners."

My mother and I turned to look at my father standing in the doorway.

"Spreading the mania."

"—wondering who, in this small quiet town, will be the first to break from the crowd of spectators and join the Runners, if indeed anyone does. Statistically, it seems to be a sure bet that one out of every forty to forty-five residents will catch 'Running Fever,' as many doctors are calling it." The voice belonged to a rather well-known lady journalist whose autobiography was crawling up the bestseller list. I was surprised the network had her tracking the Runners. And then again, perhaps it wasn't so surprising. Perhaps she had demanded it. I wondered if the doctors she'd mentioned had issued a report on Running Fever Fever yet.

"It is estimated that it may take close to three days for all of the Runners to pass through Colburn Springs, assuming that the vast majority of them don't stick to the highway. In spite of authorities' pleas for people to stay away from areas where the Runners are passing though, it seems everyone in this small Midwestern town has turned out to watch this strange migration. We now seem to be at a break in this group of Runners; only a very few are on the street right now, though observers on the interstate have told us it is clogged and positively impassable to vehicles. State police—"

I wandered away from the television. Bicycle? Somehow, it was out of the question. My parents left the TV on all day, watching it in spurts. When I came back to it later in the afternoon, the camera was inching over the crowd. I saw Jim Andros, his fresh face a study in awe and frustration. He made me think about all the people whose friends and relatives had joined the Run and left them behind. But I doubted that any of them were pacing the Runners. Or not many, anyway. Some might have, for a while, and then given up. The news had run a few interviews with relatives left behind, mostly wives and husbands. All of them had been at home.

Who will be the first Colburn Springs Runner? was the catchphrase of the day. The lady journalist's voice lost its contralto polish and turned positively salacious each time she said it. You could tell she was disappointed that it was taking so long. No one had tried to fake it, either; no one had burst onto the street in running clothes, pretending to be seized with Running Fever. If the bartender from Edith's Tap Room was trying to see how far he could run with them, he was doing it somewhere else.

The Runners hit in earnest just after noon. A helicopter hovering over the town recorded their entrance from the air. A river of Runners, live confetti from that height, pouring in from the highway. Broadway was too narrow to accommodate all of them; they spilled onto other streets, across lawns and backyards, swirling around houses and eddying around lightpoles and mailboxes.

"Flood," my father said. Something I'd learned in biology passed through my mind vaguely. What percentage of the human body was made up of water—87 percent? 90 percent? Or was it as much as 95 percent? I couldn't remember.

The people next door left sometime in the middle of the afternoon. My mother was torn between wanting to see the Runners in person and watching them on television with all the explanations and commentary. She didn't say as much, but I could tell. She and my father circled each other skittishly all day, trying to keep the length of a room between them.

I didn't see the first Colburn Springs Runner break out when it actually happened, but the network made use of instant replay several times, at regular and slow motion. A thirty-year-old bank teller named

Evie Koster. She was wearing jeans and a sweatshirt and running shoes, as though she'd come unsure whether she would end up Running or not, but wanted to be ready just in case. *Go, Evie, go!* some women were yelling in the background. Probably people she worked with. A man carrying a concealed handgun was arrested by two men in plain-clothes who had the FBI look about them. As the plainclothesmen were leading him away, the man told the journalists that he had planned to use the gun on himself if he'd gotten Running Fever.

"Drastic cure," my father said.

"Might as well," said my mother from the other room. She made a supper that none of us ate. By dark, five more people from Colburn Springs had Run away. No one knew how that stacked up statistically.

My father was asleep sitting up on the couch at 3 A.M. when I got up to ride my bike to Broadway.

The Runners had saturated Colburn Springs. There was almost no street where they weren't. I had to ride carefully. They would suddenly appear out of the darkness in twos and threes, looking mildly surprised that they would meet anything going in the opposite direction. There was no audience on the side streets, at least not at that hour of the morning, though I did see a few police cars with officers dozing in them parked at the curbs. There was no sign of the National Guard, except for one Runner in fatigues. They were probably all in the city, I realized, getting ready for the riots.

There were a surprising number of people still out on the sidewalks. I walked my bike along the street on the other side of the barricades, waiting for someone to stop me and tell me to get behind them. No one did. I stopped to buy a cup of coffee from a lunch wagon parked across a driveway.

"Hello?"

Somehow, I'd thought I'd find Jim Andros still out. I turned around and nodded at him. He looked like someone trying to fight off imminent nervous collapse. Lack of sleep and Running Fever Fever made his face too pale, his eyes too bright.

"I had to record over the conversations I had with your parents. Everyone wanted to talk to me about the Runners. I still can't get close to them." From several streets over came the sound of a big dog barking excitedly. Someone had Run through his backyard and awakened him.

"You should get some sleep." I gave Jim Andros a sip of my coffee.

"After they've gone. They're already getting into the city. I heard the reports on a radio. Someone tried to kill one of them already. Not all of them are coming through Colburn Springs. They fanned out, some of them are Running through some town north of the turnpike."

"Price's Bend," I said.

"What?"

"That's the name of the town north of the turnpike. Price's Bend."

He smiled helplessly and put a hand on my shoulder to hold himself up. "I'd have thought they'd want to stay together. But who knows, maybe as long as they're Running, they *are* together."

I leaned my bike against the front of the lunch wagon and put an arm around him. He wasn't heavy at all. "It's not like I want to stop them or hurt them. I don't. I want to Run *with* them and I can't get in." He pointed at one of the barricades with the coffee cup, as if he were toasting it. "There's a thing like that between me and Running. Can't find my way around it. I can't. I never will. Never will."

I let him finish the cup. A dozen Runners passed close enough to stir our clothes with their wind. One of them was wearing perfume, a heavy, spicy scent I recognized as Jungle Gardenia. Someone turned on a transistor radio.

"—units are removing the protestors who are lying in the middle of I-70, chanting, 'Stay here, stay here.' It seems to be an organized protest, but authorities have yet to identify a leader or leaders."

Well, that would be next, I thought. Anti-Runners. The Stayers to balance the Goers or something like that. Jim Andros was babbling. I made him sit down on the curb. A man from the first-aid station put a blanket around his shoulders and tried to make him take a pill.

"We've had a number of cases of hysteria," the man told me while Andros kept twisting his head away from him. "Maybe you should take your friend home."

"He's not from around here," I said, "and he's not my friend. Just let him alone. He'll be all right. He's been following the Runners. He's got Running Fever Fever."

The man frowned at me and then managed to get the pill between Andros's lips. He spat it out with such force it hit a passing Runner on the thigh.

The eastern sky had just begun to lighten when a new flood of Runners arrived. This time I heard them, the *pat-pat-pat* of thousands of sneakers and bare feet on asphalt. Film crews that had been dormant came to life, and floodlights went on all over the place. This group was so numerous and dense I couldn't even see across the street. It was a blanket of people, bobbing and billowing unevenly, their breathing a strange-sounding wind. The sun rose and there was no letup. They came in the thin sunlight and kept coming as though they meant

89

to cover every inch of ground with themselves. Few of them bothered to look around. It was impossible to distinguish them one from another anymore. I thought I could feel the pavement vibrate under my sneakers.

Someone touched my shoulder. Jim Andros was standing beside him, his head wagging back and forth as though he were watching a fast volley at a tennis tournament. I think I knew what he was going to do a second before he did, but I was too sluggish, moved too late. By the time I had brought my arm up, he had darted out into the midst of them.

They buffeted him back and forth as they Ran past, ignoring his outstretched arms. I couldn't hear what he was shouting to them. Perhaps he wasn't shouting at all, only opening and closing his mouth impotently. His clutching hands slipped off a large man; there was the sound of cloth tearing. Andros staggered backward into the path of three teenaged girls. Two of the girls went around him; the center girl gave him a shove, just a little one, and he went down.

I caught sight of him briefly among the flashing legs, trying to get up again before the Runners became too thick and he disappeared altogether. Several people pushed past me from behind and fought their way into the current of Runners, forcing a clear spot with their bodies. Several more followed. Someone grabbed my hand and I was in the middle of a human chain stretching into the road. The Runners were forced around us, up onto the sidewalk, knocking over the barricades. My bicycle tipped over with a clatter. Someone fell over it, recovered, and Ran on.

The man who'd been trying to feed Andros a pill earlier now waded out of the road with Andros in his arms. The rest of us retreated to the sidewalk as the Runners rushed to fill in the space we'd left. The man gave me a dirty look. Andros's nose and mouth were oozing blood. I heard someone say the man was a nurse from the county hospital. He carried Andros around the side of the lunch wagon.

Andros's camera and tape recorder were lying on the sidewalk where he'd left them. There was film in the camera; seventeen frames of a roll of thirty-six pictures had been exposed. I opened the back of the camera and exposed the rest of it before I put it down on the sidewalk again. I had to hold the tape recorder to my ear to hear it. He hadn't been very careful about recording his ersatz interviews. There were bits and pieces of different people expounding on the Runners, one recorded on top of another.

". . . escaping their responsibilities," said a woman authoritatively. "I'd like to just take off, too, but I got kids to look after, a home to keep up—and buster, if you don't think that's a job . . ." Her voice faded out and came back again. A man in pajamas Ran past me, brushing my arm. "—plete freedom of movement, but you're going to see terrible things happening in the next few days. Shortages, the TV said, and I don't know what-all. If a foreign power like the Russians wanted to attack us, now would be the time to do it with all these nuts Running like rabbits. That about sums it all up, you know, maybe you don't remember—" There was a click and then another woman was talking.

"—somewhere but *I* don't know where. Be interesting to watch them from a plane, see where they go. I don't know why they don't just grab one of them—"

"They've tried," said Jim Andros's voice neutrally. "Other Runners converge on them and knock them down."

"But surely children, if they tried grabbing a kid—"

Click. Now a young male voice.

"—get away, just get away, you know?"

Click. Another woman. "—the end. These are the last Times we're living in, in case you didn't know that, and it's probably a signal that the Rapture's about to happen. We cannot understand how God works or why He works the way He does, but this is all part of His Plan. I don't know if He will touch me and tell me to Run, but I will do His will, as we all shall. But you know, you can Run but you can't Hide, not from Him. Perhaps when they reach the Pacific ocean they'll all vanish, or they'll Run into the sea and drown themselves like the Gadarene swine, I *think* it was the Gadarene swine—"

Click. The voice was an old lady's. "Get that thing out of my face, you little punk, I'll—"

Click-click. "Lemmings," said a man. "The rat race. How is this so different from the way we've been living, go, go, go, rush, rush, rush, going nowhere and making damn good time, like the old joke says—"

A woman jounced by, and as she did, the gold necklace she was wearing dropped off onto the street. She never broke stride. I picked it up. It was a chain with a gold heart on it. The heart was inscribed *Maria*.

"—surprise me anymore," said another man's voice. "our priorities are wrong, all wrong, and if I thought I could keep up that pace, boy, you better believe I would."

"Why?" asked Jim Andros.

"Why? Why the hell not? Sick of everything, goddam IRS, goddam job, goddam inflation, goddam welfare cheaters, goddam—"

Click, click, rumble, click. Then Jim Andros's voice, all alone.

91

"—body really knows, nobody and nobody knows what will happen, and *I* don't know. I'm waiting and waiting for it to come over me and then I'll know. At last, I'll *know,* just what this one thing of all the things there are to know that I'll never know, but *this* thing, *this* thing, I don't want to be left behind. God, please don't leave me behind, I don't want to be—"

The click cut into his sob. I dropped the tape recorder on the sidewalk and it shattered.

"Miss—"

It was the nurse. He was still angry with me for not saving Jim Andros. As though I'd have been able to. A lot of people had gathered behind the barricades while I'd been listening to the tape recorder. They watched as the nurse reached for me.

I pushed aside his arm and Ran.

That was all there was to it, except for the faint ringing in my ears. I moved easily into the center of the flow, falling into Running stride as though I'd been doing it all my life. I could feel the hot sun on my back, the air parting around my face. Somewhere behind me, the lady journalist would tell a coast-to-coast audience that another Colburn Springs resident had hit the road, if she'd even noticed. A frizzy-haired man pounded along beside me, keeping his eyes straight ahead. We passed through an intersection where the light was flashing yellow. I thought I saw the bartender from Edith's Tap Room watching with envy and awe from the corner. Beside him a woman—the waitress? Yes, it was—waved and stepped into the road just as I went by. She caught up with me in the middle of the next block.

"Celia," she said.

"Pamela." And just for the hell of it, we shook hands.

"Nothing to it," she said, her voice thudding a little. "I thought it would be like a revelation, a thunderbolt in the head. But it's nothing."

"Nothing at all," I said.

"Bill's up ahead. The grouch who thought they were all nuts."

"I remember. From yesterday."

Through a gap in the Runners, I saw my parents walking along the sidewalk, close to the barricades. Not many people were lining the sidewalks here. My mother's eyes caught mine; I saw her move away from my father.

"Listen," I said to the waitress over the ringing in my ears.

"What?"

"What do you hear?"

"The sound of Running."

"What else is there?" Her oversized shirt fluttered and jounced with her breasts. "Do you think we'll get there soon? Wherever it is?"

"Soon enough," I said. "As long as we keep Running."

We went along without speaking for another block. My body was going just fine. Things inside me were changing, slowly and subtly. The waitress and I looked at each other. She could feel it, too.

I glanced over my shoulder. The Runners filled the world behind us, so that there was nothing else. My mother's face appeared briefly.

"Do you think it's gaining on us?" I asked Celia.

She looked back. "I don't know," she said. "But as long as we keep Running—"

She moved a little ahead. I matched her pace, drew even with her. Pound, pound, pound. To Run was a thankless job, but someone had to do it. Town gave way to neighborhoods; we left those behind, too.

The access road down to the next entrance to the turnpike was narrow. We stumbled through the grass, through a ditch, jumped the guardrail and met those who had stayed on the highway. Ahcad was the city. A car was broken down or abandoned on the shoulder. Someone Ran up onto the trunk, the roof, the hood, and jumped off. Others followed. The sound of metal buckling and glass breaking carried up to me. I kept going. And going. And going.

INTRODUCTION TO
MY BROTHER'S KEEPER

We've covered sex and rock'n'roll; now we're getting around to drugs.

Actually, I don't know today's drug scene and I don't want to. Because it will *get* you. They've made drugs more efficient, right along with communications, travel, commerce, war, and microwave ovens. How about that. You can now get an instantaneous high that is immediately addictive, no fooling around. Back in the good old days, you had a grace period between the first hit and the first signs of addiction, when you could consider what you were getting into. (Usually you didn't, but you could have.)

Of course, efficiency isn't perfection. It never is. Cars still get recalled, even the ones with the in-dash computers; even designer clothes unravel; there was some synthetic Demerol around that produced instant, permanent Parkinson's Disease. For God's sake, have a drink—cirrhosis takes years and you get to party while you wait.

No, no, not really. I'm *not* encouraging or advocating the abuse of any drugs. Personally, I have a broader definition of the term "drug." A drug is something that produces certain changes in the brain, resulting in gratification. Some people exercise the way others pop pills; some people shop the way others drink. There's even a support group for people addicted to sex, and they don't think that's funny.

Is it fair to compare a habit relatively free of dire consequences with a habit that shatters lives? Anyone who has ever tried to love an addict knows that's not the question.

Those of us relatively unburdened by either mundane or more exotic monkeys should not make the mistake of congratulating ourselves on having a non-addictive personality. That's a myth. If we're not addicted, we just haven't tried it yet, the receptors just haven't met the thing that activates them. But we already knew that everyone has a weakness, didn't we.

It doesn't have to be the centerpiece of your life, however. Unless you're certain you have a good reason to worry about it.

MY BROTHER'S KEEPER

*A*ll this happened a long time ago. Exactly when doesn't matter, not in a time when you can smoke your coke and Mommy and Daddy lock their grass in the liquor cabinet so Junior can't toke up at their expense. I used to think of it as a relevant episode, from a time when lots of things were relevant. It wasn't long before everyone got burned out on relevance. Hey, don't feel too ☐ guilty ☐ bad ☐ smug ☐ perplexed. There'll be something else, you know there will. It's coming in, right along with your ship.

In those days, I was still in the midst of my triumphant rise out of the ghetto (not all white chicks are found under a suburb). I was still energized and reveling at the sight of upturned faces beaming at me, saying, "Good luck, China, you're gonna be something someday!" as I floated heavenward attached to a college scholarship. My family's pride wore out sometime after my second visit home. Higher education was one thing, high-mindedness was another. I was puffed up with delusions of better and my parents kept sticking pins in me, trying to make the swelling go down so they could see me better. I stopped going home for awhile. I stopped writing, too, but my mother's letters came as frequently as ever: *Your sister Rose is pregnant again, pray God she doesn't lose this one, it could kill her; your sister Aurelia is skipping school, running around, I wish you'd come home and talk to her;* and, *Your brother Joe . . . your brother Joe . . . your brother Joe.*

My brother Joe. As though she had to identify him. I had one brother and that was Joe. My brother Joe, the original lost boy. Second oldest in the family, two years older than me, first to put a spike in his arm. Sometimes we could be close, Joe and me, squeezed between the brackets of Rose and Aurelia. He was a boner, the lone male among the daughters. Chip off the old block. Nature's middle finger to my father.

My brother Joe, the disposable man. He had no innate talents, not many learned skills other than finding a vein. He wasn't good-looking and junkies aren't known for their scintillating personalities or their sexual prowess or their kind and generous hearts. The family wasn't crazy about him; Rose wouldn't let him near her kids, Aurelia avoided him. Sometimes I wasn't sure how deep my love for him went. Junkies need love but they need a fix more. Between fixes, he could find the odd moment to wave me good-bye from the old life.

Hey, Joe, I'd say. *What the hell, huh?*

If you have to ask, babe, you don't really want to know. Already looking for another vein. Grinning with the end of a belt between his teeth.

My brother Joe was why I finally broke down and went home between semesters instead of going to suburban Connecticut with my room-mate. Marlene had painted me a bright picture of scenic walks through pristine snow, leisurely shopping trips to boutiques that sold Mucha prints and glass beads, and then, hot chocolate by the hearth, each of us wrapped in an afghan crocheted by a grandmother with prematurely red hair and an awful lot of money. Marlene admitted her family was far less relevant than mine, but what were vacations for? I agreed and was packing my bag when Joe's postcard arrived.

Dear China, They threw me out for the last time. That was all, on the back of a map of Cape Cod. Words were something else not at his command. But he'd gone to the trouble of buying a stamp and sending it to the right address.

The parents had taken to throwing him out the last year I'd lived at home. There hadn't been anything I could do about it then and I didn't know what Joe thought I could do about it now but I called it off with Marlene anyway. She said she'd leave it open in case I could get away before classes started again. Just phone so Mummy could break out the extra linens. Marlene was a good sort. She survived relevance admirably. In the end, it was hedonism that got her.

I took a bus home, parked my bag in a locker in the bus station and went for a look around. I never went straight to my parents' apartment when I came back. I had to decompress before I went home to be their daughter the stuck-up college snotnose.

It was already dark and the temperature was well south of freezing. Old snow lined the empty streets. You had to know where to look for the action in winter. Junkies wore coats for only as long as it took to sell them. What the hell, junkies were always cold anyway. I toured; no luck. It was late enough that anyone wanting to score already had and was nodding off somewhere. Streep's Lunch was one place to go after getting loaded, so I went there.

Streep's wasn't even half-full, segregated in the usual way — straights by the windows, hopheads near the jukebox and toilets, cops and strangers at the U-shaped counter in the middle. Jake Streep didn't like the junkies but he didn't bother them unless they nodded out in the booths. The junkies tried to keep the jukebox going so they'd stay awake but apparently no one had any quarters right now. The black and purple machine *(Muzik Master)* stood silent, its lights flashing on and off inanely.

97

Joe wasn't there but some of his friends were crammed into a booth, all on the nod. They didn't notice me come in any more than they noticed Jake Streep was just about ready to throw them out. Only one of them seemed to be dressed warmly enough; I couldn't place him. I just vaguely recognized the guy he was half-leaning on. I slid into the booth next to the two people sitting across from them, a lanky guy named Farmer and Stacey, who functioned more like his shadow than his girlfriend. I gave Farmer a sharp poke in the ribs and kicked one of the guys across from me. Farmer came to life with a grunt, jerking away from me and rousing Stacey.

"I'm awake, chrissakes." Farmer's head bobbed while he tried to get me in focus. A smile of realization spread across his dead face. "Oh. China. Hey, wow." He nudged Stacey. "It's China."

"Where?" Stacey leaned forward heavily. She blinked at me several times, started to nod out again and revived. "Oh. Wow. You're back. What happened?" She smeared her dark hair out of her face with one hand.

"Someone kicked me," said the guy I vaguely knew. I recognized him now, George Something-Or-Other. I'd gone to high school with him.

"Classes are out," I told Stacey.

Perplexed, she started to fade away.

"Vacation," I clarified.

"Oh. Okay." She hung on Farmer's shoulder as though they were in deep water and she couldn't swim. "You didn't quit?"

"I didn't quit."

She giggled. "That's great. Vacation. We never get vacation. We have to be us all the time."

"Shut up." Farmer made a half-hearted attempt to push her away.

"Hey. You kick me?" asked George Whoever, scratching his face.

"Sorry. It was an accident. Anyone seen Joe lately?"

Farmer scrubbed his cheek with his palm. "Ain't he in here?" He tried to look around. "I thought—" His bloodshot gaze came back to me blank. In the act of turning his head, he'd forgotten what we were talking about.

"Joe isn't here. I checked."

"You sure?" Farmer's head drooped. "Light's so bad in here, you can't see nothing, hardly."

I pulled him up against the back of the seat. "I'm sure, Farmer. Do you remember seeing him at all lately?"

His mouth opened a little. A thought was struggling through the warm ooze of his mind. "Oh. Yeah, *yeah*. Joe's been gone a coupla days." He rolled his head around to Stacey. "Today Thursday?"

Stacey made a face. "Hey, do I look like a fuckin' calendar to you?"

The guy next to George woke up and smiled at nothing. "Everybody get off?" he asked. He couldn't have been more than fifteen and still looked pretty good, relatively clean and healthy. The only one with a coat. Babe in Joyland.

"When did you see Joe last, Farmer?" I asked.

"Who?" Farmer frowned with woozy suspicion.

"Joe. My brother *Joe*."

"Joe's your brother?" said the kid, grinning like a drowsy angel. "I know Joe. He's a friend of mine."

"No, he's not," I told him. "Do you know where he is?"

"Nope." He slumped against the back of the seat and closed his eyes.

"Hey," said Stacey, "you wanna go smoke some grass? That's a college drug, ain't it? Tommy Barrow's got some. Let's all go to Tommy Barrow's and smoke grass like college kids."

"Shut *up*," said Farmer irritably. He seemed a little more alert now. "Tommy's outa town, I'm tryin' to think here." He put a heavy hand on my shoulder. "The other day, Joe was around. With this older woman. Older, you know?"

"Where?"

"You know, around. Just around. Noplace special. In here. Driving around. Just around."

I yawned. Their lethargy was contagious but I hadn't started scratching my face with sympathetic quinine itch yet. "Who is she? Anyone know her?"

"His *new* connection. His *new* connection," Stacey said in a sudden burst of lucidity. "I remember. He said she was going to set him up nice. He said she had some good sources."

"Yeah. *Yeah*," Farmer said. "That's it. She's with some distributor or something."

"What's her name?"

Farmer and Stacey looked at me. Names, sure. "Blonde," said Farmer. "Lotta money."

"And a car," George put in, sitting up and wiping his nose on his sleeve. "Like a Caddy or something."

"Caddy, shit. You think anything ain't a Volkswagen's a Caddy," Farmer said.

"It's a big white Caddy," George insisted. "I saw it."

"I saw it, too, and it ain't no Caddy."

99

"Where'd you see it?" I asked George.

"Seventeenth Street." He smiled dreamily. "It's gotta tape deck."

"*Where* on Seventeenth?"

"Like near Foster Circle, down there. Joe said she's got two speakers in the back. That's so cool."

"Okay, thanks. I guess I'll have a look around."

"Whoa." Farmer grabbed my arm. "It ain't there *now*. You kidding? I don't kr.ow where they are. Nobody knows."

"Farmer, I've got to find Joe. He wrote me at school. The parents threw him out and I've got to find him."

"Hey, he's okay. I told you, he's with this woman. Staying with her, probably."

I started to get up.

"Okay, *okay*," Farmer said. "Look, we're gonna see Priscilla tomorrow. She knows how to find him. Tomorrow."

I sighed. With junkies, everything was going to happen tomorrow. "When will you be seeing her?"

"Noon. You meet us here, okay?"

"Okay."

Streep glared at me as I left. At least the junkies bought coffee.

I thought about going down to Foster Circle anyway. It was a traffic island some idealistic mayor had decided to beautify with grass and flowers and park benches. Now it was just another junkie hang-out the straights avoided even in the daytime. It wasn't likely anyone would be hanging out there now, certainly not anyone who wanted to see me.

I trudged back to the bus station, picked up my bag and went to my parents' place.

I hadn't told my parents to expect me but they didn't seem terribly surprised when I let myself in. My father was watching TV in the living room while my mother kept busy in the kitchen. The all-American nuclear salt-of-the-earth. My father didn't look at me as I peeled off my coat and flopped down in the old green easychair.

"Decided to come home after all, did you?" he said after a minute. There was no sign of Joe in his long, square face, which had been jammed in an expression of disgust since my sister Rose had had her first baby three months after her wedding. On the television, a woman in a fancy restaurant threw a drink in a man's face. "Thought you were going to Connecticut with your rich-bitch girlfriend."

I shrugged.

"Come back to see him, didn't you?" He reached for one of the beer cans on the endtable, giving it a little shake to make sure there was something in it. "What'ud he do, call you?"

"I got a postcard." On TV the drink-throwing woman was now a corpse. A detective was frowning down at her. Women who threw drinks always ended up as corpses; if she'd watched enough TV, she'd have known that.

"A postcard. Some big deal. A postcard from a broken-down junkie. We're only your parents and we practically have to get down on our knees and beg you to come home."

I took a deep breath. "Glad to see you, too. Home sweet home."

"You watch that smart mouth on you. You coulda phoned. I'd a picked you up at the bus station. It ain't like it used to be around here." My father finished the can and parked it with the other empties. "There's a new element coming in. You don't know them and they don't know you and they don't care whose sister you are. Girl on the next block, lived here all her life—raped. On the street and it wasn't hardly dark out."

"Who was it?"

"How the hell should I know, goddamit, what am I, the Census Bureau? I don't keep track of every urchin around here."

"Then how do you know she lived here all her life?"

My father was about to bellow at me when my mother appeared in the doorway to the kitchen. "China. Come in here. I'll fix you something to eat."

"I'm not hungry."

Her face didn't change expression. "We got salami and Swiss cheese. I'll make you a sandwich."

Why not. She could make me a sandwich, I wouldn't eat it, and we could keep the enmity level up where it belonged. I heaved myself up out of the chair and went into the kitchen.

"*Did* you come home on his account?" my mother asked as I sat down at the kitchen table.

"I got a postcard from him."

"Did you." She kept her back to me while she worked at the counter. Always a soft doughy woman, my mother seemed softer and doughier than ever, as though a release had been sprung somehwere inside her, loosening everything. After a bit, she turned around holding a plate with a sandwich on it. Motherhood magic, culinary prestidigitation with ordinary salami, Swiss cheese and white bread. Behold, the family life. Too many *Leave It To Beaver* re-runs. She set the plate down in front of me.

"I did it," she said. "I threw him out."

"I figured."

She poured me a cup of coffee. "First I broke all his needles and threw them in the trash."

"Good, Ma. You know the police sometimes go through the trash where junkies are known to live?"

"So what are they going to do, bust me and your father? Joe doesn't live here any more. I wouldn't stand for him using this place as a shooting gallery. He stole. Took money out of my purse, took things and sold them. Like we don't work hard enough for anything that we can just let a junkie steal from us."

I didn't say anything. It would have been the same if he'd been staying with me. "I know, Ma."

"So?" She was gripping the back of a chair as though she didn't know whether she wanted to throw it or pull it out and sit down.

"So what," I said.

"So what do you want with him?"

"He asked for me, Ma."

"Oh, he asked for you. Great. What are you going to do, take him to live with you in your dorm room? Won't that be cozy."

I had an absurd picture of it. He'd have had a field day with all of Marlene's small valuables. "Where's Aurelia?"

"How should I know? We're on notice here—she does what she wants. I asked you to come home and talk to her. You wouldn't even answer my letters."

"What do you think I can do about her? I'm not her mother."

She gave me a dirty look. "Eat your sandwich."

I forced a bite and shoved the plate away. "I'm just not hungry."

"Suit yourself. You should have told me if you wanted something else."

"I didn't want something else. I didn't want anything." I helped myself to a cigarette. My mother's eyebrows went up but she said nothing. "When Aurelia comes home, I'll talk to her, okay?"

"*If* she comes home. Sometimes she doesn't. I don't know where she stays. I don't know if she even bothers to go to school sometimes."

I tapped ashes into the ashtray. "*I* was never able to get away with anything like that."

The look she gave me was unidentifiable. Her eyelids lowered, one corner of her mouth pulling down. For a few moments, I saw her as a stranger, some woman I'd never seen before who was waiting for me to figure something out but who was pretty sure I was too stupid to do it.

"Okay, *if* she comes home, I'll talk to her."

"Don't do me any favors. Anyway, you'll probably be out looking for *him*."

"I've always been closer to him than anyone else in the family was."

My mother made a disgusted noise. "Isn't that sweet?"

"He's still a human being, Ma. And he's still my brother."

"Don't lecture to *me* about family, you. What do you think I am, the custodian here? Maybe when you go back to college, you'd like to take Joe and Aurelia with you. Maybe you'd do better at making her come home at night and keeping him off the heroin. Go ahead. You're welcome to do your best."

"I'm not their mother or father."

"Yeah, yeah, yeah." My mother took a cigarette from the pack on the table and lit it. "They're still human beings, still your brother and sister. So what does that make me?"

I put my own cigarette out, picked my bag up in the living room and went to the bedroom I shared with Aurelia. She had started to spread out a little in it, though the division between her side and my side was still fairly evident. Mainly because she obviously wasn't spending a lot of time here.

For a long time, I sat on my bed fully clothed, just staring out the window. The street below was empty and dark and there was nothing to look at. I kept looking at it until I heard my parents go to bed. A little later, when I thought they were asleep, I opened the window a crack and rolled a joint from the stuff in the bottom drawer of my bureau. Most of the lid was still there, which meant Aurelia hadn't found it. I'd never liked grass that much after the novelty wore off, but I wanted something to blot out the bad taste the evening had left in my brain.

A whole joint to myself was a lot more than I was used to and the buzz was thick and debilitating. The smoke coiled into unreadable symbols and patterns before it was sucked out the window into the cold and dark. I thought of ragged ghosts fleeing a house like rats jumping off a sinking ship. It was the kind of dopey thought that occupies your mind for hours when you're stoned, which was fine with me. I didn't want to have to think about anything that mattered.

Eventually, I became aware that I was cold. When I could move, I reached over to shut the window and something down on the street caught my eye. It was too much in the shadows close to the building to see very well if it was even there at all. Hasher's delirium, or in this case, grasser's delirium. I tried to watch it anyway. There was a certain strength of definition and independence from the general fuzziness of my stoned eyesight, something that suggested there was more to it than the dope in my brain. Whatever it was—a dope exaggeration of a cat or a dog or a big rat—I didn't like it. Unbidden, my father's words about a new element moving in slid into my head. Something about the thing made me think of a reptile, stunted evolution or evolution reversed, and a sort of evil that might have lain thickly in pools of decay millions of years ago, pre-dating warm-blooded life. Which was ridiculous, I thought, because human beings brought the distinction between good and evil into the world. Good and evil, and stoned and not stoned. I was stoned. I went to bed.

But remember, said my still-buzzing mind as I was drifting into stupor-sleep, in order to make distinctions between any two things like good and evil, they first have to exist, don't they.

This is what happens when would-be intellectuals get stoned, I thought and passed out.

The sound of my father leaving for work woke me. I lay listening to my mother in the kitchen, waiting for the sound of bacon and eggs frying and her summons to get up and have a good breakfast. Instead, I heard water running briefly in the sink and then her footsteps going back to the bedroom and the door closing. That was new—my mother going back to bed after my father went to work, in spite of the fact that the college kid was home. I hadn't particularly wanted to talk to her anyway, especially if it were just going to be a continuation of the previous night but it still made me feel funny.

I washed and dressed, taking my time, but my mother never re-emerged. Apparently she was just not going to be part of my day. I left the house far earlier than I'd intended to, figuring I'd go find something to do with myself until it was time to meet Farmer and the others.

In the front vestibule of the apartment building, I nearly collided with my sister Rose, who seemed about ready to have her baby at any moment. She had dyed her hair blonde again, a cornsilk yellow color already brassing at the ends and showing dark roots.

"What are you doing home?" she asked, putting her hands protectively over her belly, protruding so much she couldn't button her coat.

"Vacation," I said. "How are you?"

"How am I ever? Pregnant."

"There *is* such a thing as birth control."

"Yeah, and there is such a thing as it not working. So?"

"Well. This is number five, isn't it?"

"I didn't know *you* were keeping score." She tried pulling her coat around her front but it wouldn't go. "It's cold down here. I'm going up to Ma."

"She went back to bed."

"She'll get up for me."

"Should you be climbing all those stairs in your condition?"

Rose lifted her plucked-to-nothing eyebrows. "You wanna carry me?" She pushed past me and slowly started up the first flight of steps.

"Come on, Rose," I called after her, "what'll happen if your bag of waters breaks or something while you're on the stairs?"

She turned to look at me from seven steps up. "I'll scream, what do you think I'll do?" She resumed her climb.

"Well, do you want me to walk up with you?" I asked, starting after her. She just waved a hand at me and kept going. Annoyed and amused, I waited until she had made the first landing and begun the next flight, wondering if I shouldn't run up after her anyway or at least stay there until I heard my mother let her in. Then I decided Rose probably knew what she was doing, in a half-assed way. My theory was that she had been born pregnant and waited sixteen years until she found someone to act as father. She hadn't been much smaller than she was now when she and Roger had gotten married, much to my parents' dismay. It hadn't bothered Rose in the least.

The sun was shining brightly but there was no warmth to it. The snow lining the curb was dirtier than ever, pitted and brittle. Here and there on the sidewalk, old patches of ice clung to the pavement like frozen jellyfish left after a receding tide. It wasn't even 10:30 but I went over to Streep's Lunch, in case anyone put in an early appearance. That wasn't very likely but there wasn't much else to do.

Streep had the place to himself except for a couple of old people sitting near the windows. I took a seat at the counter and ordered breakfast to make up for the night before. My atonement didn't exactly

104

impress him but he surprised me by actually speaking to me as he poured my coffee. "You home on vacation?"

"That's right," I said, feeling a little wary as I added cream from an aluminum pitcher.

"You like college?"

"It would be heaven if it weren't for the classes."

Streep's rubbery mouth twitched, shaking his jowls. "I thought that was what you went for, to go to classes and get smart."

I shrugged.

"Maybe you think you're already smart."

"Some people would say so." I smiled, thinking he should have asked my father.

"You think it's smart to keep coming around here and hanging out with junkies?"

I blinked at him. "I didn't know you cared."

"Just askin' a question."

"You haven't seen my brother Joe lately, have you?"

Streep made a fast little noise that was less than a laugh and walked away. Someone had left a newspaper on one of the stools to my right. I picked it up and read it over breakfast just for something to do. An hour passed, with Streep coming back every so often to refill my cup without any more conversation. I bought a pack of cigarettes from the machine just to have something else to do and noticed one of the old people had gone to sleep before finishing breakfast. She was very old, with frizzy grey hair and a sagging hawk nose. Her mouth had dropped open to show a few long, stained teeth. I had a half-baked idea of waking her when she gave an enormous snore. Streep didn't even look at her. What the hell, her hash browns were probably stone cold anyway. I went back to my newspaper.

When the clock over the grill said 12:10, I left some money on the counter and went outside. I should have known they'd be late, I thought. I'd probably have to stand around until close to dark, when they'd finally remember they were supposed to meet me here and not show, figuring I'd split.

A horn honked several times. George poked his head out the driver's side window of a car parked across the street. I hurried over as the back door swung open.

"Christ, we been waiting for you," Farmer said irritably as I climbed in. "You been in there the whole time?"

"I thought you were meeting Priscilla here."

"Change of venue, you should pardon the expression," Farmer said. "Streep won't give you a cup of water to go." He was in front with

George. Stacey and the kid were in the back with me. The kid didn't look so good today. He had dark circles under his eyes and wherever he'd spent the night hadn't had a washroom.

"Why aren't you in school?" I asked him.

"Screw it, what's it to you?" he said flippantly.

"Haven't been home yet, have you?"

"Chrissakes, what are you, his probation officer?" said Farmer. "Let's go, she's waiting."

The car pulled away from the curb with a jerk. George swore as he eased it into the light noon-time traffic. "I ain't used to automatics," he complained to no one.

Farmer was rummaging in the glove compartment. "Hey, there's no works in here. You got any?"

"I got them, don't worry. Just wait till we pick up Priscilla, okay?"

"Just tell me where they are."

"Don't sweat it, I told you I got them."

"I just want to know where."

"Up my ass, all right? Now let me drive."

"I'll give you up your ass," Farmer said darkly.

Stacey tapped him on the back of the head. "Come on, take it easy, Farmer. Everybody's gonna get what they need from Priscilla."

"Does Priscilla know where Joe is?" I asked.

"Priscilla knows everything," said Stacey, believing it.

Priscilla herself was standing on the sidewalk in front of a beauty parlor, holding a big styrofoam cup. She barely waited for the car to stop before she yanked the door open and got into the front seat next to Farmer.

"You got works?" he asked as she handed him the cup. "This asshole won't tell me if he's got any."

"In a minute, Farmer. I have to say hello to China." She knelt on the front seat and held her arms out to me. Obediently, I leaned forward over the kid so she could hug me. She was as bizarre-looking as ever, with her pale pancake make-up, frosted pink lipstick, heavily-outlined eyes, and flat-black hair. The junkie version of Elizabeth Taylor. She was a strange little girl in a puffy woman's body and she ran hot and cold with me, sometimes playing my older sister, then snubbing me outright, depending on Joe. They'd been on and off for as long as he'd been shooting, with her as the pursuer unless Joe knew for sure that she had a good connection.

Today she surprised me by kissing me lightly on the lips. It was like being kissed by a crayon. "How's our college kid?" she asked tenderly.

"Fine, Priscilla. Have you—"

"I haven't seen you since the fall," she went on, gripping the back of the seat as George pulled into the street again. "How do you like school? Are you doing real well?"

Farmer pulled her around. "This is very sweet, old home week and all, but do you have anything?"

"No, Farmer, I always stand around on the street with a cup of water. Don't spill it."

"I've got a spoon," said the kid, holding one up. Stacey took it from him.

"Me first?" she said hopefully.

Priscilla turned around and stared down her nose at her, junkie aristocracy surveying the rabble. "I understand I'm not the only one in this car with works?"

George was patting himself down awkwardly as he drove, muttering, "Shit, shit, shit."

"Asshole," said Farmer. "I knew you didn't have any."

"I *had* some, but I don't know where they are now."

"Try looking up your ass. Priscilla?"

Priscilla let out a noisy sigh. "I'm not going to do this any more. Someday we're all going to get hep and die."

"Well, *I'm* clean," the kid announced proudly.

"Keep borrowing works, you'll get a nice case of hepatitis," I said. "Joe got the clap once, using someone else's."

"Bullshit."

"Tell him whose spike it was, Stacey," I said, feeling mean. Stacey flushed.

"And you want to go first?" Priscilla said. "No way."

"That was last year, I'm cured now, honest. I don't even have a cold." She glared at me. "Please, Priscilla. Please."

Priscilla sighed again and passed her a small square of foil and a plastic syringe. "You give me anything and I'll fucking kill you, I swear."

"Here, hold this." Stacey dumped everything in the kid's lap and took the water from Farmer. "Who's got a belt?"

Somehow everyone looked at everyone else and ended up looking at me.

"Shit," I said and slipped it off. Stacey reached for it and I held it back. "Somebody tell me where Joe is or I'll throw this out the window right now."

"China, don't be like that. You're holding things up," said Priscilla chidingly, as though I were a bratty younger sister.

"I want to know where Joe is."

"Just let us fix first, okay? Now give Stacey your belt."

Stacey snatched the belt away from me before I could say anything else and shoved her shirt and sweater sleeves high up on her arm. "Wrap it on me," she said to the kid. Her voice was getting shaky. The kid got the belt around her upper arm and pulled it snug. He had to pour a little water into the bowl of the spoon for her, too, and shake the heroin out of the foil. Someone had a ragged piece of something that had to pass for cheesecloth. Stacey fidgeted with it while the kid held a match under the spoon. When the mix in the bowl started to bubble, Stacey laid the cloth over the surface and drew some solution into the syringe. Her hands were very steady now. She held the syringe up and flicked it with her finger.

"Will you hurry it up?" Farmer snapped. "There's other people besides you."

"Keep your shirt on, I'm trying to lose some bubbles. Help me," Stacey said. "Tighten that belt."

The kid pulled the belt tighter for her as she straightened her arm. She felt in the fold of her elbow with her pinky. "There he is. Old Faithful. He shoulda collapsed long ago but he just keeps on truckin'. I heard about this guy, you know? Who shot an air bubble and he saw it in his vein just as he was nodding out, you know?" She probed with the needle, drew back the plunger and found blood. "That poor guy just kept stroking it down and stroking it down and would you believe—" her eyelids fluttered. I reached over the kid to loosen the belt on her arm. "He actually got rid of it. He's still shooting." She started to say something else and passed out.

"Jesus, Priscilla." I took the needle out of Stacey's arm. "What kind of stuff have you got?"

"Only the best. Joe's new connection. You next?" she asked the kid.

"He's not an addict yet," I said. "He can pass this time."

"Who asked you?" said the kid. "You're not my fucking mother."

"You have to mainline for two weeks straight to get a habit," I said. "Take the day off."

But he already had the belt around his arm. "No. Give me the needle."

I plunged the syringe into the cup he was holding. "You have to clean it first, jerk-off." I cranked down the window and squirted a thin stream of water into the air. "If you're going to do this anyway, you might as well do it right."

Suddenly he looked unsure of himself. "I never shot myself up before. Stacey always did me."

I looked at her, sprawled out on his other side. "She's a big help, that girl. Looks like you're on your own. I don't give injections."

But I flicked the bubbles out of the syringe for him. It was better than watching him shoot an air bubble. He had veins like power cables.

Priscilla went next. I barely had time to clean the needle and spoon for her. Farmer fixed after her. The spoon was looking bad. I was scrubbing the mess out of it with a corner of my shirt when I noticed it was real silver. The kid's spoon. Probably stolen out of his mother's service for eight. Or maybe it was the one they'd found lodged in his mouth when he'd been born. I looked at him slumped next to Stacey, eyes half-closed, too ecstatic to smile. Was this part of the new element moving in that my father had mentioned, a pampered high school kid?

"Priscilla, are you awake?" I asked, squirting water from the needle out the window while Farmer cooked his load.

"Mmm," she said lazily.

"Do you really know where Joe is?"

She didn't answer. I dipped the needle into the water one last time and squirted a stream out the window again. It arched gracefully into the air and splattered against the passenger side window of the police car that had pulled up even with us. I froze, still holding the needle up in plain sight. Farmer was telling me to hand him the fucking spike but his voice seemed to be coming through miles of cotton batting. I was back in the buzz of the night before, the world doing a slow-motion underwater ballet of the macabre while I watched my future dribble down the window along with the water. The cop at the wheel turned his head for a year before his eyes met mine. Riding all alone, must be budget-cutting time, my mind babbled. His face was flat and I could see through the dirty glass that his skin was rough and leathery. His tongue flicked out and ran over his lips as we stared at each other. He blinked once, in a funny way, as though the lower lids of his color-less eyes had risen to meet the upper ones. A kind of recognition passed between us. Then he turned away and the police car accelerated, passing us.

"Did you see that?" I gave the needle to Farmer, who was calling me nine kinds of bastard.

"Nope," George said grimly. "And he didn't see us, neither."

I tried to laugh, as though I were in on the joke. "Oh, man. I thought for sure we were all busted."

"Times are changing."

"Don't tell me the junkies are pooling their money to buy off the cops."

Priscilla came to and sighed happily. "Somebody is. We got all the conveniences. Good dope, bad cops. Things ain't so bad around here these days."

The kid was pulling himself up on me. I sat him up without thinking about it. "Priscilla? Do you know where Joe is? Priscilla?"

"Joe? Oh, yeah. He's at my place."

"I thought he was going around with his connection."

"He's at my place. Or he was."

George pulled the car over again as Farmer woozily began cooking his shot for him. "Let me fix and I'll drive you over there, okay?" he said, smiling thinly over his shoulder at me.

The kid threw himself over my lap and fumbled the car door open. "Wanna go for a walk," he mumbled, crawling over my legs and hauling himself upright on the door. He stood swaying and tried a few tentative steps. "Can't make it. Too loaded." I caught him and pulled him back in, shoving him over next to Stacey. He smiled at me. "You're a real nice girl, you know that? You're a real nice girl."

110 "Shit!" George slammed his hand against the steering wheel. "It broke, the fucking needle broke!"

"Did you fix?" asked Farmer.

"Yeah, just in time. Sorry, Priscilla." George turned to look at her and nearly fell across Farmer. "I'll find mine and give it to you. Never been used, I swear."

Priscilla made a disgusted noise.

"Hey, if everybody's happy, let's go over to Priscilla's place now," I said.

George wagged his head. "Not yet. Can't get that far, stuff was too strong. I gotta let it wear off some first. Where are we?" He opened his door and nearly fell out. "Hey, we're back near Streep's. Go there for awhile, okay?" No one answered. "Okay? Go to Streep's, get some coffee, listen to some music. Okay?" He nudged Farmer. "Okay?"

"Shit." I got out, hauled the kid out after me and left him leaning on the door while I dragged Stacey out. She woke up enough to smile at me. Farmer and Priscilla found their way around the car, stumbling over each other. I looked around. A few cars passed, no one paying any attention. Here we are in scenic Junk City in the Land of Nod, where five loaded hopheads can attract no interest. What's wrong with this picture?

George reeled past me and I grabbed him, patting his pants pockets. "What?" he said dreamily.

"Let me borrow your car."

"It's not my car. It's—" His voice trailed off as his head drooped. "That's okay," I said, shaking him, "just give me the keys." I dug them out of his right pants pocket, giving him a thrill he was too far gone to appreciate. George wasn't wearing any underwear. "Priscilla."

She had managed to go nearly half a block unassisted. At the sound of her name, she swiveled around, hugging herself against a cold she probably wasn't really feeling.

"Is Joe really at your place?"

She shrugged elaborately. "Hurry, you might catch him." Farmer went by and yanked her along with him. I watched them all weaving and staggering away from me, a ragged little group minus one, who was still leaning against the car.

"My name's Tad," he said. Probably short for tadpole, I thought. "Take me with you."

I went to call out to Farmer and the rest of them but they had already turned the corner. I was stuck with their new friend unless I chose to leave him in some doorway. He was grinning at me as he swayed from side to side. The coat was dirty now but it was still pretty nice. His gloves looked like kidskin and the boots were brand new. If I left him, I'd come back and find him up on blocks, nude. I shoved him into the back seat.

"Lie down, pass out and don't give me any trouble."

"You're a real nice girl," he mumbled.

"Yeah, we could go to the prom together in a couple of years."

The front seat was too far back for me and wouldn't move up. I perched on the edge of the broken-down cushion and just managed to reach the pedals. I got the car started but pulling out was the tricky part. I'd never learned to drive. The car itself wasn't in terrific running condition—it wanted either to stall or race. I eased it down the street in half a dozen jerks that pushed me against the steering wheel and sent the kid in back off the seat and onto the floor. He didn't complain.

Priscilla had an apartment in one of the tenements near the railroad yard. The buildings looked abandoned at first glance; at second glance, they still looked abandoned. I steered the car off the road into an unpaved area that served as a parking lot and pulled up in front of the building nearest to the tracks. In the back, my companion pulled himself up on the seat, rubbing his eyes. "Where are we?"

"Wait here," I said, getting out of the car.

He shook his head emphatically. "No, I was here last night. This is Priscilla's. It ain't safe. I should go with you." He stumbled out of the car and leaned against it, trying to look sober. "I'm okay, now. I'm just high."

"I'm not going to wait for you." I headed toward the building with

him staggering after me. The heroin in his system had stabilized somewhat and he fell only three times. I kept going.

He gave up on the first flight. I left him hanging on the railing
muttering to himself while I trotted up to Priscilla's place on the second
floor. The door was unlocked, I knew—the lock had been broken ages
ago and Priscilla wasn't about to spend good junk money on getting
it fixed—but the sagging screen door, was latched. I found a torn place
in the screen and reached in to unhook it.

"Joe?" I called, stepping into the filthy kitchen. An odor of something long dead hit me square in the face, making me gag. "Joe?" I
tiptoed across the room. On the sink was a package of hamburger
Priscilla had probably left out to thaw and then forgotten about, three
weeks before, it seemed like. I wondered how she could stand it and
then remembered how she liked to brag that coke had destroyed her
nose. The rest of them wouldn't care as long as they could get fixed.
My stomach leaped and I heaved on the floor. It was just a bit of bile
in spite of the breakfast I'd eaten but I couldn't take any more and
headed for the porch.

"Whaddaya want?"

I whirled, holding my hand over my mouth and nose as my gag
reflex went into action again. A large black man wearing only a pair
of pajama bottoms was standing in the doorway to the bedroom. We
stared at each other curiously.

"Whaddaya want?" he asked me again.

"I'm looking for Joe," I said from behind my hand.

"I'm Joe." He scratched his face and I saw a thin line of blood
trickling from the corner of his mouth.

"Wrong Joe," I said, cursing Priscilla. She knew goddam well,
the con artist. What did she think, that I'd forget about finding Joe
and curl up with this guy instead? Yeah, that was Priscilla all over.
A Joe for a Joe, fair deal. "The Joe I'm looking for is my brother."

"I'm a brother."

"Yeah, you are. You're bleeding."

He touched his mouth and looked dully at his fingers. "I'm blood."

I nodded. "Well, if you see a white guy named Joe, he's *my* brother.
Tell him China was looking for him."

"China."

"Right. China."

"China's something real fragile. Could break." His expression
altered slightly and that same kind of recognition that had passed between me and the cop in the patrol car seemed to pass between us
now in Priscilla's stinking kitchen.

112

I glanced at the rotting hamburger on the counter and suddenly it didn't look like rotting meat any more than the man standing in the doorway of Priscilla's bedroom looked like another junkie, or even a human being. He tilted his head and studied me, his eyes narrowing, and it all seemed to be going in slow motion, that underwater feeling again.

"If you ain't in some kinda big hurry, why don't you hang around," he said. "Here all by myself. Not too interesting, nobody to rap with. Bet you got a lot of stuff you could rap about."

Yeah, he was probably craving to find out if I'd read any good books lately. I opened my mouth to say something and the stink hit me again in the back of the throat.

"Whaddaya say, you stick around here for awhile. I don't bite. 'Less I'm invited to."

I wanted to ask him what he'd bitten just recently. He touched his lip as though he'd been reading my mind and shrugged. I took a step back. He didn't seem so awfully junked-up any more and it occurred to me that it was strange that he wasn't with Priscilla instead of here, all by himself.

Maybe, I thought suddenly, he was waiting for someone. Maybe Joe was supposed to be here after all, maybe he was supposed to come here for some reason and I'd just arrived ahead of him.

I swallowed against the stink, almost choked again, and said, "Hey, did Priscilla tell you she had a friend coming by, a guy named Joe, or just a guy maybe? I mean, have you been waiting for someone?"

"Just you, babe."

I'd heard that line once or twice but it never sounded so true as it did just then. The kid's words suddenly came back to me. *This is Priscilla's. I was here last night.* Farmer must have run right over after I'd seen him, to tell her I was looking for Joe. So she decided to send me on a trip to nowhere, with Farmer and the rest of them in on it, playing out the little charade of meeting her today so I could ask her about Joe and she could run this ramadoola on me. But why? What was the point?

"No, man," I said, taking another step back. "Not me."

"You sure about that?" The voice was smooth enough to slip on, like glare ice. Ice. It was chilly in the apartment, but he didn't seem to feel it. "Must be something I can . . . help you with."

Outside, there was the sound of a train approaching in the distance. In a few moments, you wouldn't be able to hear anything for the roar of the train passing.

I turned and fled out to the porch. The deadmeat smell seemed

113

to follow me as I galloped back down the stairs and woke the kid still hanging on the bannister. "Let's go, let's get out of here."

The train was thundering past as I shoved him back into the car and pulled out.

"You find Joe?" he shouted as we bounced across the parking lot.

"Yeah, I found him. I found the wrong fucking Joe."

The kid giggled a little. "There's lots of guys named Joe."

"Thanks for the information. I'll keep it in mind." I steered the car onto the street again, unsure of what to do next. Maybe just cruise around, stopping random junkies and asking them if they'd seen Joe, or look for the white Caddy or whatever it was. A white luxury car would stand out, especially if a pretty blonde woman were driving it.

The junkies were starting to come out in force now, appearing on the sidewalks and street corners. A few of them waved at the car and then looked confused when they saw me at the wheel. It seemed to me there were more new faces among the familiar ones, people I didn't even know by sight. But that would figure, I thought—had I really expected the junkie population to go into some kind of stasis while I was away at college? Every junkie's got a friend and eventually the friend's got a habit. Like the jailbait in the backseat.

I glanced in the rear view mirror at him. He was sitting up with his head thrown back, almost conscious. If I were going to find Joe or at least his ladyfriend, I'd have to dump the kid.

"Wake up," I said, making a right turn onto the street that would take me past Foster Circle and down to Streep's. "I'm going to leave you off at the restaurant with everyone else. Can you handle that?"

He struggled forward and leaned over the front seat. "But we ain't found Joe yet."

" 'Haven't found Joe yet.' What's the matter, do you just nod out in English class?"

He giggled. "Yeah. Don't everyone?"

"Maybe. I can't be hauling your ass all over with me. There's no end-of-class bell around here. You're on your own." I took another look at him as he hung over the seat, grinning at me like God's own fool. "You don't know that, do you?"

"Know what." He ruffled my hair clumsily.

"Quit that. You don't know that you're on your own."

"Shit, I got *lots* of friends."

"You've got junkies is what you've got. Don't confuse them with friends."

"Yeah?" He ruffled my hair again and I slapped his hand away. "So why are you so hot to find Joe?"

"Joe isn't my friend, he's my brother."

"Jeez, no kidding? I thought you were like his old lady or something."

How quickly they forget, junkies. I was about to answer him when I saw it, gleaming like fresh snow in the afternoon sunlight, impossibly clean, illegally parked right at the curb at Foster Circle. George had been right—it was a Caddy after all. I looked for a place to pull over and found one in front of a fire hydrant.

"Wait here," I said, killing the engine. "If I'm not back in ten minutes, you're free to go."

"Unh-unh," the kid said, falling back and fumbling for the door handle. "I'm coming with you."

"Fuck off." I jumped out of the car and darted across two lanes of on-coming traffic, hoping the kid would pass out again before he solved the mystery of the door handle. The Caddy was unoccupied; I stepped over the low thorny bushes the ex-mayor had chosen for their red summer blooms and looked around wildly.

At the time, it didn't seem strange that I almost didn't see her. She was sitting on a bench fifty feet away looking as immaculate as her car in a thick brown coat and spike-heeled boots. Her pale blonde hair curved over her scarf in a simple, classy pageboy, like a fashion model's. But even from where I stood, I could see she was just a bit old for a fashion model. More like an ex-fashion model, from the careful, composed way she was sitting with her ankles crossed and her tidy purse resting on her knees, except the guy on the bench next to her wasn't material for the Brut ad campaign. It was Farmer. He still looked pretty bleary but he raised one arm and pointed at me. She turned to look and her elegantly made-up face broke into that sort of cheery smile some stewardesses reserve for men who drink heavily in first class.

She beckoned with a gloved hand and I went over to them.

"Hello," she said in a warm contralto. "We've been waiting for you."

"Oh, yeah?" I said casually. "Seems like there's always someone waiting for me these days. Right, Farmer?" He was too busy staring at the woman to answer. "I thought you didn't know how to find her."

"I don't," Farmer said and smiled moonily at the woman, which pissed me off. "She found me. Kind of."

"At *Streep's?*" I didn't look right at her but I could see she was following the exchange with that same cheery smile, completely unoffended that we were talking about her in the third person.

115

"Nah. After you left us off, I left everybody at Streep's and came down here, figuring maybe I could find somebody who'd get in touch with Joe for you."

"Sure. Except Priscilla told me Joe was at her place. Only he wasn't. What about that, Farmer? You wanna talk about that a little? Like how you were there last night?"

Farmer could have cared less, though it was hard to see how. "Yeah, we was there. She wouldn't let us in, said she'd meet us today like we planned." He shrugged. "Anyway, I came down here and there was her car going down the street, so I flagged her down and told her you were looking for Joe. So then we came here. I figured you'd look here sooner or later because this was where I told you I saw her and Joe. And, you know, Streep's, shit, it's not a good place."

Sure wasn't, especially if you thought you could make your own connection and not have to let the rest of your junkie pals in on it directly. "So you decided to sit out in the cold instead." I blew out a short, disgusted breath. "I'd have gone back to Streep's, eventually."

"Well, if it got too cold, we was gonna get in the car." Farmer looked uncomfortable. "Hey, what are you bitching at me for? I found her, didn't I?"

I turned to the woman. "Where's Joe?"

Her eyes were deep blue, almost navy. "He's at my place. I understand you're his sister, China?" She tilted her head like game show women do when they're showing you the year's supply of Turtle Wax behind door number three. "I had no idea Joe had a sister in college. But I see the resemblance, you have the same eyes, the same mouth. You're very close to Joe?"

"I'd like to see him."

She spread her hands. "Then we'll go see him. All of us." She smiled past me and I turned around. The kid was standing several feet behind me, still doped up and a little unsteady but looking eager and interested in that way junkies have when they smell a possibility of more heroin. Fuck the two weeks; he'd been a junkie all his life, just like Joe.

I turned back to the woman, intending to tell her the kid was only fifteen and surely she didn't want that kind of trouble but she was already on her feet, helping Farmer up, her expensive gloves shining incongruously against his worn, dirty denim jacket.

But then again, she didn't have to touch him with her bare hands.

She made no objection when I got into the front seat with her and jerked my thumb over my shoulder instead of moving over so Farmer could get in next to me. He piled into the back with the kid and we drove off just as a meter maid pulled up next to George's car. I looked over my shoulder at the Cushman.

"Looks like we're leaving just in time," I said.

"They never ticket my car." She pushed a Grateful Dead 8-track into the tape deck and adjusted the volume on the rear speakers.

"That's funny," I said, "you don't seem like the Grateful Dead type. I'd have thought you were more of a Sinatra fan. Or maybe Tony Bennett."

"Actually, my own taste runs to chamber music," she said smoothly. "But it has very limited appeal with most of our clients. The Grateful Dead have a certain rough charm, especially in their ballads, though I will never have the appreciation for them that so many young people do. I understand they're quite popular among college students."

"Yeah, St. Stephen with a rose," I said. "Have another hit and all that. Except that's Quicksilver Messenger Service."

"I have one of their tapes, too, if you'd prefer to hear that instead."

"No, the Dead will do."

She almost looked at me. Then Farmer called out, "This is *such* a great *car!*" and she turned up the volume slightly.

"They can't hear us," she said.

"They sure can't."

Her face should have been tired from smiling so much but she was a true professional. Don't try this at home. Suddenly I wished I hadn't. My father was right; cocky snotnosed college know-it-all. I hadn't had the first idea of what I'd gotten into here with this white Cadillac and this ex-fashion model who referred to junkies as clients but I was beginning to get a clue. We were heading for the toll bridge over the river. The thing to do was jump out as soon as she stopped, jump out and run like hell and hope that would be fast enough.

There was a soft, metallic click. Power locks.

"Such a bad area," she said. "Must always keep the doors secure when you drive through."

And then, of course, she blinked. Even with her in profile, I could see her lower eyelid rise to meet the upper one.

She used the exact change lane, barely slowing as she lowered the window and reached toward the basket. For my benefit only, I guessed; her hand was empty.

She took us to a warehouse just on the other side of the river, one of several in an industrial cluster. Some seemed to be abandoned, some not. It wasn't quite evening yet but the place was shadowy. Still, I was willing to make a run for it as soon as we stopped and fuck whatever was in the shadows, I'd take my chances that I'd be able to get away, maybe come back with the cops. After I'd given them a blink test. But she had some arrangement; no stops. While the Dead kept on trucking, she drove us right up a ramp to a garage door, which automatically rumbled upward. We drove onto a platform that had chicken wire fencing on either side. Two bright lamps hanging on the chicken wire went on. After a moment, there was a jerk and the platform began to lift slowly. Really some arrangement.

"Such a bad area," she said. "You take your life in your hands if you get out of the car."

Yeah, I thought, I just bet you did.

After a long minute, the elevator thumped to a stop and the doors in front of us slid open. We were looking into a huge, elegantly furnished living room. *House and Garden* conquers the universe.

"This is it," she said gaily, killing the engine and the Dead. "Everybody out. Careful when you open the door, don't scratch the paint. Such a pain getting it touched up."

I waited for her to release the locks and then I banged my door loudly against the chicken wire. What the hell, I figured; I'd had it anyway. Only a cocky snotnosed college know-it-all would think like that.

But she didn't say anything to me about it, or even give me a look. She led the way into the living room and gestured at the long beige sofa facing the elevator doors, which slid closed just as Farmer and the kid staggered across the threshold.

"Make yourselves comfortable," she said. "Plenty of refreshments on the table."

"Oh, man," said Farmer, plumping down on the couch. "Can we play some more music, maybe some more Dead?"

"Patience, Farmer," she said as she took off her coat and laid it on one of the stools in front of a large mahogany wet bar. It had a mirror behind it and, above that, an old-fashioned picture of a plump woman in bloomers and a corset lounging on her side eating chocolates from a box. It was like a stage set. She watched me staring at it.

"Drink?" she said. "I didn't think people your age partook in that very much nowadays but we have a complete stock for those who can appreciate vats and vintages and whatnot."

"I'll take a shot of twenty-year-old scotch right after you show me where Joe is."

The woman chuckled indulgently. "Wouldn't you prefer a nice cognac?"

"Whatever you think is best," I said.

"I'll be right back." She didn't move her hips much when she walked but in that cream-colored cashmere dress, she didn't have to. This was real refinement, real class and taste. Smiling at me over her shoulder one more time, she slipped through a heavy wooden door at the far end of the room next to an enormous antique secretary.

I looked at Farmer and the kid, who were collapsed on the sofa like junkie versions of Raggedy Andy.

"Oh, *man,*" said Farmer, "this is *such* a *great place!* I never been in such a *great place!*"

"Yeah," said the kid. "It's so far out."

There were three silver boxes on the coffee table in front of them. I went over and opened one; there were several syringes in it, all clean and new. The box next to it held teaspoons and the one next to that, white powder. That one was next to the table lighter. I picked it up. It was an elaborately carved silver dragon coiled around a rock or a monolith or something, its wings pulled in close to its scaly body. You flicked the wheel in the middle of its back and the flame came out of its mouth. All I needed was a can of aerosol deodorant and I'd have had a flame thrower. Maybe I'd have been able to get out with a flame thrower. I doubted it.

"Jeez, will you look at that!" said the kid, sitting up in delayed reaction to the boxes. "What a set-up!"

"This is such a *great place!*" Farmer said, picking up the box of heroin.

"Yeah, a real junkie heaven," I said. "It's been nice knowing you."

Farmer squinted up at me. "You going?"

"We're all going."

He sat back, still holding the box while the kid eyed him nervously. "You go ahead. I mean, this isn't exactly your scene anyway. But I'm hanging in."

"You just don't get it, do you? You think Blondie is just going to let you wander back out across the river with all the horse you can carry?"

Farmer smiled. "Shit, maybe she wants me to move in. I think she likes me. I get that very definite feeling."

"Yeah, and the two of you could adopt Tadpole here, and Stacey and Priscilla and George can come over for Sunday roast."

The kid shot me a dirty look. Farmer shrugged. "Hey, somebody's gotta be out there, takin' care of the distribution."

"And she throws out Joe to make room for you, right?" I said.

"Oh, yeah, Joe." Farmer tried to think. "Well, hell, this is a big place. There's room for three. More, even." He giggled again.

"*Farmer.* I don't think many people see this place and live."

He yawned widely, showing his coated tongue. "Hey, ain't we all lucky, then."

"No. We're not lucky."

Farmer stared at me for a long moment. Then he laughed. "Shit. You're crazy."

The door at the far end of the room opened again and the woman came out. "Here he is!" she announced cheerfully and pulled Joe into the room.

My brother Joe, the original lost boy, the disposable man in an ankle-length bathrobe knotted loosely at the waist, showing his bony chest. The curly brown hair was cleaner than it had been the last time I'd seen him but duller and thinner, too. His eyes seemed to be sunk deep in the sockets and his skin looked dry and flaky. But he was steady on his bare feet as he came toward me.

"Joe," I said. "It's me, Chi—"

"I know, babe, I know." He didn't even change expression. "What the fuck?"

"I got your card."

"Shit. I told you, it was for the last time."

I blinked at him. "I came home because I thought—" I stopped, looking at the woman who was still smiling as she moved behind the bar and poured a little cognac into a glass.

"Well, go on," she said. "Tell him what you thought. And have your cognac. You should warm the bowl between your hands."

I shook my head slightly, looking down at the plush carpet. It was also beige. Not much foot traffic around here. "I thought you needed me to do something. Help you or something."

"I was saying good-bye, babe. That's all. I thought I should, you know, after everything you seen me through. I figured, what the hell, one person in the world who ever cared what happened to me, I'd say good-bye. Fucking parents don't care if they never see me again. Rose, Aurelia—like, forget it."

I looked up at him. He still hadn't changed expression. He might have been telling me it was going to snow again this winter.

"Have your cognac," the woman said to me again. "You warm the bowl between your hands like this." She demonstrated and then held the glass out to me. When I didn't move to take it, she put it down on the bar. "Perhaps you'll feel like it later." She hurried over to the couch where Farmer and the kid were rifling the syringes and the spoons. Joe took a deep breath and let it out in a not-quite sigh.

"I can tell her to let you go," he said. "She'll probably do it."

"Probably?" I said.

He made a helpless, impotent gesture with one hand. "What the fuck did you come here for?"

"For you, asshole. What the fuck did *you* come here for?"

Bending over the coffeetable, the woman looked back at us. "Are you going to answer that, Joe? Or shall I?"

Joe turned toward her slightly and gave a little shrug. "Will you let her go?"

That smile. "Probably."

Farmer was holding up a syringe. "Hey, I need some water. And a cooker. You got a spoon? And some cloth."

"Little early for your next fix, isn't it?" I said.

"Why wait?" He patted the box of junk cuddled in his lap.

The woman took the syringe from him and set it on the table. "You won't need any of that. We keep it around for those who have to be elsewhere—say, if you had an appointment to keep or if Joe were running an errand—but here we do it differently."

"Snort?" Farmer was disgusted. "Lady, I'm way past the snort stage."

She gave a refined little laugh and moved around the coffeetable to sit down beside him. "Snort. How revolting. There's no snorting here. Take off your jacket."

Farmer obeyed, tossing his jacket over the back of the couch. She pushed up his left shirt sleeve and studied his arm.

"Hey, China," Farmer said, watching the woman with junkie avidity, "gimme your belt."

"No belt," said the woman. "Sit back, relax. I'll take care of everything." She touched the inside of his elbow with two fingers and then ran her hand up to his neck. "Here is actually a lot better."

Farmer looked nervous. "In the neck? You sure you know what you're doing? Nobody does it in the neck."

"It's not an easy technique to master but it's far superior to your present methods. Not to mention faster and far more potent."

"Well, hey." Farmer laughed, still nervous. "More potent, sure, I'm for that."

"Relax," the woman said, pushing his head back against the couch. "Joe's done it this way a lot of times, haven't you, Joe?"

I looked at his neck but I didn't see anything, not even dirt.

The woman loosened Farmer's collar and pushed his hair back, ignoring the fact that it was badly in need of washing. She stroked his skin with her fingertips, making a low, crooning noise, the kind of sound you'd use to calm a scared puppy. "There, now," she murmured close to Farmer's neck. "There it is, there's our baby. All nice and strong. That's a good one."

121

Farmer moaned pleasurably and reached for her but she caught his hand and held it firmly on his thigh.

"Don't squirm around now," she said. "This won't take long. Not very long."

She licked his neck.

I couldn't believe it. Farmer's dirty old neck. I'd have licked the sidewalk first. And *this* woman—I looked at Joe but he was watching the woman run her tongue up Farmer's neck and still no expression on him, as though he were watching a dull TV program he'd already seen.

Farmer's eyelids were at half-mast. He gave a small laugh. "Tickles a little."

The woman pulled back and then blew on the spot gently. "There now. We're almost ready." She took the box of heroin from his lap.

I didn't want to see this. I looked at Joe again. He shook his head slightly, keeping his gaze on the woman. She smiled at me, scooped up a small amount of heroin and put it in her mouth.

"Fucking lowlife," I said, but my voice sounded far away. The woman nodded, as if to tell me I had it right and then, fast, like a snake striking, she clamped her mouth on Farmer's neck.

Farmer jumped slightly, his eyes widening. Then he went completely slack, only the woman's mouth on him holding him up.

I opened my mouth to yell, but nothing came out. As though there was a field around me and Joe that kept us still.

She seemed to stay like that on Farmer's neck forever. I stood there, unable to look away. I'd watched Farmer and Joe and the rest of them fix countless times. The scene played in my brain, the needle sliding into skin, probing, finding the vein and the blood tendriling in the syringe when it hit. Going for the boot because it made the rush better. Maybe this made the rush better for both of them.

Time passed and left us all behind. I'd thought it was too soon to fix again, but yeah, it would figure that she'd have to get them while they were still fucked up, so they'd just sit there and take it. Hey, was that last fix a little strange? —Strange? What's strange? Nod.

Then the woman drew her head back a little and I saw it. A living needle, like a stinger. I wished I were a fainter so I could have passed out, shut the picture off, but she held my gaze as strongly as she held Farmer. I'd come to see Joe and this was part of it, package deal. In another part of my mind, I was screaming and yelling and begging Joe to take us both out of there, but that place was too far away, in some other world where none of this was possible.

She brought her mouth down to Farmer's neck again, paused, and lifted her head. There was a small red mark on Farmer's skin, like a vaccination. She swallowed and gave me that professional smile.

"That's what he came here for," she said. "Now, shall I do the next one, Joe, or would you like to?"

"Oh, Jesus, Joe," I said. "Oh, *Jesus.*"

"I don't like boys," he said. And blinked.

"Oh, *Jesus—*"

"Well, there's only one girl here for you." She actually crinkled her nose.

"No. *No,* oh, Jesus, *Joe—*" I grabbed two fistfuls of his bathrobe and shook him. He swayed in my grasp and it felt like I was shaking a store mannequin. Even in his deepest junked-out stupor, he'd been a million times more alive than he was now. My late brother Joe, the original lost boy now lost for all time, the disposable man finally disposed of.

He waited until I stopped shaking him and looked down at me. I took a step back. A dull television program he'd already seen. "Let her go, okay?"

"Now, Joe," she said, admonishing.

I bolted for the elevator but the doors didn't open. She had the power over them, over everything, junkies, me, even tollbooths. I just stood there until I felt Joe's hands on my shoulders.

"China—"

I jumped away from him and backed up against the elevator doors. There was a buzzing in my ears. Hyperventilating. In a moment, I was going to pass out and they could do whatever they liked. Standing between Farmer comatose on the couch and the kid, who was just sitting like a junked-up lump, the woman looked bored.

"China," my brother repeated, but he didn't reach for me again.

I forced myself to breathe more slowly. The buzzing in my ears receded and I was almost steady again. "Oh, Jesus, Joe, where did you *find* these—these whatever-they-are. They're not people."

"I didn't really find them," he said. "One day I looked around and they were just there. Where they've always been."

"I never saw them before."

"You never had to. People like me and Farmer and whatsisname over there, the kid, we're the ones they come for. Not you."

"Then why did *I* find them?"

"I don't like to think about that. It's—" he fumbled for a moment. "I don't know. Contagious, I guess. Maybe someday they'll come for everyone."

"Well, that *is* in the plan," the woman said. "There are only so many Joes and Farmers in the world. Then you have to branch out. Fortunately, it's not hard to find new ways to reach new receptors." She ran a finger along the collar of her dress. "The damnedest things come into fashion and you know how that is. Something can just sweep the country."

"Let her go now," Joe said.

"But it's close to time for you, dear one."

"Take her back to Streep's. Stacey and George'll be there, maybe Priscilla. You can bring them here, leave her there."

"But, *Joe,*" she said insistently, "she's *seen* us."

"So you can get her later."

I began to shake.

"Joe." The stewardess smile went away. "There are *rules*. And they're not just arbitrary instructions designed to keep the unwashed multitude moving smoothly through intersections during rush hour." She came around the coffeetable to him and put her hand on his arm. I saw her thumb sink deeply into the material of his bathrobe. "You *chose* this, Joe. You *asked* for it, and when we gave it to you, you agreed. And this is part of the deal."

He pried her hand off his arm and shoved it away. "No, it's not. My sister isn't a junkie. It wouldn't go right, not now. You know it wouldn't. You'd just end up with a troublesome body to dispose of and the trail would lead directly to me. Here. Because everyone probably knows she's been looking for me. She's probably asked half the city if they've seen me. Isn't that right, China."

I nodded, unable to speak.

"You know we've got the cops."

"Not all of them. Not even enough of them."

The woman considered it. Then she shook her head at him as though he were a favored, spoiled pet. "I wouldn't do this for anyone else, I hope you know that."

"I know it," said Joe.

"I mean, in spite of everything you said. I might have decided just to work around the difficulties. It's just that I like you so much. You fit in so well. You're just so — *appropriate.*" She glanced back at the kid on the couch. "Well, I hope this can wait until I take care of our other matter."

"Whatever you like," Joe said.

She turned her smile on me again but there was a fair amount of sneer in it. "I'll be with you shortly."

I turned away as she went back to the couch so I wouldn't have to see her do the kid. Joe just stood there the whole time, making no

124

move toward me or away from me. I was still shaking a little; I could see my frizzy bangs trembling in front of my eyes. The absurd things you notice, I thought, and concentrated on them, out of focus against the background of the fabulous antique bar, trying to make them hold still. If they stopped trembling then I would have stopped shaking. The kid on the couch made a small noise, pleasure or pain or both, and I looked up at Joe, wanting to scream at him to make her stop it but there was nothing there to hear that kind of scream. The kid was on his own; *I* was the one who really hadn't known that. We were all on our own, now.

The dead eyes stared at me, the gaze as flat as an animal's. I tried to will one last spark of life to appear, even just that greedy, gotta-score look he used to get, but it wouldn't come. Whatever he'd had left had been used up when he'd gotten her to let me go. Maybe it hadn't even been there then; maybe he'd been genuinely concerned about the problem of getting rid of my corpse. Junkies need love but they need a fix more.

125

Eventually, I heard the kid slump over on the couch.

"Well, come on," the woman said, going over to the bar to pick up her coat. The elevator doors slid open.

"Wait," Joe said.

I paused in the act of going toward the car and turned back to him.

"She goes back to Streep's," Joe said. "Just like I told you. And you pick up Stacey and George and Priscilla and whoever else is around if you want. But you fucking leave her off. Because I'll know if you don't."

I wanted to say his name but I still couldn't make a sound.

Hey, Joe. What the hell.

If you have to ask, babe, you don't really want to know.

"All right, Joe," the woman said amiably. "I told you I'd do it your way."

His lower lids rose up and stayed shut. *Good-bye Joe.*

"Too bad you never got to drink your cognac," the woman said to me as she put on her coat. She nodded at the snifter where it still stood on the bar. "It's VSOP, you know."

Night was already falling as she took me back across the river. She put on the Quicksilver Messenger Service tape for me. Have another hit. Neither of us said anything until she pulled up in front of Streep's.

"Run in and tell them I'm waiting, will you?" she asked cheerfully.

I looked over at her. "What should I say?"

"Tell them Joe and I are having a party. They'll like that."

"You and Joe, huh? Think you'll be able to handle such an embarrassment of riches, just the two of you?"

"Oh, there'll be a few others by the time I get back. You don't think we need all that space for just the two of us, do you?"

I shrugged. "What do I know?"

"You know enough." We stared at each other in the faint light from the dashboard. "Sure you don't want to ride back? Priscilla's friend will undoubtedly have arrived by the time we get there."

I took a deep breath. "I don't know what she told him about me, but it wasn't even close."

"Are you sure about that?"

"Real sure."

She stared at me a moment longer, as though she were measuring me for something. "Then I'll see you later, China."

I got out of the car and went into Streep's.

After that, I went home just long enough to pack my bag again while my father bellowed at me and my mother watched. I phoned Marlene from the bus station. She was out but her grandmother sounded happy to hear from me and told me to come ahead, she'd send Marlene out with the car.

So that was all. I went home even less after that, so I never saw Joe again. But I saw them. Not her, not Joe's blonde or the cop or the guy from Priscilla's apartment, but others. Apparently once you'd seen them, you couldn't not see them. They were around. Sometimes they would give me a nod, like they knew me. I kept on trucking, got my degree, got a job, got a life, and saw them some more.

I don't see them any more frequently but no less, either. They're around. If I don't see them, I see where they've been. A lot of the same places I've been. Sometimes I don't think about them and it's like a small intermission of freedom, but it doesn't last, of course. I see them and they see me and someday they'll find the time to come for me. So far, I've survived relevance and hedonism and I'm not a Yuppie. Nor my brother's keeper.

But I'm something. I was always going to be something someday. And eventually, they're going to find out what it is.

INTRODUCTION TO
PRETTY BOY CROSSOVER

Video, video. Do you want to be in a video? Or would you rather go it one better and *be* a video?

When I was four months pregnant, I had my brush with the Manhattan club scene. Ellen Datlow took me to a place called AREA, where the two-and-a-half-of-us waited 45 minutes past the announced opening time in the January cold, barred by velvet ropes. Every so often, someone would come out of the crowd and try to climb over the ropes in a casual, I'm-supposed-to-do-this way. The people on the door occasionally suffered one or two of them to be allowed in, except they didn't go in—they stood on the steps grinning at the rest of us who weren't so lucky to have someone know we were that important. I found out later that even our having invitations was no guarantee we'd be allowed inside—you were supposed to be on a list, too. That New York club scene—it's full of kidders.

(In Kansas City, we know how to handle this kind of thing; we file lawsuits for discrimination and we close those suckers down until they learn the meaning of *public place.*)

Well, we did get inside without begging, and it was the opening night of Science Fiction Theme Time. The decor was suitably impressive—a construction of the scene edited out of *Alien* (the first movie) and two people stuck for the night in 3-D glasses as part of a display, and a woman wearing a body-baggie over two sequins and a cork, armed with a ray-gun. But the real show was the crowd. They'd walked out of the pages of *Interview*. A few of them would start dancing, look around, stop, look around again, dance some more, take another look around, stop, look around, dance again, in an indefinite cycle. Seen at the scene.

Two nights later, we went in a small party to a punk club, where any-one with the price of admission could come in and pogo their brains out. Different decor—naked mannequin torsos in silvery barbed armor, dim light, but the real show was still the crowd. I stepped into the tiny bathroom at one point and came face to face with a very big punk re-slicking her hair spikes. I thought, *This woman will kill me and stuff my body behind the toilet.* Instead, she grinned at my already-protruding stomach and said, "When are you due?"

It wasn't my last surprise of the night. Back on the dance floor, a kid with an angel's face and full body leather asked me to dance. I had to give him a polite no—I really don't think he meant to pogo with somebody's mother. Eventually, I got tired and caught a cab back to Ellen's, where I started the story.

Every so often, I go back to New York and Ellen and I go dancing in a club, but not anywhere that we, or anyone else, would have to beg for admission. Never mind the humiliation of being turned down; it's what you could start believing if they let you in. You might think, for instance, you're a video.

PRETTY BOY CROSSOVER

> First you see video. Then you wear video.
> Then you eat video. Then you *be* video.
> *The Gospel According To Visual Mark*

Watch or Be Watched.
> *Pretty Boy Credo*

"*W*ho made you?"

"You mean recently?"

Mohawk on the door smiles and takes his picture. "You in. But only you, okay? Don't try to get no friends in, hear that?"

"I hear. And I ain't no fool, fool. I got no friends."

Mohawk leers, leaning forward. "Pretty Boy like you, no friends?"

"Not in this world." He pushes past the Mohawk, ignoring the kissy-kissy sounds. He would like to crack the bridge of the Mohawk's nose and shove bone splinters into his brain but he is lately making more effort to control his temper and besides, he's not sure if any of that bone splinters in the brain stuff is really true. He's a Pretty Boy, all of sixteen years old, and tonight could be his last chance.

The club is Noise. Can't sneak into the bathroom for quiet, the

Noise is piped in there, too. Want to get away from Noise? Why? No reason. But this Pretty Boy has learned to think between the beats. Like walking between the raindrops to stay dry, but he can do it. This Pretty Boy thinks things all the time—*all* the time. Subversive (and he thinks so much that he knows that word *subversive,* sixteen, Pretty, or not). He thinks things like *how many Einsteins have died of hunger and thirst under a hot African sun* and *why can't you remember being born* and *why is music common to every culture* and especially *how much was there going on that he didn't know about and how could he find out about it.*

And this is all the time, one thing after another running in his head, you can see by his eyes. It's for def not much like a Pretty Boy but it's one reason why they want him. That he *is* a Pretty Boy is another and one reason why they're halfway home getting him.

He knows all about them. Everybody knows about them and everybody wants them to pause, look twice, and cough up a card that says, Yes, we see possibilities, please come to the following address during regular business hours on the next regular business day for regular further review. Everyone wants it but this Pretty Boy, who once got five cards in a night and tore them all up. But here he is, still a Pretty Boy. He thinks enough to know that this is a failing in himself, that he likes being Pretty and chased and that is how they could end up getting him after all and that's b-b-b-bad. When he thinks about it, he thinks it with the stutter. B-b-b-bad. B-b-b-bad for him because he doesn't God help him want it, no, no, n-n-n-no. Which may make him the strangest Pretty Boy still live tonight and every night.

Still live and standing in the club where only the Prettiest Pretty Boys can get in any more. Pretty Girls are too easy, they've got to be better than Pretty and besides, Pretty Boys like to be Pretty all alone, no help thank you so much. This Pretty Boy doesn't mind Pretty Girls or any other kind of girls. Lately, though, he has begun to wonder how much longer it will be for him. Two years? Possibly a little longer? By three it will be for def over and the Mohawk on the door will as soon spit in his face as leer in it.

If they don't get to him.

And if they *do* get to him, then it's never over and he can be wherever he chooses to be and wherever that is will be the center of the universe. They promise it, unlimited access in your free hours and endless hot season, endless youth. Pretty Boy Heaven, and to get there, they say, you don't even really have to die.

He looks up to the dj's roost, far above the bobbing, boogieing crowd on the dance floor. They still call them djs even though they aren't discs any more, they're chips and there's more than just sound on a lot of them. The great hyper-program, he's been told, the ultimate of ultimates, a short walk from there to the fourth dimension. He suspects this stuff comes from low-steppers shilling for them, hoping they'll get auditioned if they do a good enough shuck job. Nobody knows what it's really like except the ones who are there and you can't trust them, he figures. Because maybe they *aren't*, any more. Not really.

The dj sees his Pretty upturned face, recognizes him even though it's been awhile since he's come back here. Part of it was wanting to stay away from them and part of it was that the thug on the door might not let him in. And then, of course, he *had* to come, to see if he could get in, to see if anyone still wanted him. What was the point of Pretty if there was nobody to care and watch and pursue? Even now, he is almost sure he can feel the room rearranging itself around his presence in it and the dj confirms this is true by holding up a chip and pointing it to the left.

They are squatting on the make-believe stairs by the screen, reminding him of pigeons plotting to take over the world. He doesn't look too long, doesn't want to give them the idea he'd like to talk. But as he turns away, one, the younger man, starts to get up. The older man and the woman pull him back. He pretends a big interest in the figures lining the nearest wall. Some are Pretty, some are female, some are undecided, some are very bizarre, or wealthy, or just charity cases. They all notice him and adjust themselves for his perusal.

Then one end of the room lights up with color and new noise. Bodies dance and stumble back from the screen where images are forming to rough music.

It's Bobby, he realizes.

A moment later, there's Bobby's face on the screen, sixteen feet high, even Prettier than he'd been when he was loose among the mortals. The sight of Bobby's Pretty-Pretty face fills him with anger and dismay and a feeling of loss so great he would strike anyone who spoke Bobby's name without his permission.

Bobby's lovely slate-grey eyes scan the room. They've told him senses are heightened after you make the change and go over but he's not so sure how that's supposed to work. Bobby looks kind of blind up there on the screen. A few people wave at Bobby—the dorks they let in so the rest can have someone to be hip in front of—but Bobby's eyes move slowly back and forth, back and forth, and then stop, looking right at him.

"Ah . . ." Bobby whispers it, long and drawn out. "Aaaaaaahhhhhh."

He lifts his chin belligerently and stares back at Bobby.

"You don't have to die any more," Bobby says silkily. Music bounces under his words. "It's beautiful in here. The dreams can be as real as you want them to be. And if you want to be, you can be with me."

He knows the commercial is not aimed only at him but it doesn't matter. This is *Bobby*. Bobby's voice seems to be pouring over him, caressing him, and it feels too much like a taunt. The night before Bobby went over, he tried to talk him out of it, knowing it wouldn't work. If they'd actually refused him, Bobby would have killed himself, like Franco had.

But now Bobby would live forever and ever, if you believed what they said. The music comes up louder but Bobby's eyes are still on him He sees Bobby mouth his name.

"Can you really see me, Bobby?" he says. His voice doesn't make it over the music but if Bobby's senses are so heightened, maybe he hears it anyway. If he does, he doesn't choose to answer. The music is a bumped-up remix of a song Bobby used to party-till-he-puked to. The giant Bobby-face fades away to be replaced with a whole Bobby, somewhat larger than life, dancing better than the old Bobby ever could, whirling along changing scenes of streets, rooftops, and beaches. The locales are nothing special but Bobby never did have all that much imagination, never wanted to go to Mars or even to the South Pole, always just to the hottest club. Always he liked being the exotic in plain surroundings and he still likes it. He always loved to get the looks. To be watched, worshipped, pursued. Yeah. He can see this is Bobby-heaven. The whole world will be giving him the looks now.

The background on the screen goes from street to the inside of a club; *this* club, only larger, better, with an even hipper crowd, and Bobby shaking it with them. Half the real crowd is forgetting to dance now because they're watching Bobby, hoping he's put some of them into his video. Yeah, that's the dream, get yourself remixed in the extended dance version.

His own attention drifts to the fake stairs that don't lead anywhere. They're still perched on them, the only people who are watching *him* instead of Bobby. The woman, looking overaged in a purple plastic sacsuit, is fingering a card.

He looks up at Bobby again. Bobby is dancing in place and looking back at him, or so it seems. Bobby's lips move soundlessly but so precisely he can read the words: *This can be you. Never get old, never get tired, it's never last call, nothing happens unless you want it to and it could be you. You. You.* Bobby's hands point to him on the beat. *You. You. You.*

Bobby. Can you really see me?

Bobby suddenly breaks into laughter and turns away, shaking it some more.

He sees the Mohawk from the door pushing his way through the crowd, the real crowd, and he gets anxious. The Mohawk goes straight for the stairs, where they make room for him, rubbing the bristly red strip of hair running down the center of his head as though they were greeting a favored pet. The Mohawk looks as satisfied as a professional glutton after a foodrace victory. He wonders what they promised the Mohawk for letting him in. Maybe some kind of limited contract. Maybe even a try-out.

Now they are all watching him together. Defiantly, he touches a tall girl dancing nearby and joins her rhythm. She smiles down at him, moving between him and them purely by chance but it endears her to him anyway. She is wearing a flap of translucent rag over second-skins, like an old-time showgirl. Over six feet tall, not beautiful with that nose, not even pretty, but they let her in so she could be tall. She probably doesn't know that; she probably doesn't know anything that goes on and never really will. For that reason, he can forgive her the hard-tech orange hair.

A Rude Boy brushes against him in the course of a dervish turn, asking acknowledgement by ignoring him. Rude Boys haven't changed in more decades than anyone's kept track of, as though it were the same little group of leathered and chained troopers buggering their way down the years. The Rude Boy isn't dancing with anyone. Rude Boys never do. But this one could be handy, in case of an emergency.

The girl is dancing hard, smiling at him. He smiles back, moving slightly to her right, watching Bobby possibly watching him. He still can't tell if Bobby really sees anything. The scene behind Bobby is still a double of the club, getting hipper and hipper if that's possible. The music keeps snapping back to its first peak passage. Then Bobby gestures like God and he sees *himself.* He is dancing next to Bobby, Prettier than he ever could be, just the way they promise. Bobby doesn't look at the phantom but at him where he really is, lips moving again. *If you want to be, you can be with me. And so can she.*

His tall partner appears next to the phantom of himself. She is also much improved, though still not Pretty, or even pretty. The real girl turns and sees herself and there's no mistaking the delight in her face. Queen of the Hop for a minute or two. Then Bobby sends her image away so that it's just the two of them, two Pretty Boys dancing the night away, private party, stranger, go find your own good time. How it used to be sometimes in real life, between just the two of them. He remembers hard.

"B-b-b-bobby!" he yells, the old stutter reappearing. Bobby's image seems to give a jump, as though he finally heard. He forgets everything, the girl, the Rude Boy, the Mohawk, them on the stairs, and plunges through the crowd toward the screen. People fall away from him as though they were re-enacting the Red Sea. He dives for the screen, for Bobby, not caring how it must look to anyone. What would they know about it, any of them. He can't remember in his whole sixteen years ever hearing one person say, *I love my friend.* Not Bobby, not even himself.

He fetches up against the screen like a slap and hangs there, face pressed to the glass. He can't see it now but on the screen, Bobby would seem to be looking down at him. Bobby never stops dancing.

The Mohawk comes and peels him off. The others swarm up and take him away. The tall girl watches all this with the expression of a woman who lives upstairs from Cinderella and wears the same shoe size. She stares longingly at the screen. Bobby waves bye-bye and turns away.

"Of course, the process isn't reversible," says the older man. The steely hair has a careful blue tint; he has sense enough to stay out of hip clothes.

They have laid him out on a lounger with a tray of refreshments right by him. Probably slap his hand if he reaches for any, he thinks.

"Once you've distilled something to pure information, it just can't be reconstituted in a less efficient form," the woman explains, smiling. There's no warmth to her. *A less efficient form.* If that's what she really thinks, he knows he should be plenty scared of these people. Did she say things like that to Bobby? And did it make him even *more* eager?

"There may be no more exalted a form of existence than to live as sentient information," she goes on. "Though a lot more research must be done before we can offer conversion on a larger scale."

"Yeah?" he says. "Do they know that, Bobby and the rest?"

"Oh, there's nothing to worry about," says the younger man. He looks as though he's still getting over the pain of having outgrown his boogie shoes. "The system's quite perfected. What Grethe means is we want to research more applications for this new form of existence."

"Why not go over yourselves and do that, if it's so *exalted*."

"There are certain things that need to be done on this side," the woman says bitchily. "Just because —"

"Grethe." The older man shakes his head. She pats her slicked-back hair as though to soothe herself and moves away.

"We have other plans for Bobby when he gets tired of being featured in clubs," the older man says. "Even now, we're educating him, adding more data to his basic information configuration—"

"That would mean he ain't really *Bobby* any more, then, huh?"

The man laughs. "Of course he's Bobby. Do you change into someone else every time you learn something new?"

"Can you prove I *don't?*"

The man eyes him warily. "Look. You *saw* him. Was that Bobby?"

"I saw a video of Bobby dancing on a giant screen."

"That *is* Bobby and it will remain Bobby no matter what, whether he's poured into a video screen in a dot pattern or transmitted the length of the universe."

"That what you got in mind for him? Send a message to nowhere and the message is him?"

"We could. But we're not going to. We're introducing him to the concept of higher dimensions. The way he is now, he could possibly break out of the three-dimensional level of existence, pioneer a whole new plane of reality."

"Yeah? And how do you think you're gonna get Bobby to do *that?*"

"We convince him it's entertaining."

He laughs. "That's a good one. Yeah. Entertainment. You get to a higher level of existence and you'll open a club there that only the hippest can get into. It figures."

The older man's face gets hard. "That's what all you Pretty Boys are crazy for, isn't it? Entertainment?"

He looks around. The room must have been a dressing room or something back in the days when bands had been live. Somewhere overhead he can hear the faint noise of the club but he can't tell if Bobby's still on. "You call this entertainment?"

"I'm tired of this little prick," the woman chimes in. "He's thrown away opportunities other people would kill for—"

He makes a rude noise. "Yeah, we'd all kill to be someone's data chip. You think I really believe Bobby's real just because I can see him on a *screen?*"

The older man turns to the younger one. "Phone up and have them pipe Bobby down here." Then he swings the lounger around so it faces a nice modern screen implanted in a shored-up cement-block wall.

"Bobby will join us shortly. Then he can tell you whether he's real or not himself. How will that be for you?"

He stares hard at the screen, ignoring the man, waiting for Bobby's image to appear. As though they really bothered to communicate regularly with Bobby this way. Feed in that kind of data and memory and

Bobby'll believe it. He shifts uncomfortably, suddenly wondering how far he could get if he moved fast enough.

"My *boy*," says Bobby's sweet voice from the speaker on either side of the screen and he forces himself to keep looking as Bobby fades in, presenting himself on the same kind of lounger and looking mildly exerted, as though he's just come off the dance floor for real. "Saw you shakin' it upstairs awhile ago. You haven't been here for such a long time. What's the story?"

He opens his mouth but there's no sound. Bobby looks at him with boundless patience and indulgence. So Pretty, hair the perfect shade now and not a bit dry from the dyes and lighteners, skin flawless and shining like a healthy angel. Overnight angel, just like the old song.

"My *boy*," says Bobby. "Are you struck, like, shy or *dead?*"

He closes his mouth, takes one breath. "I don't like it, Bobby. I don't like it this way."

"Of course not, lover. You're the Watcher, not the Watchee, that's why. Get yourself picked up for a season or two and your disposition will *change*."

"You really like it, Bobby, being a blip on a chip?"

"Blip on a chip, your ass. I'm a universe now, I'm, like, *everything*. And, hey, dig—I'm on every channel." Bobby laughs. "I'm happy I'm sad!"

"S-A-D," comes in the older man. "Self-Aware Data."

"Ooo-eee," he says. "Too clever for me. Can I get out of here now?"

"What's your hurry?" Bobby pouts. "Just because I went over you don't love me any more?"

"You always were screwed up about that, Bobby. Do you know the difference between being loved and being watched?"

"Sophisticated boy," Bobby says. "So wise, so learned. So fully packed. On this side, there *is* no difference. Maybe there never was. If you love me, you watch me. If you don't look, you don't care and if you don't care, I don't matter. If I don't matter, I don't exist. Right?"

He shakes his head.

"No, my boy, I *am* right." Bobby laughs. "You believe I'm right, because if you *didn't,* you wouldn't come shaking your Pretty Boy ass in a place like *this,* now, would you? You *like* to be watched, get seen. You see me, I see you. Life goes on."

He looks up at the older man, needing relief from Bobby's pure Prettiness. "How does he see me?"

"Sensors in the equipment. Technical stuff, nothing you care about."

He sighs. He should be upstairs or across town, shaking it with everyone else, living Pretty for as long as he could. Maybe in another few months, this way would begin to look good to him. By then they might be off Pretty Boys and looking for some other type and there he'd be, out in the cold-cold, sliding down the other side of his peak and no one would *want* him. Shut out of something going on that he might want to know about after all. Can he face it? He glances at the younger man. All grown up and no place to glow. Yeah, but can *he* face it?

He doesn't know. Used to be there wasn't much of a choice and now that there is, it only seems to make it worse. Bobby's image looks like it's studying him for some kind of sign, Pretty eyes bright, hopeful.

The older man leans down and speaks low into his ear. "We need to get you before you're twenty-five, before the brain stops growing. A mind taken from a still-growing brain will blossom and adapt. Some of Bobby's predecessors have made marvelous adaptation to their new medium. Pure video: there's a staff that does nothing all day but watch and interpret their symbols for breakthroughs in thought. And we'll be taking Pretty Boys for as long as they're publicly sought-after. It's the most efficient way to find the best performers, go for the ones everyone wants to see or be. The top of the trend is closest to heaven. And even if you never make a breakthrough, you'll still be entertainment. Not such a bad way to live for a Pretty Boy. Never have to age, to be sick, to lose touch. You spent most of your life young, why learn how to be old? Why learn how to live without all the things you have now—"

He puts his hands over his ears. The older man is still talking and Bobby is saying something and the younger man and the woman come over to try to do something about him. Refreshments are falling off the tray. He struggles out of the lounger and makes for the door.

"Hey, my *boy*," Bobby calls after him. "Gimme a minute here, gimme what the *problem* is."

He doesn't answer. What can you tell someone made of pure information anyway?

There's a new guy on the front door, bigger and meaner than His Mohawkness, but he's only there to keep people out, not to keep anyone *in*. You want to jump ship, go to, you poor un-hip asshole. Even if you are a Pretty Boy. He reads it in the guy's face as he passes from Noise into the three A.M. quiet of the street.

They let him go. He doesn't fool himself about that part. They *let* him out of the room because they know all about him. They know he lives like Bobby lived, they know he loves what Bobby loved—the clubs, the admiration, the lust of strangers for his personal magic. He

137

can't say he doesn't love that, because he *does*. He isn't even sure if he loves it more than he ever loved Bobby, or if he loves it more than being alive. Than being live.

And here it is, three A.M., prime clubbing time, and he is moving toward home. Maybe he *is* a poor un-hip asshole after all, no matter what he loves. Too stupid even to stay in the club, let alone grab a ride to heaven. Still he keeps moving, unbothered by the chill but feeling it. Bobby doesn't have to go home in the cold any more, he thinks. Bobby doesn't even have to get through the hours between club-times if he doesn't want to. All times are now prime time for Bobby. Even if he gets unplugged, he'll never know the difference. Poof, it's a day later, poof, it's a year later, poof, you're out for good. Painlessly.

Maybe Bobby has the right idea, he thinks, moving along the empty sidewalk. If he goes over tomorrow, who will notice? Like when he left the dance floor—people will come and fill up the space. Ultimately, it wouldn't make any difference to anyone.

He smiles suddenly. Except *them*. As long as they don't have him, he makes a difference. As long as he has flesh to shake and flaunt and feel with, he makes a pretty goddam big difference to *them*. Even after they don't want him any more, he will still be the one they didn't get. He rubs his hands together against the chill, feeling the skin rubbing skin, really *feeling* it for the first time in a long time, and he thinks about sixteen million things all at once, maybe one thing for every brain cell he's using, or maybe one thing for every brain cell yet to come.

He keeps moving, holding to the big thought, making a difference, and all the little things they won't be making a program out of. He's lightheaded with joy—he doesn't know what's going to happen.

Neither do they.

INTRODUCTION TO
TWO

You had the super-power fantasy once, especially if you read comic books; but even if you didn't, you probably had it anyway. This is why *Superman* is so enduring. We all just *knew* that if we had some extraordinary power, nobody would be able to push us around, or exploit us in any trashy or stupid damned way.

We were wrong.

I keep threatening to write Sarah Jane's story at novel-length. One of these days. And I've never been happy with the title. Sometimes I think I should have called it "One."

TWO

*H*e seldom touched her.

Lying on the bed on her left side, Sarah Jane thought about that. She heard the newspaper crackle as he turned the pages. If she rolled over, she would see him sitting at the small table under the hanging light, almost a solid shadow in front of the bright drapes screening out the early afternoon glare. It would be—was—a sight so familiar she called it a variation on the theme of their existence.

It might have been different if he touched her.

She had read in the magazines he was always buying her that people needed to be touched physically. Children needed hugs to thrive, married people who cuddled were happiest. Sometimes she wanted him to touch her so badly it was like pain.

"Michael?" Her voice was small and powerless in the room. He didn't answer but she knew he had looked up from the paper. "Could we get married?"

He laughed briefly, without humor. "No. No, we can't get married."

She hadn't thought so. After a moment, she pushed up from the bed and wandered into the clean, clean bathroom to unwrap one of the water glasses. Her reflection in the mural-sized mirror looked peaked. The funny fluorescent lighting they used in hotel bathrooms sucked all the color out of her, leaving her like an old color photograph about to turn black-and-white. She patted her long, light brown hair and curled the ends around her fingers. Her face was bony, just like the rest of her, as though she were treading on the sunny side of starvation. It was her thinness, she decided, that made her look sometimes so much older and sometimes so much younger than twelve.

Behind the drapes was a sliding glass door that opened onto a balcony. Michael went on reading the newspaper as she stepped outside and stood in the sunlight with her hands clasped behind her back and her feet apart. A slight wind flapped her shirttails. Not exactly a portrait of a lady, she thought. But she had never figured on being a lady, not her. No chance. Ladies had graceful, refined forms, not bony bodies that were still growing, and they didn't wear thrift shop shirts and faded jeans, and they didn't stand like they had a plank between their legs. And they didn't live in and out of hotel rooms with men like Michael.

She leaned on the wrought-iron railing and looked down at the hotel parking lot, which was beginning to fill up with cars. The cars belonged mostly to middle-aged married couples, coming in for the hotel's Weekend Mini-Honeymoon Special. She had read all about it on a stand-up card by the telephone. Three days, two nights, complimentary champagne the first night and a special buffet brunch on Sunday morning, $90 a couple. She wondered how all those people would react to having her and Michael in their respectable midst. She imagined them walking through the crowded lounge together during the special buffet brunch on Sunday morning, while the husbands and wives stared. *It's okay,* she might say to them as they passed, *he never touches me. I'm twelve and he's almost thirty and we're just good friends.* Right. Michael would slap her silly if she told anyone he was closing in on thirty. He could pass for 22 or 23. But a slap was a touch, anyway.

141

Inside the room, the phone rang. She closed her eyes. Michael picked it up on the third ring. She didn't listen in. That was one of the rules Michael had laid down in the beginning. He said when she could listen and when she couldn't and if she didn't abide by them, he would leave her. A strand of hair blew across her face. She dragged it away with two fingers and threw it over her shoulder. Even though she wasn't listening, she knew when he had put the phone down and she felt him coming to the open glass door.

"Sarah Jane?"

She turned around. He was smiling. For the millionth time, she thought of how handsome he was.

"I got it set up for tonight. A game. It's safe and it's heavy sugar."

She gave him a split-second, mirthless smile.

"It's not gonna be any different than the other times. Clean pickings." He stared at her. When she didn't say anything, his smile broadened defiantly. "I'm gonna catch a nap now. Wake me up at 6:30. I'll take a shower and then we'll get some supper before the game, okay?"

"Okay, Michael."

His mouth twitched with annoyance. "Practice calling me Uncle Mike or they'll know something's up."

"Okay. Uncle Mike."

"Right." He took a deep breath and let it out. His dark hair showed mahogany lights in the sun. "No funny stuff while I'm asleep, got it?"

She blinked at him solemnly.

"I mean it." He pointed his finger at her through the screen. "I really mean it, Sarah Jane. I don't like any funny stuff, you know that."

Her gaze roamed over his body. He wasn't a big man. She was nearly as tall as he was but he was solid, perfectly formed, without a bit of fat to him.

142

"Hey, why don't you put on your bathing suit and go down to the pool," he said, his voice softening. "Get a little sun. You could use some."

She shrugged. "Maybe. I don't know. I don't like being out in public in a bathing suit, you know that."

"Jesus. You're the only female I know who thinks she's too skinny. I know broads that're living on celery sticks and water trying to get a shape like yours."

"I don't have a shape." She turned away and looked down at the parking lot. "Even if I did, I still don't think I'd want to go out in a bathing suit."

"You oughta get some sun, for chrissakes. You're a kid. You're supposed to go out and play sometimes."

She looked over her shoulder at him sourly. Was he kidding?

His gaze dropped to his feet. "Yeah. Well. Do whatever the hell you want, take some money and go have an ice cream sundae or something, I don't care. Just be sure you wake me up at 6:30. And *no funny stuff*."

Her face was expressionless now. "OK. Uncle Mike."

She didn't go back into the room until she knew he was asleep. He had pulled the heavier drape behind the light one to dim the room and he was lying fully-clothed on top of his bed with one arm thrown over his eyes.

Michael was the only person she had ever known who could sleep at his own command. If he decided he needed a nap so he could stay up all night, he would just lie down and be out in a few minutes. It was just another of his extraordinary features. Except he always needed her to wake him up.

She stood over him, wishing he'd move his arm so she could see his face. Michael's face did something to her; she never got tired of looking at him.

You're a kid. Twelve years old and hopelessly in love? Anyone else would laugh in her face if she said it out loud. Michael would laugh in her face but the laughter would be nervous because he'd know it was the truth. She couldn't help it. Michael was the only one, the only one she had ever found, maybe the only one in the world. All her life she had hoped to find someone like him. She had been afraid for a long time that perhaps no one like him existed, or even if one did, the person might not want her.

Michael rolled over, putting his back to her. She tensed but he was deeply asleep, unaware of her. She wanted to lie down next to him, just to be near him but if she did, she wouldn't be able to resist touching him and she knew what would happen then. He wouldn't have it; he was very firm. *No funny stuff.*

Would it have been any worse if he'd been, say, a married bank teller with three kids? She probably wouldn't have been able to get near him then. If he'd been a woman—well, that would have been completely different. Some nice woman, who would maybe have liked being kind of a mother or older sister to her. That would have been best of all. But Michael was what she had.

Michael. She mouthed his name. *Roll over facing me.* Without really meaning to, she pushed out a little and he obeyed in his sleep. His expression was peaceful, all his concerns set aside while he rejuvenated himself for the evening's game. She could see his eyeballs moving back and forth behind the lids. Dreaming. *Michael,* she implored silently, *share your dreams with me.* Because she had already pushed out once, she couldn't stop herself from doing it again. Her eyes closed and she had the sensation of drifting downward through still air, floating toward a region of fog and shadow. As she sank closer to it, it began to take on dark colors and there was a flickering of something like heat lightning playing in clouds.

Then she was with him. A jumble of images like animated balloons assailed her: Michael broke, Michael flush, Michael humiliated in school for some petty sin against classroom protocol. Michael meeting her for the first time in the laundromat. Michael and a woman—she turned away from that one. Michael when she had tried to touch him. When he hit her. Michael discovering she was telling him the truth—

143

Okay, little sister, if you can really do that, tell me what that guy over there is thinking. Standing on a sidewalk near a diner, Michael jerked his head at a man holding a flat paper bag under one arm while he waited for the light to change so he could cross the street.

He's thinking when is the goddam light going to change.

Michael laughed at her. *Brilliant, Sherlock. I'm no mind reader and I could have guessed that.*

She stared up at him evenly. *I wasn't finished.* And then she really gave it to him, not orally but direct, right between the eyes. He's-thinking-I-wonder-when-this-goddam-light-is-gonna-change-I-wanna-get-back-to-the-office-nobody-there-now-lunch-get-some-peace-piece-magazine-nice-one-all-women-crawling-all-over-each-other-oily-women-tongues-skin-oily-hard-oh—

Michael froze, unable to move while she gave it all to him, dictating the man's thoughts while he waited for the goddam light to change. Then the light did change and he was striding across the street quickly, swinging his arms, the small brown paper bag in his right hand moving like a pendulum.

Where's he going? Michael asked.

Back to his office.

Where's that?

I don't know.

You don't know?!

I can only hear what people are actively thinking about. I can't get into their minds. They can't receive me. Nobody can. But you.

He didn't give her time to tell him how lonely she had been, how she had run away from home six weeks before, how hollowly she had profited from the ability and how she had tried to give up using it and couldn't. But he took her back to his place, one room in a shabby building called the Hotel Cosmo (By the Day, Week, or Month, In Advance).

Something stirred in his mind. She'd been in almost too long; if she stayed much longer, he would become aware of her and wake up. But she needed the contact, God, how she needed it. Michael knew that. He kept her on short rations, letting her in only for a few minutes. He didn't like her crawling around in his head, it was a dirty thing to him. Except when it was useful.

Like for the games.

They might have done anything else. At twelve, she knew more about people than anyone should have known at any age and they might have done something grand, even if Michael insisted on keeping her out most of the time. Instead—

Her head filled with an unimaginably bright light and she was whirling in sudden disorientation. There was a feeling of falling and acceleration and it was as if she were plummeting past a thousand bulky objects, hitting every one of them—

When she opened her eyes, she was on the floor. Michael had hit her with the telephone book.

"What did I tell you, little sister?" He threw the slim volume at her. It bounced off her breastbone and one sharp corner dug into her stomach. "Did I say no funny stuff or what." He crouched over her, wrapping one hand in her hair. It was safe for him to touch her hair; hair was dead. "Did I tell you no funny stuff? Answer me!" He jerked her head back.

"Michael, I couldn't help it." Her voice came out in a high-pitched whisper. "You know I've got to have—"

"You can *wait,* you understand that, you can *wait* until later when *I* say!" He forced her to her feet and shoved her at the bed. Her hair was still tangled around his hand and she cried out. He shoved her again, freeing himself from her roughly as she tumbled down onto the mattress. She got up, reaching for him but he had the phone book again and he batted her hand away.

"Michael—"

"Back! I mean it, girl, get back! I don't have to touch you to hit you!" He stepped forward and she threw one arm up defensively. For a moment, she thought he would strike her. Then he rolled the thin directory into a tight tube.

"OK. Great. You just stay there on the bed and don't move." He ambled around to the foot of the bed, watching her. She began to bring her arm down and he swatted it. "I said, don't move!"

"No, Michael, OK, I won't." Her eyes burned, wanting to fill with tears but she wouldn't let them come. If she could just touch him, it would stop. The contact was instantaneous if they were physically touching but Michael was careful about that because she could paralyze him with it.

"Did I warn you about the funny stuff? Answer me!"

"Yes, Michael, you warned me."

"But you did it anyway. Why."

"I couldn't help it—"

"You *can* help it!" He slammed the phone book down on the bed inches from her other hand. "You *can* help it, you've got the control and we both know it. You can keep from listening in on me or anyone else. *Why* did you do what I told you not to."

Her throat seemed to be twisted as tightly as the phone directory

145

in Michael's hands. "I wanted to—" Tears filled her eyes after all and overflowed. "I'm so lonely, you don't know—"

He slammed the directory down on the bed in front of her, nearly grazing her cheek. "Don't you ever," he said, low and gravelly and dangerous, "don't you ever come inside me without I tell you to again. Don't you *ever. Don't you ever*—because I swear I'll really hurt you bad. And you'll never see me again. Now you think you can remember that?"

She nodded.

"You'll be goddam lucky if I let you in tonight after the game. That's when you get yours, girly, when *I* let you in. I can keep you out, you know I can. And I still might do that."

"Please," she whispered.

"Shut up. You better do right tonight, little sister. You better be on your best all night because if you're not, I might decide I like my old scams better. Are you taking this in?"

146

"Yes, Michael. Can I put my arm down?"

He stepped back. "Get out."

She scuttled across the bed, watching him warily, and backed toward the door. "I—I need some money, Michael."

He threw a crumpled ten dollar bill at her. "Get your skinny ass *out.*"

Moving quickly, she crouched to pick the money up off the carpet, still keeping her wide eyes on him.

"Little sister."

She paused halfway out of the room, holding the door in front of her like a shield.

"Be back here to wake me at 6:30 or don't bother coming back." She dipped her head in a nod and slipped out into the hall.

She spent nearly an hour in the tacky gift shop off the lobby, drifting among the shelves while the clerk behind the counter tried to decide whether she was a shoplifter and wondered why, on his salary, he should have cared.

Out of boredom, she bought a *Vogue* magazine and a small bag of pistachio nuts with her crumpled ten dollar bill and went out to the patio near the pool to sit at one of the umbrella tables. There weren't many people around and she was left to herself to methodically pry each nut open with her teeth and suck the meat out, staining her fingertips and mouth magenta while she stared at fierce-faced models cavorting in unlikly places in even unlikelier clothes. The pistachio shells made an untidy little pile on the metal table and the wind threatened to scatter them. Deliberately, she held herself tight and would not tune in on the few people who walked by and gave her curious glances. She didn't want to know what they were thinking, she didn't want to know what anyone was thinking ever again. She might be better off if she just walked away from the hotel, let Michael sleep until he woke up, whenever that would be, and tried to forget about him. Her own parents didn't want her back but maybe she could find a family to take her in. She could try to live like regular people, suppress the ability (she had never called it a gift) and maybe it would atrophy and disappear.

A woman advertising purple lipstick offered her a kiss from a glossy page. She turned it over, working a pistachio nut open on her bottom teeth. She might as well try to alter the basic rhythm of her heart or glue her eyes permanently shut as attempt to give up using the ability. It was still useful and having lived with it, she could not live without it.

Live without Michael? Go back to the way things had been before, having no one to get close to in the special way she needed? No one to provide the complement to the ability, to receive her, bind with her in a union that transcended the separateness of two minds in two bodies—

But Michael would never let things go quite that far with them. He opened up to her only so much but when he felt the start of the process that would have melded them together, he forced her out again.

In the beginning, she had tried to convince him it was the right thing to let the process continue to its conclusion. *Don't you see, Michael? It's supposed to be that way. Maybe we're not really two people—maybe we're one person who came apart somehow—*

But he didn't want to hear about that. If she didn't know who she was, *he* knew who *he* was and he wasn't half a man and half a twelve year old girl. If she didn't like the way things were, she could walk, he wouldn't stop her.

Whether he actually would let go of his meal-ticket she didn't know. He managed to keep a lot of his motivations hidden from her, even when she was inside him. Sometimes she thought if she ran away, he would come after her; other times, she was afraid he'd carry through on his threat to leave her.

And in the meantime, they were getting closer, whether Michael liked it or not. Every time her let her in, even just a little bit during the games or afterward, they drew that much closer. Someday he would have to let her all the way in. Either that or never let her in again.

She looked at her reddened fingers and tried to wipe them on her shirttail. The stain would have to wear off. She wished Michael would wear off, that he would somehow lose his capacity to receive her. There wouldn't be anything she could do if he just lost it. Then she wouldn't feel so desperately drawn to him, her compulsive, helpless love would fade and she could search for someone else. And if there wasn't anyone else, she wouldn't be any worse off than she'd been before she'd found him. Would she?

The last pistachio nut in the bag refused to open. She held it up to examine it. The shell was perfectly smooth all over, with no hint of an opening or even a seam where she could split it open. Licking her stained lips, she put the nut between her back molars and bit down, crushing both the shell and the meat inside to pulp.

She stayed by the pool, looking through the *Vogue* over and over again until it was time to go upstairs and wake Michael. He said little to her beyond telling her to change her clothes but his anger seemed to have passed. She kept thumbing through the magazine while he showered and when they went down to the dining room, she carried it with her without thinking about it.

"Why'd you bring that?" Michael said after they were seated in a corner booth.

She shrugged one shoulder. "I don't know."

"It's not exactly bright enough for reading in here. All this candle-light crap." He looked around the dim, almost full dining room. "Mr. and Mrs. America, getting away for a weekend from the kids they wish they'd never had. Isn't that right, little sister?"

"I don't know," she said again.

"You don't know?" He had a sip of beer. "Don't tell me you've been wandering around loose all afternoon and you didn't listen in on anybody?"

"I didn't feel like it."

"You just read a magazine and ate those watchamacallit nuts."

"Pistachio." She looked down at her lap.

"You look like hell. You got red all over your mouth. What's the matter with you? Girls your age are supposed to be all uptight about how they look and you go around like that." He blew out his breath disgustedly. "*Vogue* magazine, for crying out loud. I give you money for clothes and you go to the Salvation Army and come home with somebody's old rag they don't want any more."

She didn't look up. She couldn't tell him she went to the charity stores because the thoughts of the people who worked in those places were usually warm and comforting and permeated by something that lay in a grey area between kindness and love. Not like the thoughts of the people she met with Michael.

"All right, so what do you want to eat? You ain't even looked at the menu."

"A cheeseburger."

"A cheeseburger. Jesus. Come on, eat something real for a change. A cheeseburger. We're in a nice place here."

"I want a cheeseburger," she said firmly.

"A cheeseb—have a steak."

She shook her head. This was Michael trying to be nice to her now, except he didn't really know how. She had to clench her teeth to keep from pushing out to him, to taste his mind and his self and show him how to love.

"You're having a steak. You gotta eat good stuff if you're going to keep your strength up. And coffee. I don't want you falling asleep on me tonight. I probably should have made you take a nap."

"I can't sleep during the day."

"Yeah, yeah, yeah." He made a disgusted noise. "You won't do this and you can't do that and you don't like to do the other thing. You're a major pain in the ass, Sarah Jane. You can't appreciate a goddam thing I do for you. If it weren't for me, you'd still be camping out in laundromats and parking garages, eating whatever you could steal. And you wouldn't have anybody for that funny stuff you're so hot to do. And what do *I* get for it? A big long face and crazy questions about can we get married. Cut me a break, little sister."

"What do you want me to do?" she asked miserably, twisting the ends of her hair around her fingers.

Michael leaned forward with a nasty grin. "Tell me what's going on with those two over there." He jerked his head to her left. She turned to look and saw a middle-aged couple at another table. They were scowling down at their place settings, not looking or speaking to each other.

"What about them?"

"Tell me what's eating them."

And this, she thought, was Michael offering to let her back into his good graces. She sighed. "They're just a couple of married people here for the weekend."

"Yeah, but look at them. I mean, take a good look at them. Listen in."

She made a pained face.

"Listen in and maybe I'll let you stay in longer than usual after the game tonight."

"You alway say that but you don't mean it."

"Don't give me a hard time, little sister." His smile was flat and counterfeit. "The harder you make it on me, the harder I can make it on you."

She didn't answer.

"Come on. Call it practice for later."

"I don't need to practice."

"Are you gonna keep pushing it?" Michael leaned forward. "What do you care if we know what they're thinking. They won't know it. Come on."

Her eyes narrowed. Michael watched her eagerly. He was expecting her to tell him out loud. She waited several seconds until she saw a hint of impatience in his face and then sent a stream of thought at him, directly instead of speaking. *—telephone-call-from-the-sitter-one-of-the-kids-is-sick-she-wants-to-check-out-and-go-home-and-he-doesn't-and—*

Michael fell against the padded back of the booth, shutting himself off from her. His face reddened with the effort. She had a sudden feeling that if she had persisted, she could have forced her way through his barrier and stayed inside him whether he liked it or not. But she let him break the contact.

"You little—" Michael sat up straight and pointed a finger at her. "I oughta—"

"Sorry," she said coolly. "Just practicing for tonight."

He reached for his beer. "You just better do me right, little sister. You just better."

"I will." She looked over at the couple again. They were still staring unhappily at the table. She actually had no idea what their problem was; she had just made the whole thing up.

She insisted on buying another bag of pistachio nuts before she and Michael drove across town to a dark, rundown neighborhood and a bar that seemed to be nothing more than a hole in the wall. Michael parked the car on the street and told her to wait in it with the doors locked and the windows rolled up while he went in. A minute later he came out and took her around the corner to a side entrance.

"They run the game in the store-room," he told her. But she was already listening, thoughts from several different people jumbling together in her mind. She followed Michael through a dim hallway and into a small room full of boxes and crates. Under a bare, hanging bulb, a round table had been set up and four men were already seated at it. Cigar and cigarette smoke slithered in the air over their heads. They looked up from their cards and one of them, a sandy-haired man with a florid complexion said, "You're late, Mr., ah, Jones." Then all the men caught sight of her.

"What the hell is this?" asked the sandy-haired man. "You think this is some kinda tea party we're having here?"

Michael spread his hands. "Hey, what can I do? At the last minute, my sister comes over and dumps the kid on my doorstep. She's going to the Ozarks for a week with her boyfriend and somebody's got to keep an eye on Sarah Jane." Michael looked around at the stony faces of the men. Standing behind him, she clutched the *Vogue* and the bag of pistachios to her chest. The men's thoughts jabbered like an open telephone switchboard. *Guy's crazy what the hell does he think bring a kid here busted we all take a fall how old is she* and then Michael cutting through everything: *Do they believe me, Sarah Jane? Answer me! Are they buying it?*

She trembled. *They think you're nuts bringing me here.*

Michael seemed to relax. "Hey, you guys. Really. What could I do?"

The sandy-haired man walked around Michael to have a look at   *151* her. She hunched her shoulders and tried to make herself smaller. "Thought you were new in town," he said to Michael but staring at her.

"I am. But my sister lives here. Moved here with her boyfriend."

"Kid looks old enough to stay home alone."

"Yeah, but she's afraid to," Michael said and shrugged. "She's kind of a big baby, you know what I mean?"

The man gave Michael a disgusted look. *Sleazeball scumbag dragging a kid to a place like this some people no decency—*

She couldn't help smiling.

"Something funny?" the man asked her.

She put her hand to her mouth as Michael turned to look at her. "Sarah Jane's kinda, hey, you know. Sometimes she smiles at nothing, sometimes she laughs. You know?"

"So what are you saying here? Is she gonna create a disturbance or something?"

"Nah, nah, she's OK. She'll be real quiet, won't make a sound. She can sit on those boxes over there, look at her magazine, eat her nuts, she won't bother anyone. Right, Sarah Jane? You won't bother your Uncle Mike while he plays cards with his friends, will you, honey?"

She gave him a moron's stare with her mouth hanging open before she wandered over to some boxes against the far wall and sat down. The men's thoughts babbled as their eyes followed her. *—a hundred pounds stripped crazy or dumb call my kid tomorrow throw him out and her too christ are we babysitters or what no meat on her big girl—*

"She reads magazines?" the sandy-haired man said to Michael suspiciously.

"She looks at the pictures, big deal. Look, you don't want me here, fine, I'm out. But I came a long way for a good game and I got friends in this town. They like me to have a good time."

The man gave a sharp little laugh. "So take a seat, who's stopping you?"

Michael looked at her and nodded almost imperceptibly before seating himself at the table. Now it began, the worst part of living with Michael. She tore open the bag of pistachios, pretending to be absorbed in the pictures of the improbable models. She knew them all by heart now. The men's thoughts rumbled and churned in her head under the sound of the cards being shuffled and she began sorting them out. The man to Michael's right was some kind of repairman, he didn't trust Michael, didn't like him and wished he hadn't come. His thoughts were like heavy persistent drumbeats. The man next to him had trouble concentrating. Memories of insignificant things constantly rolled through his thoughts, interrupting them or enhancing them as though he couldn't stop free-associating. He cared the least about Michael having brought her but she recognized him as the one who was going to call his kid the next day. Now he was thinking about food.

The man with his back to her didn't like the idea of her sitting directly behind him. It meant he wouldn't know when she was looking at him. He was the one who kept wondering how old she was.

And the sandy-haired man with the red face. He showed flashes of concern for her but it was the kind he had for dumb, not particularly useful animals: don't hurt them but keep them well out of the way.

The circle came back to Michael, who was grinning at the cards piling up in front of him. The harsh overhead light threw strange shadows onto his face. She put a pistachio nut to her mouth and pushed out, touching Michael's mind.

Let's go, little sister. What's the story?

She sighed. A thousand ways they could have used their respective abilities and Michael insisted on using them to cheat at poker. She directed her attention around the table, listening in as each man evaluated his hand and then dutifully reported to Michael.

Three nines; pair of eights and possible straight, seven low, ten high; one seven and possible straight ace through four; pair of fives and an ace, queen, jack. Michael had taught her everything, coaching her over and over until she sounded to herself like she thought a Vegas croupier must sound. Michael's own hand had only a pair of threes. *So far, not so good,* she thought at him.

Just report on their cards, little sister.

She paid close attention as each player asked for one or two or three cards. Michael ended up with a pair of kings along with the pair of threes, but the three nines took the pot. Michael's disappointment oozed through her like the taste of something rancid.

See, Michael? Even cheating can't help, sometimes.

Just you do what you're supposed to do and let me play. I'm getting the feel of them.

Miraculously during the third hand, Michael was dealt a straight, seven through jack. He stood pat while the others took two or three cards from the sandy-haired man — Harvey, they were calling him — and then began to bet. Michael's triumph thrummed in her, making her hand shake as she reached into the bag for another pistachio. The money in the center of the table increased.

This is ideal, little sister. They'll believe every bluff I lay on them from now on.

She squirmed. *The heavy man across from you doesn't believe you have anything, Michael. He doesn't trust you. He thinks you're cheating.*

Chill out, little sister, and let me play it.

Agitated, she cracked a nut between her teeth. The heavy man who thought Michael was cheating twisted around to glare at her.

"Does she have to do that? It's driving me bugfuck!" He turned to Michael but his anger pounded incoherently in her mind like a jack-hammer; she passed that on to Michael. His mouth twisted down at the corners.

"Knock it off, Sarah Jane. No more nuts. We can't concentrate here."

She set the bag quietly aside and listened as the betting continued. The angry man held a pair of kings; the rest of the hands were cold. Only Harvey attempted to stay in for awhile. Then he, too, folded his cards and sat back to observe the duel between Michael and the man opposite. Sarah Jane's head began to throb.

"Ten bucks," said the man.

"See you and raise you another five." *Bluff his ass out of the water. How far will he go, Sarah Jane?*

He's thinking about cutting your throat.

That's why they call it cutthroat, babe.

For real, Michael. With a knife.

The man — Klemmer was the name he identified himself with, not Albert, which was his first name — folded his five dollar bill in half the long way and then set it like a tent on top of the other bills. "Call," he said.

153

"You first," Michael told him.

The man wagged his greying head from side to side. "I paid for 'em, I get to see 'em."

Don't show off, Michael, she begged. But he laid his cards down showily, one at a time in descending order, until he came to the seven. He appeared to hesitate and then put it on the table face down.

"How much you bet it's a seven, Klemmer?"

A jolt of terror almost loosened Sarah Jane's bowels. *You're not supposed to know his name, Michael! He never told you!*

Michael smiled defiantly at the man, whose thoughts had flattened into a low hum of suspicion. But mercifully, he hadn't noticed Michael's use of his name.

It's too early to pull this, Michael! Stop it!

"How much?" Michael prodded.

The other man was about to answer — *twenty* — when Harvey leaned forward and turned the seven over. Michael's thoughts flared angrily but before he could say anything, the sandy-haired man just laughed.

"You even had me going there for awhile, Slick, but I knew that had to be a seven. Forget it, the pot's big enough for anyone. Right?"

Michael's anger died; he picked his winnings up bill by bill. "Yeah. Sure. Big enough for anyone. I play sincere poker."

Don't be a big shot, Michael. That man saved you.

Lay off, little sister. They'd take me for everything in a minute if they could.

You're the stranger, they don't trust you!

"Hey, Sarah Jane," Michael said aloud. "Go ahead. Have a few nuts. We concentrate just fine, don't we?"

The heavy man's anger seared her mind and brought tears to her eyes. She sat with her head bent, pretending to be in a light doze.

Michael's cards went dead for the next few hands but the tension between him and the heavy man increased steadily. The sandy-haired man, Harvey, kept watching him, undecided as to whether Michael was honest.

Sarah Jane felt herself settle into a weird calm. Michael bought the table a round of beer, brought in to them by a fat, bored bartender whose mind seemed to be on automatic pilot. The sight of her stirred no new thoughts, as though she were just a blurry photograph to him.

The game continued, the cards running cold almost without a break. Someone produced a new deck, which was examined and pronounced acceptable. It didn't do any of them much good. She ceased to pay attention to anything except the contents of each man's hand, reporting the information mechanically to Michael. Sometimes it helped,

154

sometimes not. The heavy man's anger had subsided but remained ready. The others were nondescript in her mind, colorless entities who neither lost nor won large amounts of money, players Michael referred to as chairwarmers, there only to fill out the pot.

The time crawled past, leaving her with a feeling of weighty exhaustion. The smoke in the air turned her stomach and hurt her eyes. In front of Michael, the pile of money increased and then decreased but he continued to run ahead, consulting her as though she were just another part of his mind. And she seemed to be just that. In her inner eye, she could see the cards he held; she could taste the alcoholic maltiness of beer in his mouth, feel the air going in and out of his lungs. She slid in further, wincing at the ache in his back and the hardness of the chair. Michael's gaze flickered to her and she saw herself sitting on the boxes with her head bowed and her hair hanging down. Then she was all the way inside him and she saw her body go limp. There was a roaring in her/Michael's ears and the sensation of something about to give way. She began to topple over.

"Sarah Jane!"

The faces of the other men flashed before her dizzyingly and then the floor was rushing at her.

Moments later, she was blinking up at Michael who was bending over her, his face white with fury.

"I'd say it's past your little mascot's bedtime," said the sandy-haired man. "Either that or she's pitching a fit. Which is it?"

"Get up," Michael growled at her, "and don't pull that shit again, Sarah Jane."

"Being a little hard on her, aren't you?" said the heavy man sarcastically.

Michael looked at him. "What's it to you? She's just a dumb kid."

"Yeah. Sure. Your sister's kid, right?"

Sarah Jane sat up with her back against the boxes. *Michael, let's get out of here.*

"That's what I said." Michael straightened up slowly. "What about it?"

Michael, please! Something's going to happen!

"She always faint when you're about to lose big?"

"What are you trying to say?" Michael asked.

"What is it you got going, some kind of signaling system maybe?"

"Hey, come on—" said the sandy-haired man stepping forward but the heavy man shoved him back.

Michael, we have to run. Now!

"Yeah, that's what it is, isn't it? Your little mascot signals to you and you signal back what you've got, right?"

"Bullshit in a bag, man, she's been sitting right over here on these boxes all night reading her goddam magazine and eating her nuts."

"Eating *my* nuts, pal, looking over my shoulder and telling you what I got!"

Sarah Jane pushed away from them, crawling toward the corner.

"She can't see what you got from where she's sitting," Michael said. "And she sure as hell couldn't see what the other guys were holding. You're crazy."

"Don't call me that, buddy."

Michael sneered at him. "Oh, *sorry,* Klemmer."

Michael, don't! I told you, you're not supposed to know his name! Sarah Jane thought at him just as he turned to her and yelled, "Will you shut up, you little bitch!"

The men looked at Sarah Jane and then at Michael. "You're the one who's crazy," said the sandy-haired man to Michael. "The kid hasn't said a word."

"It's their signaling system!" said Klemmer furiously. "That's how she talks to him without saying a word! Isn't it, little girl?" He lunged for her but the other two men caught him and held him back.

"Hey, come on, now," said one of them, the man who was going to call his kid. "You don't want to hurt her."

"I wanna *kill* her!" said the heavy man. "I'm down three bills because of her!"

"Forget it, she's just a kid," said the sandy-haired man. "Who knows where he got her. I bet if we let her out right now, we'd probably never see her again. Would we, kid?"

Michael looked around at the men just as the sandy-haired man took hold of his upper arm. *Sarah Jane? What's going on, they can't believe that shit, can they? Sarah Jane? Answer me, goddamit!*

Sarah Jane pulled herself up and stood facing them all with her arms clutching herself. *It's too late, Michael. I tried to warn you. They know there's something going on, they just don't know what. But they don't like you because you were winning all their money and now—*

The sandy-haired man jerked his head at the door. "Get out. And keep going."

She opened her mouth to say something.

"I mean *now,* kid!" said the sandy-haired man. "Beat it. And don't ever come around here again."

"What are you going to do?" Michael said as she backed around the table. "Hey, come on, we weren't cheating—"

"'We' weren't, huh?" said the heavy man. "Sure, buddy."

Oh, Michael—

Get the cops, Sarah Jane. Go get them right now!

"Out!" yelled the sandy-haired man and she fled out the door into the hallway.

"Hey, Klemmer, Harvey, come on—" came Michael's voice through the door.

"And how the hell do you know our names?" the heavy man said. "We never told you our names!"

"Hey, come on, now," Michael said desperately, "you don't want to do anything—"

"We're just going to check your honesty a little," said the sandy-haired man. "Make sure it's still there."

The men's thoughts rose to an incoherent roar in her head and over it all was Michael screaming to her to get help. Then the pain came, so white-hot and overpowering that she never heard the blows.

She was unable to think of anything except getting out of range of the agony pounding in her skull.

She came to herself crouched in an alleyway behind a trash dumpster, her forehead pressed against her knees. The awful noise in her mind had faded away a long time before and something like general background babble had rushed in to fill the void. She had been resting open, like a microphone that had been left on and forgotten. Distant thoughts faded in and out of her mind, mixing together unintelligibly.

Slowly, she lifted her head, forcing the mind-babble down into silence. It was like trying to close an enormous, heavy steel door that had been stuck open. She concentrated, pressing her own thoughts against the others, filling her mind with her own awareness until there wasn't room for anything else.

Peace. For a few moments. And then she remembered Michael.

Michael?

For the first time in months, there was no answer.

She stood up unsteadily and found her way around the dumpster to the mouth of the alley. The street was unfamiliar, dingy under the yellowish streetlamps. She had no idea where she was in relation to the bar or the hotel and she couldn't feel Michael at all. Feeling suddenly weary and light all at once, she leaned against a brick-walled building and looked up at the night sky. This was it. She was free. She hadn't been out of range of Michael since she'd found him and now she was. She could go now if she wanted to, just go, and not look back.

And then it came, so faintly she almost thought she was imagining it: *Sarah Jane. Sarah Jane . . .*

She wiped her hands over her face. No, she could never be out of range of Michael. Not while he lived.

They had tossed him out of a car into the shadow of an abandoned warehouse on the other side of the freeway, perhaps a mile away from where she'd come to. She found him without any awareness of where she was going, only that she was going to him. Weak at first, his thoughts grew stronger as they hooked onto her, drawing her to him. The pain was curiously remote to her; she could feel it but she could keep it fenced off so it wouldn't take her over. She could also feel Michael's relief and joy at having found her but that, too, was fenced off with the pain. It was peculiar. She'd never done that before with Michael.

Sarah Jane.

He was lying on the broken pavement of what had once been a parking lot. She closed her eyes, not wanting to see the gleam of blood in the faint light of a streetlamp a block away. She got it from him all at once: they had not intended to kill him, just to beat him badly, teach him a lesson. Except they'd beaten him too badly and he was dying after all.

Won't they freak when they hear about it on the news, how my body was found here. They'll shit their frigging pants over it.

She crouched down a few feet away from his head, still not looking at him. *Yeah, Michael. They'll freak. They'll shit their frigging pants.*

And they'll be worried about you, Sarah Jane. They'll be afraid you'll go to the cops about it.

Yeah, Michael. They sure will.

So we'll have to hide for awhile. And then, when they think they're secure, we'll go to the cops and nail their asses.

Her mind stopped cold for a moment. *We?*

Yeah. We. You and me, Sarah Jane. The way you always wanted it.

But you —

And then she saw what he meant to do as clearly as a movie in her head. She could even see him as though in a waking dream, standing before her with his arms open, ready to catch her up in a big, never-ending hug.

Come to me now, Sarah Jane. It's the only way. You can save me and I'll be with you for good, the way you always wanted me to be with you.

She felt herself moving toward him in her mind.

Just reach down and put your hand on my head, Sarah Jane. Just touch me. You were always wanting to touch me. Touch me now, Sarah Jane. I know you still want to.

She could see it—Michael wrapping himself around her, stepping out of the painful, dying body on the ground and into her young one, living with her, melding with her the way she had known he would have to someday. Either meld or—not.

Come on, Sarah Jane. Touch me and we'll have it made. I'm not strong enough to come to you now, you have to bring me in. Save me, Sarah Jane, save me for yourself. Remember what you said about how maybe we weren't really two people but one that got split up somehow? That's the way it'll be for us, for always, if you'll just touch me now.

Her hand trembled in the air. Horrifed, she snatched it back and pressed it to her chest. In her mind, Michael's image receded a little.

Sarah Jane? Underneath his hurt and confusion, she could sense the undertone of the old anger. *What's the matter?*

You are, Michael, she thought wearily. *How can we be sure you'd come into me and I wouldn't come into you instead and die with you?*

He didn't even hesitate. *Because you're the one with the power, Sarah Jane—the real power. I was always just your receiver. Right? You've got the power. You can keep us both alive.*

He was reaching for her now with his last bit of strength. She imagined the fence that kept out his pain growing up higher between them. Chicken wire, she imagined, like so many fences she'd seen. Chicken wire and barbed wire.

Sarah Jane? What are you doing?

I can't, Michael.

Can't what?

Can't take you.

You always wanted this!

When you were alive. The fence thickened, chicken wire crisscrossing barbed wire; he was disappearing behind the snarls. *When there was no alternative.*

There's no alternative now!

Not for you.

The fence shut him completely out of sight. *Sarah Jane! I thought you loved me!*

I love you, Michael, she thought miserably. *But I don't want to be you.*

His thoughts became a howl of outrage and betrayal. *I'll haunt you, little sister, if I can find a way, I swear I'll come after you, I swear*

*I'll get you, you'll be cursed all your life and I'll be waiting for you
when you die —*

The most amazing thing, she thought, was that he'd called her *little
sister* at the end instead of something like *you bitch.*

She didn't take much from the hotel room, just one small bag of
clothes and Michael's emergency stash of money. The clerk sitting alone
at the desk in the lobby gave her an odd look as she passed him on
the way in and on the way out again. The lateness of the hour. It was
so late even the little store was closed. No more fashion magazines
or pistachio nuts tonight.

Amazingly, she found a cab sitting a little ways from the hotel
entrance, the driver dozing behind the wheel. She got in and told him
to take her to the airport, ignoring his sleepy curiosity about her. There
was enough cash to get her a one-way ticket to the coast. After that —
well, there was the ability. She'd be able to listen in so she'd know
when she could lift an unguarded purse or a few small food items.
She'd get by. She'd done it before.

It was a long ride to the airport. She sat back and let her mind
drift. She hadn't even felt him die. So strange; she'd have thought she'd
have felt something that marked the ending of Michael's life but there'd
been nothing. Was that all there was to it?

"Huh? What'd you say?"

Sarah Jane sat up with a start. "What?"

"Did you just say something to me?" asked the cab-driver.

She swallowed, forcing herself to breathe normally. "No. I didn't
say a word. Nothing."

"Oh. Musta been the radio I heard."

She sat back again and smiled. "Yeah. It must have been."

The man picked up the microphone and murmured something in
cab-driver to it. "So, what's a young girl like you doing going to the
airport so late at night?" he asked as he put the microphone back in
its holder.

"I'm going home," she said. "Death in the family."

"Oh," the cab-driver said. She let his thoughts ramble lazily through
her mind. He was wondering what she could have been doing here
and families today, Jesus, how could they let their kids go traveling
by themselves, didn't they know awful things could happen, especially
to the really sweet ones, didn't they care . . .

And then, without warning, she was in.

The contact lasted barely half a second but it was dizzying; his
name was Tom Cheney and he had a wife and three sons, he was

working long hours for the oldest boy's college tuition and it wasn't the greatest life but at least they all had a home to go to and—

Sarah Jane wrenched away from him, shaking. They rode a mile on the highway in silence and then the cab-driver gave a long sigh. "Jeez, I'm tireder than I thought. After I drop you off, I better call it a night."

She sank against the seat cushions. Of course, he wouldn't know what it was. How could he? She wanted to laugh and cry with relief and dismay. Of all the crazy things, to find another receiver so soon after Michael—

Except he wasn't another receiver. She could tell by the aftertaste in her mind. He was just a normal person. It was her ability that had changed.

After all those months with Michael, pushing out to him, getting into him, it had been like exercising a muscle. It had strengthened the ability so that now, she could make anyone her receiver.

Anyone.

"Huh? Did you just say something?" asked the cab-driver.

"No, I—no. I didn't."

"Damn. Sorry. I guess I must be going nuts or something, hearing voices."

"The radio," she said, smiling.

"No, it wasn't the radio," the man said, troubled. "It was real weird. I thought I heard someone say, 'little sister.'"

Sarah Jane's smile faded. "'Little sister'?"

"Yeah. Just like that. 'Little sister.'"

She wiped her hands over her face. "Did you—did you hear anything else?"

The man shrugged. "I dunno. Why? You hearin' the same voices or something?" He laughed. "You psychic?"

Sarah Jane hesitated. "I think everyone is. Just a little, I mean."

"I don't much believe in that stuff. My wife does, though. She reads her horoscope every day in the paper, says she knows when one of the kids is in some kinda trouble. Me, I figure that's part of being a good parent. Intuition, you know. Say, what about your parents? They must be nuts, letting you run around in the middle of the night so far from home."

"They're okay," she said noncommittally. She pushed out with her mind. *Michael?*

Nothing. He could reach someone receiving her but he wasn't quite strong enough to reach her. Yet. How long before he was?

It didn't matter, she decided. Because she would find someone before then, and together, they'd keep him out. Two live people would be stronger than one dead Michael.

"Huh?" said the cab-driver. "I *swear* you said something that time."

"Like what?" she asked.

"I swear I heard you say 'better hurry.'"

"Oh," said Sarah Jane. "Yeah. I guess we should. I don't want to miss the last flight out. I want to find my family as fast as possible."

"Find them?"

"You know, at the airport."

"Oh, yeah." The cab sped up slightly. "Don't worry, little sister. I'll get you there."

"You'll try," she muttered, but the cab-driver didn't hear her.

INTRODUCTION TO
ANGEL

This story was nominated for the Nebula, the Hugo, and the World Fantasy Award, and it won the *Locus* Reader's Poll in 1988, in the short story category. I'm highly gratified, but puzzled as hell. At the risk of sounding as if I'm making salacious—and untrue—claims, it's a story that involves a truly unnatural act.

This is what I've always loved about science fiction—there are many more dimensions to a term like "unnatural act" than you would find in any other kind of literature.

I didn't realize what I was writing about right away. In fact, I started the story back in 1981, kept getting three-fourths of the way through it only to hit a blank wall. Disgusted, I tore it up and threw it out. Years later, when I was between drafts of *Mindplayers* (Bantam-Spectra, 1987), I reconstructed the story from handwritten drafts and tossed it up on the computer. And there was the ending, where it had been all along, I guess.

And it still took my husband's pointing out to me that I had written a homage to "Under The Hollywood Sign" by Tom Reamy before I finally caught on.

ANGEL

Stand with me awhile, Angel, I said and Angel said he'd do that. Angel was good to me that way, good to have with you on a cold night and nowhere to go. We stood on the street corner together and watched the cars going by and people and all. The streets were lit up like Christmas, streetlights, store lights, marquees over the all-night movie houses and bookstores blinking and flashing; shank of the evening in east midtown. Angel was getting used to things here and getting used to how I did, nights. Standing outside, because what else are you going to do. He was my Angel now, had been since that other cold night when I'd been going home, because where are you going to go, and I'd found him and took him with me. It's good to have someone to take with you, someone to look after. Angel knew that. He started looking after me, too.

Like now. We were standing there awhile and I was looking around at nothing and everything, the cars cruising past, some of them stopping now and again for the hookers posing by the curb, and then I saw it, out of the corner of my eye. Stuff coming out of the Angel, shiny like sparks but flowing like liquid. Silver fireworks. I turned and looked all the way at him and it was gone. And he turned and gave a little grin like he was embarrassed I'd seen. Nobody else saw it, though; not the short guy who paused next to the Angel before crossing the street against the light, not the skinny hype looking to sell the boom-box he was carrying on his shoulder, not the homeboy strutting past us with both his girlfriends on his arms, nobody but me.

The Angel said, Hungry?

Sure, I said. I'm hungry.

Angel looked past me. Okay, he said. I looked, too, and here they came, three leather boys, visor caps, belts, boots, keyrings. On the cruise together. Scary stuff, even though you know it's not looking for you.

I said, them? *Them?*

Angel didn't answer. One went by, then the second, and the Angel stopped the third by taking hold of his arm.

Hi.

The guy nodded. His head was shaved. I could see a little grey-black stubble under his cap. No eyebrows, disinterested eyes. The eyes were because of the Angel.

I could use a little money, the Angel said. My friend and I are hungry.

The guy put his hand in his pocket and wiggled out some bills, offering them to the Angel. The Angel selected a twenty and closed the guy's hand around the rest.

This will be enough, thank you.

The guy put his money away and waited.

I hope you have a good night, said the Angel.

The guy nodded and walked on, going across the street to where his two friends were waiting on the next corner. Nobody found anything weird about it.

Angel was grinning at me. Sometimes he was the Angel, when he was doing something, sometimes he was Angel, when he was just with me. Now he was Angel again. We went up the street to the luncheonette and got a seat by the front window so we could still watch the street while we ate.

Cheeseburger and fries, I said without bothering to look at the plastic-covered menus lying on top of the napkin holder. The Angel nodded.

Thought so, he said. I'll have the same, then.

The waitress came over with a little tiny pad to take our order. I cleared my throat. It seemed like I hadn't used my voice in a hundred years. "Two cheeseburgers and two fries," I said, "and two cups of—" I looked up at her and froze. She had no face. Like, nothing, blank from hairline to chin, soft little dents where the eyes and nose and mouth would have been. Under the table, the Angel kicked me, but gentle.

"And two cups of coffee," I said.

She didn't say anything—how could she?—as she wrote down the order and then walked away again. All shaken up, I looked at the Angel but he was calm like always.

She's a new arrival, Angel told me and leaned back in his chair. Not enough time to grow a face.

But how can she breathe? I said.

Through her pores. She doesn't need much air yet.

Yah, but what about—like, I mean, don't other people notice that's she's got nothing there?

No. It's not such an extraordinary condition. The only reason you notice is because you're with me. Certain things have rubbed off on you. But no one else notices. When they look at her, they see whatever face they expect someone like her to have. And eventually, she'll have it.

But you have a face, I said. You've always had a face.

I'm different, said the Angel.

You sure are, I thought, looking at him. Angel had a beautiful face. That wasn't why I took him home that night, just because he had a beautiful face—I left all that behind a long time ago—but it was there, his beauty. The way you think of a man being beautiful, good clean lines, deep-set eyes, ageless. About the only way you could describe him—look away and you'd forget everything except that he was beautiful. But he did have a face. He did.

Angel shifted in the chair—these were like somebody's old kitchen chairs, you couldn't get too comfortable in them—and shook his head, because he knew I was thinking troubled thoughts. Sometimes you could think something and it wouldn't be troubled and later you'd think the same thing and it would be troubled. The Angel didn't like me to be troubled about him.

Do you have a cigarette? he asked.

I think so.

I patted my jacket and came up with most of a pack that I handed over to him. The Angel lit up and amused us both by having the smoke come out his ears and trickle out of his eyes like ghostly tears. I felt my own eyes watering for his; I wiped them and there was that stuff again, but from me now. I was crying silver fireworks. I flicked them on the table and watched them puff out and vanish.

Does this mean I'm getting to be you, now? I asked.

Angel shook his head. Smoke wafted out of his hair. Just things rubbing off on you. Because we've been together and you're—susceptible. But they're different for you.

Then the waitress brought our food and we went on to another sequence, as the Angel would say. She still had no face but I guess she could see well enough because she put all the plates down just where you'd think they were supposed to go and left the tiny little check in the middle of the table.

Is she—I mean, did you know her, from where you—

Angel gave his head a brief little shake. No. She's from somewhere else. Not one of my—people. He pushed the cheeseburger and fries in front of him over to my side of the table. That was the way it was done; I did all the eating and somehow it worked out.

I picked up my cheeseburger and I was bringing it up to my mouth when my eyes got all funny and I saw it coming up like a whole series of cheeseburgers, whoom-whoom-whoom, trick photography, only for real. I closed my eyes and jammed the cheeseburger into my mouth, holding it there, waiting for all the other cheeseburgers to catch up with it.

167

You'll be okay, said the Angel. Steady, now.

I said with my mouth full, That was—that was weird. Will I ever get used to this?

I doubt it. But I'll do what I can to help you.

Yah, well, the Angel *would* know. Stuff rubbing off on me, he could feel it better than I could. He was the one it was rubbing off from.

I had put away my cheeseburger and half of Angel's and was working on the french fries for both of us when I noticed he was looking out the window with this hard, tight expression on his face.

Something? I asked him.

Keep eating, he said.

I kept eating but I kept watching, too. The Angel was staring at a big blue car parked at the curb right outside the diner. It was silvery blue, one of those lots-of-money models and there was a woman kind of leaning across from the driver's side to look out the passenger window. She was beautiful in that lots-of-money way, tawny hair swept back from her face and even from here I could see she had turquoise eyes. Really beautiful woman. I almost felt like crying. I mean, jeez, how did people get that way and me too harmless to live.

But the Angel wasn't one bit glad to see her. I knew he didn't want me to say anything, but I couldn't help it.

Who is she?

Keep eating, Angel said. We need the protein, what little there is.

I ate and watched the woman and the Angel watch each other and it was getting very—I don't know, very *something* between them, even through the glass. Then a cop car pulled up next to her and I knew they were telling her to move it along. She moved it along.

Angel sagged against the back of his chair and lit another cigarette, smoking it in the regular, unremarkable way.

What are we going to do tonight? I asked the Angel as we left the restaurant.

Keep out of harm's way, Angel said, which was a new answer. Most nights we spent just kind of going around soaking everything up. The Angel soaked it up, mostly. I got some of it along with him, but not the same way he did. It was different for him. Sometimes he would use me like a kind of filter. Other times he took it direct. There'd been the big car accident one night, right at my usual corner, a big old Buick running a red light smack into somebody's nice Lincoln. The Angel had had to take it direct because I couldn't handle that kind of stuff. I didn't know how the Angel could take it but he could. It carried him for days afterwards, too. I only had to eat for myself.

It's the intensity, little friend, he'd told me, as though that were supposed to explain it.

It's the intensity, not whether it's good or bad. The universe doesn't know good or bad, only less or more. Most of you have a bad time reconciling this. *You* have a bad time with it, little friend, but you get through better than other people. Maybe because of the way you are. You got squeezed out of a lot, you haven't had much of a chance at life. You're as much an exile as I am, only in your own land.

That may have been true, but at least I belonged here, so that part was easier for me. But I didn't say that to the Angel. I think he liked to think he could do as well or better than me at living—I mean, I couldn't just look at some leather boy and get him to cough up a twenty dollar bill. Cough up a fist in the face or worse, was more like it.

Tonight, though, he wasn't doing so good and it was that woman in the car. She'd thrown him out of step, kind of.

Don't think about her, the Angel said, just out of nowhere. Don't think about her any more.

Okay, I said, feeling creepy because it was creepy when the Angel got a glimpse of my head. And then, of course, I couldn't think about anything else hardly.

Do you want to go home? I asked him.

No. I can't stay in now. We'll do the best we can tonight but I'll have to be very careful about the tricks. They take so much out of me and if we're keeping out of harm's way, I might not be able to make up for a lot of it.

It's okay, I said. I ate. I don't need anything else tonight, you don't have to do any more.

Angel got that look on his face, the one where I knew he wanted to give me things, like feelings I couldn't have any more. Generous, the Angel was. But I didn't need those feelings, not like other people seem to. For awhile, it was like the Angel didn't understand that but he let me be.

Little friend, he said, and almost touched me. The Angel didn't touch a lot. I could touch him and that would be okay but if he touched somebody, he couldn't help doing something to them, like the trade that had given us the money. That had been deliberate. If the trade had touched the Angel first, it would have been different, nothing would have happened unless the Angel touched him back. All touch meant something to the Angel that I didn't understand. There was touching without touching, too. Like things rubbing off on me. And sometimes, when I did touch the Angel, I'd get the feeling that it was maybe more his idea than mine, but I didn't mind that. How many people were going their whole lives never being able to touch an Angel?

169

We walked together and all around us the street was really coming to life. It was getting colder, too. I tried to make my jacket cover more. The Angel wasn't feeling it. Most of the time hot and cold didn't mean much to him. We saw the three rough trade guys again. The one Angel had gotten the money from was getting into a car. The other two watched it drive away and then walked on. I looked over at the Angel.

Because we took his twenty, I said.

Even if we hadn't, Angel said.

So we went along, the Angel and me, and I could feel how different it was tonight than it was all the other nights we'd walked or stood together. The Angel was kind of pulled back into himself and it seemed to be keeping a check on me, pushing us closer together. I was getting more of those fireworks out of the corners of my eyes but when I'd turn my head to look, they'd vanish. It reminded me of the night I'd found the Angel standing on my corner all by himself in pain. The Angel told me later that was real talent, knowing he was in pain. I never thought of myself as any too talented but the way everyone else had been just ignoring him, I guess I must have had something to see him after all.

The Angel stopped us several feet down from an all-night bookstore. Don't look, he said. Watch the traffic or stare at your feet, but don't look or it won't happen.

There wasn't anything to see right then but I didn't look anyway.

That was the way it was sometimes, the Angel telling me it made a difference whether I was watching something or not, something about the other people being conscious of me being conscious of them. I didn't understand but I knew Angel was usually right. So I was watching traffic when the guy came out of the bookstore and got his head punched.

I could almost see it out of the corner of my eye. A lot of movement, arms and legs flying and grunty noises. Other people stopped to look but I kept my eyes on the traffic, some of which was slowing up so they could check out the fight. Next to me, the Angel was stiff all over. Taking it in, what he called the expenditure of emotional kinetic energy. No right, no wrong, little friend, he'd told me. Just energy, like the rest of the universe.

So he took it in and I felt him taking it in and while I was feeling it, a kind of silver fog started creeping around my eyeballs and I was in two places at once. I was watching the traffic and I was in the Angel watching the fight and feeling him charge up like a big battery.

It felt like nothing I'd ever felt before. These two guys slugging it out—well, one guy doing all the slugging and the other skittering around trying to get out from under the fists and having his head punched but good and the Angel drinking it like he was sipping at an empty cup and somehow getting it to have something in it after all. Deep inside him, whatever made the Angel go was getting a little stronger.

I kind of swung back and forth between him and me, or swayed might be more like it was. I wondered about it, because the Angel wasn't touching me. I really was getting to be him, I thought; Angel picked that up and put the thought away to answer later. It was like I was traveling by the fog, being one of us and then the other, for a long time, it seemed, and then after awhile I was more me than him again and some of the fog cleared away.

And there was that car, pointed the other way this time and the woman was climbing out of it with this big weird smile on her face, as though she'd won something. She waved at the Angel to come to her.

Bang went the connection between us dead and the Angel shot past me, running away from the car. I went after him. I caught a glimpse of her jumping back into the car and yanking at the gear shift.

Angel wasn't much of a runner. Something funny about his knees. We'd gone maybe a hundred feet when he started wobbling and I could hear him pant. He cut across a Park & Lock that was dark and mostly empty. It was back-to-back with some kind of private parking lot and the fences for each one tried to mark off the same narrow strip of lumpy pavement. They were easy to climb but Angel was too panicked. He just *went* through them before he even thought about it; I knew that because if he'd been thinking, he'd have wanted to save what he'd just charged up for when he really needed out bad enough.

I had to haul myself over the fences in the usual way and when he heard me rattling on the saggy chainlink, he stopped and looked back.

Go, I told him. Don't wait on me!

He shook his head sadly. Little friend, I'm a fool. I could stand to learn from you a little more.

Don't stand, run! I got over the fences and caught up with him. Let's go! I yanked his sleeve as I slogged past and he followed at a clumsy trot.

Have to hide somewhere, he said, camouflage ourselves with people.

I shook my head, thinking we could just run maybe four more blocks and we'd be at the freeway overpass. Below it were the butt-ends of old roads closed off when the freeway had been built. You could hide there the rest of your life and no one would find you. But Angel made me turn right and go down a block to this rundown crack-in-the-wall called Stan's Jigger. I'd never been in there—I'd never made it a practice to go into bars—but the Angel was pushing too hard to argue.

171

Inside it was smelly and dark and not too happy. The Angel and I went down to the end of the bar and stood under a blood-red light while he searched his pockets for money.

Enough for one drink apiece, he said.

I don't want anything.

You can have soda or something.

The Angel ordered from the bartender, who was suspicious. This was a place for regulars and nobody else, and certainly nobody else like me or the Angel. The Angel knew that even stronger than I did but he just stood and pretended to sip his drink without looking at me. He was all pulled into himself and I was hovering around the edges. I knew he was still pretty panicked and trying to figure out what he could do next. As close as I was, if he had to get real far away, he was going to have a problem and so was I. He'd have to tow me along with him and that wasn't the most practical thing to do.

Maybe he was sorry now he'd let me take him home. He'd been so weak then and now what with all the filtering and stuff I'd done, he couldn't just cut me off without a lot of pain.

I was trying to figure out what I could do for him when the bartender came back and gave us a look that meant order or get out and he'd have liked it better if we got out. So would everyone else there. The few other people standing at the bar weren't looking at us but they knew right where we were, like a sore spot. It wasn't hard to figure out what they thought about us, either, maybe because of me or because of the Angel's beautiful face.

We got to leave, I said to the Angel but he had it in his head this was good camouflage. There wasn't enough money for two more drinks so he smiled at the bartender and slid his hand across the bar and put it on top of the bartender's. It was tricky doing it this way; bartenders and waitresses took more persuading because it wasn't normal for them just to give you something.

The bartender looked at the Angel with his eyes half-closed. He seemed to be thinking it over. But the Angel had just blown a lot going through the fence instead of climbing over it and the fear was scuttling his concentration and I just knew that it wouldn't work. And maybe my knowing that didn't help, either.

172

The bartender's free hand dipped down below the bar and came up with a small club. "Faggot!" he roared and caught Angel just over the ear. Angel slammed into me and we both crashed to the floor. Plenty of emotional kinetic energy in here, I thought dimly as the guys standing at the bar fell on us and I didn't think anything more as I curled up into a ball under their fists and boots.

We were lucky they didn't much feel like killing anyone. Angel went out the door first and they tossed me out on top of him. As soon as I landed on him, I knew we were both in trouble; something was broken inside him. So much for keeping out of harm's way. I rolled off him and lay on the pavement, staring at the sky and trying to catch my breath. There was blood in my mouth and my nose and my back was on fire.

Angel? I said, after a bit.

He didn't answer. I felt my mind get kind of all loose and runny, like my brains were leaking out my ears. I thought about the trade we'd taken the money from and how I'd been scared of him and his friends and how silly that had been. But then, I was too harmless to live.

The stars were raining silver fireworks down on me. It didn't help. Angel? I said again.

I rolled over onto my side to reach for him and there she was. The car was parked at the curb and she had Angel under the armpits, dragging him toward the open passenger door. I couldn't tell if he was conscious or not and that scared me. I sat up.

She paused, still holding the Angel. We looked into each other's eyes and I started to understand.

"Help me get him into the car," she said at last. Her voice sounded hard and flat and unnatural. "Then you can get in, too. In the *back* seat."

I was in no shape to take her out. It couldn't have been better for her than if she'd set it up herself. I got up, the pain flaring in me so bad that I almost fell down again and sort of took the Angel's ankles. His ankles were so delicate, almost like a woman's, like hers. I didn't really help much except to guide his feet in as she sat him on the seat and strapped him in with the shoulder harness. I got in the back as she ran around to the other side of the car, her steps real light and peppy, like she'd found a million dollars lying there on the sidewalk.

We were out on the freeway before the Angel stirred in the shoulder harness. His head lolled from side to side on the back of the seat. I reached up and touched his hair lightly, hoping she couldn't see me do it.

Where are you taking me, the Angel said.

"For a ride," said the woman. "For the moment."

Why does she talk out loud like that? I asked the Angel.

Because she knows it bothers me.

"You know I can focus my thoughts better if I say things out loud," she said. "I'm not like one of your little pushovers." She glanced at me in the rear view mirror. "Just what have you gotten yourself into since you left, darling? Is that a boy or a girl?"

I pretended I didn't care about what she said or that I was too harmless to live or any of that stuff but the way she said it, she meant it to sting.

Friends can be either, Angel said. It doesn't matter which. Where are you taking us?

Now it was *us*. In spite of everything, I almost could have smiled.

"Us? You mean, you and me? Or are you really referring to your little pet back there?"

My friend and I are together. You and I are *not*.

The way the Angel said it made me think he meant more than not together; like he'd been with her once the way he was with me now. The Angel let me know I was right. Silver fireworks started flowing slowly off his head down the back of the seat and I knew there was something wrong about it. There was too much all at once.

"Why can't you talk out loud to me, darling?" the woman said with fakey-sounding petulance. "Just say a few words and make me happy. You have a lovely voice when you use it."

That was true, but the Angel never spoke out loud unless he couldn't

173

get out of it, like when he'd ordered from the bartender. Which had probably helped the bartender decide about what he thought we were, but it was useless to think about that.

"All right," said Angel, and I knew the strain was awful for him. "I've said a few words. Are you happy?" He sagged in the shoulder harness.

"Ecstatic. But it won't make me let you go. I'll drop your pet at the nearest hospital and then we'll go home." She glanced at the Angel as she drove. "I've missed you so much. I can't stand it without you, without you making things happen. Doing your little miracles. You knew I'd get addicted to it, all the things you could do to people. And then you just took off, I didn't know what had happened to you. And it *hurt*." Her voice turned kind of pitiful, like a little kid's. "I was in *real* pain. You must have been, too. Weren't you? Well, *weren't* you?"

Yes, the Angel said. I was in pain, too.

I remembered him standing on my corner where I'd hung out all that time by myself until he came. Standing there in pain. I didn't know why or from what then, I just took him home and after a little while, the pain went away. When he decided we were together, I guess.

The silvery flow over the back of the car seat thickened. I cupped my hands under it and it was like my brain was lighting up with pictures. I saw the Angel before he was my Angel in this really nice house, the woman's house, and how she'd take him places, restaurants or stores or parties, thinking at him real hard so that he was all filled up with her and had to do what she wanted him to. Steal sometimes; other times, weird stuff, make people do silly things like suddenly start singing or taking their clothes off. That was mostly at the parties, though she made a waiter she didn't like burn himself with a pot of coffee. She'd get men, too, through the Angel, and they'd think it was the greatest idea in the world to go to bed with her. Then she'd make the Angel show her the others, the ones that had been sent here the way he had for crimes nobody could have understood, like the waitress with no face. She'd look at them, sometimes try to do things to them to make them uncomfortable or unhappy. But mostly she'd just stare.

It wasn't like that in the very beginning, the Angel said weakly and I knew he was ashamed.

It's okay, I told him. People can be nice at first, I know that. Then they find out about you.

The woman laughed. "You two are so sweet and pathetic. Like a couple of little children. I guess that's what you were looking for, wasn't it, darling? Except children can be cruel, too, can't they? So you got this—creature for yourself." She looked at me in the rear view

mirror again as she slowed down a little and for a moment I was afraid
she'd seen what I was doing with the silvery stuff still pouring out of
the Angel. It was starting to slow now. There wasn't much time left.
I wanted to scream but the Angel was calming me for what was coming
next. "What happened to you, anyway?"

Tell her, said the Angel. To stall for time, I knew, keep her occupied.

I was born funny, I said. I had both sexes.

"A hermaphrodite!" she exclaimed with real delight.

She loves freaks, the Angel said but she didn't pay any attention.

There was an operation but things went wrong. They kept trying
to fix it as I got older but my body didn't have the right kind of chem-
istry or something. My parents were ashamed. I left after awhile.

"You poor thing," she said, not meaning anything like that. "You
were just what darling, here, needed, weren't you? Just a little nothing,
no demands, no desires. For anything." Her voice got all hard. "They
could probably fix you up now, you know."

I don't want it. I left all that behind a long time ago, I don't need it.

"Just the sort of little pet that would be perfect for you," she said
to the Angel. "Sorry I have to tear you away. But I can't get along
without you now. Life is so boring. And empty. And—" She sounded
puzzled. "And like there's nothing more to live for since you left me."

That's not me, said the Angel. That's you.

"No, it's a lot of you, too, and you know it. You know you're
addictive to human beings, you knew that when you came here—when
they *sent* you here. Hey, you, pet, do you know what his crime was,
why they sent him to this little backwater penal colony of a planet?"

Yeah, I know, I said. I really didn't, but I wasn't going to tell
her that.

"What do you think about that, little pet neuter?" she said gleefully,
hitting the accelerator pedal and speeding up. "What do you think of
the crime of refusing to mate?"

The Angel made a sort of an out loud groan and lunged at the
steering wheel. The car swerved wildly and I fell backwards, the
silvery stuff from the Angel going all over me. I tried to keep scooping
it into my mouth the way I'd been doing but it was flying all over the
place now. I heard the crunch as the tires left the road and went onto
the shoulder. Something struck the side of the car, probably the guard
rail, and made it fishtail, throwing me down on the floor. Up front
the woman was screaming and cursing and the Angel wasn't making
a sound but in my head, I could hear him sort of keening. Whatever
happened, this would be it. The Angel had told me all that time ago

after I'd taken him home that they didn't last long after they got here, the exiles from his world and other worlds. Things tended to happen to them, even if they latched on to someone like me or the woman. They'd be in accidents or the people here would kill them. Like antibodies in a human rejecting something or fighting a disease. At least I belonged here, but it looked like I was going to die in a car accident with the Angel and the woman both. I didn't care.

The car swerved back onto the highway for a few seconds and then pitched to the right again. Suddenly there was nothing under us and then we thumped down on something, not road but dirt or grass or something, bombing madly up and down. I pulled myself up on the back of the seat just in time to see the sign coming at us at an angle. The corner of it started to go through the windshield on the woman's side and then all I saw for a long time was the biggest display of silver fireworks ever.

176

It was hard to be gentle with him. Every move hurt but I didn't want to leave him sitting in the car next to her, even if she was dead. Being in the back seat had kept most of the glass from flying into me but I was still shaking some out of my hair and the impact hadn't done much for my back.

I laid the Angel out on the lumpy grass a little ways from the car and looked around. We were maybe a hundred yards from the highway, near a road that ran parallel to it. It was dark but I could still read the sign that had come through the windshield and split the woman's head in half. It said, CONSTRUCTION AHEAD, REDUCE SPEED. Far off on the other road, I could see a flashing yellow light and at first I was afraid it was the police or something but it stayed where it was and I realized that must be the construction.

"Friend," whispered the Angel, startling me. He'd never spoken aloud to me, not directly.

Don't talk, I said, bending over him, trying to figure out some way I could touch him, just for comfort. There wasn't anything else I could do now.

"I have to," he said, still whispering. "It's almost all gone. Did you get it?"

Mostly, I said. Not all.

"I meant for you to have it."

I know.

"I don't know that it will really do you any good." His breath kind of bubbled in his throat. I could see something wet and shiny on his mouth but it wasn't silver fireworks. "But it's yours. You can do as you like with it. Live on it the way I did. Get what you need when you need it. But you can live as a human, too. Eat. Work. However, whatever."

I'm not human, I said. I'm not any more human than you, even if I do belong here.

"Yes you are, little friend. I haven't made you any less human," he said, and coughed some. "I'm not sorry I wouldn't mate. I couldn't mate with my own. It was too, I don't know, too little of me, too much of them, something. I couldn't bond, it would have been nothing but emptiness. The Great Sin, to be unable to give, because the universe knows only less or more and I insisted that it would be good or bad. So they sent me here. But in the end, you know, they got their way, little friend." I felt his hand on me for a moment before it fell away. "I did it after all. Even if it wasn't with my own."

The bubbling in his throat stopped. I sat next to him for awhile in the dark. Finally I felt it, the Angel stuff. It was kind of fluttery-churny, like too much coffee on an empty stomach. I closed my eyes and lay down on the grass, shivering. Maybe some of it was shock but I don't think so. The silver fireworks started, in my head this time, and with them came a lot of pictures I couldn't understand. Stuff about the Angel and where he'd come from and the way they mated. It was a lot like how we'd been together, the Angel and me. They looked a lot like us but there were a lot of differences, too, things I couldn't make out. I couldn't make out how they'd sent him here, either — by light, in, like, little bundles or something. It didn't make any sense to me but I guessed an Angel could be light. Silver fireworks.

177

I must have passed out or something because when I opened my eyes, it felt like I'd been laying there a long time. It was still dark, though. I sat up and reached for the Angel, thinking I ought to hide his body.

He was gone. There was just a sort of wet sandy stuff where he'd been.

I looked at the car and her. All that was still there. Somebody was going to see it soon. I didn't want to be around for that.

Everything still hurt but I managed to get to the other road and start walking back toward the city. It was like I could feel it now, the way the Angel must have, as though it were vibrating like a drum or ringing like a bell with all kinds of stuff, people laughing and crying and loving and hating and being afraid and everything else that happens to people. The stuff that the Angel took in, energy, that I could take in now if I wanted.

And I knew that taking it in that way, it would be bigger than anything all those people had, bigger than anything I could have had if things hadn't gone wrong with me all those years ago.

I wasn't so sure I wanted it. Like the Angel, refusing to mate back where he'd come from. He wouldn't, there, and I couldn't, here. Except now I could do something else.

I wasn't so sure I wanted it. But I didn't think I'd be able to stop it, either, any more than I could stop my heart from beating. Maybe it wasn't really such a good thing or a right thing. But it was like the Angel said: the universe doesn't know good or bad, only less or more.

Yeah. I heard *that*.

I thought about the waitress with no face. I could find them all now, all the ones from the other places, other worlds that sent them away for some kind of alien crimes nobody would have understood. I could find them all. They threw away their outcasts, I'd tell them, but here, we kept ours. And here's how. Here's how you live in a universe that only knows less or more.

I kept walking toward the city.

178

IT WAS THE HEAT

In 1986, I visited New Orleans for the first time and fell completely in love. With the *city*. I spent five days there as part of the research group my then-employer Hallmark Cards sent to the American Booksellers Association national convention, and I devoted just about all my free time to walking around the French Quarter. Walking around the French Quarter is a pretty tame way to have a wild time, provided you keep moving and don't stop, except perhaps to replenish your go-cup.

At that point, I had spent almost ten years working full-time in the sanitized-for-your-protection, climate-controlled-for-your-comfort corporate vivarium, and even as a member of the eccentrics division — aka creative — I was familiar with the burdens of the corporate, dressed-for-success career woman, who is allowed very little in the way of margin for error, no false moves, and no judgment calls that would indicate she is a mere mortal. It's a jungle in there. My mind kept making a double-exposure (no pun intended, *really*) of the two milieus — the crisp, dry corporate world and the ornate, sultry French Quarter.

A little over a year later, I called it quits with Hallmark, and I arrived home after my last climate-controlled day to find a letter from Tim Sullivan telling me he had sold the *Tropical Chills* anthology: "Get to work." To commemorate my years in bondage, I took the weekend off and got to work bright and early the following Monday morning, and the story became my first sale as a full-time freelance writer, as well as my love letter to the city of New Orleans. Um, maybe it's more of a mash-note.

If your company ever offers you a business trip to New Orleans, by all means go. But take it easy, and watch out for heat-stroke.

IT WAS THE HEAT

*I*t was the heat, the incredible heat that never lets up, never eases, never once gives you a break. Sweat till you die; bake till you drop; fry, broil, burn, baby, burn. How'd you like to live in a fever and never feel cool, never, never, never.

Women think they want men like that. They think they want some-one to put the devil in their Miss Jones. Some of them even lie awake at night, alone, or next to a silent lump of husband or boyfriend or friendly stranger, thinking, *Let me be completely consumed with fire. In the name of love.*

Sure.

Right feeling, wrong name. Try again. And the thing is, they do. They try and try and try, and if they're very, very unlucky, they find one of them.

I thought I had him right where I wanted him—between my legs. Listen, I didn't always talk this way. That wasn't me you saw storm-ing the battlements during the Sexual Revolution. My ambition was liberated but I didn't lose my head, or give it. It wasn't me saying, *Let them eat pie.* Once I had a sense of propriety but I lost it with my inhibitions.

You think these things happen only in soap operas—the respectable, thirty-five-year-old wife and working mother goes away on a business trip with a suitcase full of navy blue suits and classy blouses with the bow at the neck and a briefcase crammed with paperwork. Product management is not a pretty sight. Sensible black pumps are a must for the run on the fast track and if your ambition is sufficiently liberated, black pumps can keep pace with perforated wing-tips, even outrun them.

But men know the secret. Especially businessmen. This is why management conferences are sometimes held in a place like New Orleans instead of the professional canyons of New York City or Chicago. Men know the secret and now I do, too. But I didn't then, when I arrived in New Orleans with my luggage and my paperwork and my inhibitions, to be installed in the Bourbon Orleans Hotel in the French Quarter.

The room had all the charm of home—more, since I wouldn't be cleaning it up. I hung the suits in the bathroom, ran the shower, called home, already feeling guilty. Yes, boys, Mommy's at the hotel now and she has a long meeting to go to, let me talk to Daddy. Yes, dear, I'm fine. It was a long ride from the airport, good thing the corporation's paying for this. The hotel is very nice, good thing the corporation's paying for this, too. Yes, there's a pool but I doubt I'll have time to use it and anyway, I didn't bring a suit. Not that kind of suit. This isn't a pleasure trip, you know, I'm not on vacation. No. Yes. No. Kiss the boys for me. I love you, too.

If you want to be as conspicuous as possible, be a woman walking almost late into a meeting room full of men who are all gunning to be CEOs. Pick out the two or three other female faces and nod to them even though they're complete strangers, and find a seat near them. Listen to the man at the front of the room say, *Now that we're all here, we can begin* and know that every man is thinking that means you. Imagine what they are thinking, imagine what they are whispering to each other. Imagine that they know you can't concentrate on the opening presentation because your mind is on your husband and children back home instead of the business at hand when the real reason you can't concentrate is because you're imagining they must all be thinking your mind is on your husband and children back home instead of the business at hand.

Do you know what *they're* thinking about, really? They're thinking about the French Quarter. Those who have been there before are thinking about jazz and booze in go-cups and bars where the women are totally nude, totally, and those who haven't been there before are wondering if everything's as wild as they say.

Finally the presentation ended and the discussion period following the presentation ended (the women had nothing to discuss so as not to be perceived as the ones delaying the after-hours jaunt into the French Quarter). Tomorrow, nine o'clock in the Hyatt, second floor meeting room. Don't let's be too hung over to make it, boys, ha, ha. Oh, and girls, too, of course, ha, ha.

The things you hear when you don't have a crossbow.

Demure, I took a cab back to the Bourbon Orleans, intending to leave a wake-up call for 6:30, ignoring the streets already filling up. In early May, with Mardi Gras already a dim memory? Was there a big convention in town this week, I asked the cab driver.

No, ma'am, he told me (his accent—Creole or Cajun? I don't know—made it more like *ma'ahm*). De Quarter always be jumpin', and de weather be so lovely.

182

This was lovely? I was soaked through my drip-dry white blouse and the suitcoat would start to smell if I didn't take it off soon. My crisp, boardroom coiffure had gone limp and trickles of sweat were tracking leisurely along my scalp. Product management was meant to live in air conditioning (we call it climate control, as though we really could, but there is no controlling this climate).

At the last corner before the hotel, I saw him standing at the curb. Tight jeans, red shirt knotted above the navel to show off the washboard stomach. Definitely not executive material; executives are required to be doughy in that area and the area to the south of that was never delineated quite so definitely as it was in this man's jeans.

Some sixth sense made him bend to see who was watching him from the back seat of the cab.

"Mamma, mamma!" he called and kissed the air between us. "You wanna go to a party?" He came over to the cab and motioned for me to roll the window all the way down. I slammed the lock down on the door and sat back, clutching my sensible black purse.

"C'mon, mamma!" He poked his fingers through the small opening of the window. "I be good to you!" The golden hair was honey from peroxide but the voice was honey from the comb. The light changed and he snatched his fingers away just in time.

"I'll be waiting!" he shouted after me. I didn't look back.

"What was all that about?" I asked the cab driver.

"Just a wild boy. Lotta wild boys in the Quarter, ma'am." We pulled up next to the hotel and he smiled over his shoulder at me, his teeth just a few shades lighter than his coffee-colored skin. "Any time you want to find a wild boy for yourself, this is where you look." It came out more like *dis is wheah you look*. "You got a nice company sends you to the Quarter for doin' business."

I smiled back, overtipped him, and escaped into the hotel.

It wasn't even a consideration, that first night. Wake-up call for six-thirty, just as I'd intended, to leave time for showering and breakfast, like the good wife and mother and executive I'd always been.

Beignets for breakfast. Carl had told me I must have beignets for breakfast if I were going to be New Orleans. He'd bought some beignet mix and tried to make some for me the week before I'd left. They'd come out too thick and heavy and only the kids had been able to eat them, liberally dusted with powdered sugar. If I found a good place for beignets, I would try to bring some home, I'd decided, for my lovely, tolerant, patient husband, who was now probably making thick, heavy pancakes for the boys. Nice of him to sacrifice some of his vacation time to be home with the boys while Mommy was out of town. Mommy had never gone out of town on business before. Daddy had, of course; several times. At those times, Mommy had never been able to take any time away from the office, though, so she could be with the boys while Daddy was out of town. Too much work to do; if you want to keep those sensible black pumps on the fast track, you can't be putting your family before the work. Lots of women lose out that way, you know, Martha?

I knew.

No familiar faces in the restaurant, but I wasn't looking for any. I moved my tray along the line, took a beignet and poured myself some of the famous Louisiana chicory coffee before I found a small table under a ceiling fan. No air-conditioning and it was already up in the eighties. I made a concession and took off my jacket. After a bite of the beignet, I made another and unbuttoned the top two buttons of my blouse. The pantyhose already felt sticky and uncomfortable. I had a perverse urge to slip off to the ladies' room and take them off. Would anyone notice or care? That would leave me with nothing under the half-slip. Would anyone guess? There goes a lady executive with no pants on. In the heat, it was not unthinkable. No underwear at all was not unthinkable. Everything was binding. A woman in a gauzy caftan breezed past my table, glancing down at me with careless interest. Another out-of-towner, yes. You can tell—we're the only ones not dressed for the weather.

"All right to sit here, ma'am?"

I looked up. He was holding a tray with one hand, already strad-
dling the chair across from me, only waiting my permission to sink
down and join me. Dark, curly hair, just a bit too long, darker eyes,
smooth skin the color of over-creamed coffee. Tank top over jeans.
He eased himself down and smiled. I must have said yes.

"All the other tables're occupied or ain't been bussed, ma'am. Hope
you don't mind, you a stranger here and all." The smile was as slow
and honeyed as the voice. They all talked in honey tones here. "Eatin'
you one of our nice beignets, I see. First breakfast in the Quarter,
am I right?"

I used a knife and fork on the beignet. "I'm here on business."

"You have a very striking face."

I risked a glance up at him. "You're very kind." Thirty-five and
up is striking, if the world is feeling kind.

"When your business is done, shall I see you in the Quarter?"

"I doubt it. My days are very long." I finished the beignet quickly,
gulped the coffee. He caught my arm as I got up. It was a jolt of heat,
like being touched with an electric wand.

"I have a husband and three children!" It was the only thing I could
think to say.

"You don't want to forget your jacket."

It hung limply on the back of my chair. I wanted to forget it badly,
to have an excuse to go through the day of meetings and seminars
in shirtsleeves. I put the tray down and slipped the jacket on. "Thank
you."

"Name is Andre, ma'am." The dark eyes twinkled. "My heart will
surely break if I don't see you tonight in the Quarter."

"Don't be silly."

"It's too hot to be silly, ma'am."

"Yes. It is," I said stiffly. I looked for a place to take the tray.

"They take it away for you. You can just leave it here. Or you
can stay and have another cup of coffee and talk to a lonely soul."
One finger plucked at the low scoop of the tank top. "I'd like that."

"A cab driver warned me about wild boys," I said, holding my
purse carefully to my side.

"I doubt it. He may have told you but he didn't warn you. And
I ain't a boy, ma'am."

Sweat gathered in the hollow between my collarbones and spilled
downward. He seemed to be watching the trickle disappear down into
my blouse. Under the aroma of baking breads and pastries and coffee,
I caught a scent of something else.

184

"Boys stand around on street corners, they shout rude remarks, they don't know what a woman is."

"That's enough," I snapped. "I don't know why you picked me out for your morning's amusement. Maybe because I'm from out of town. You wild boys get a kick out of annoying the tourists, is that it? If I see you again, I'll call a cop." I stalked out and pushed myself through the humidity to hail a cab. By the time I reached the Hyatt, I might as well not have showered.

"I'm skipping out on this afternoon's session," the woman whispered to me. Her badge said she was Frieda Fellowes, of Boston, Massachusetts. "I heard the speaker last year. He's the biggest bore in the world. I'm going shopping. Care to join me?"

I shrugged. "I don't know. I have to write up a report on this when I get home and I'd better be able to describe everything in detail."

She looked at my badge. "You must work for a bunch of real hardasses up in Schenectady." She leaned forward to whisper to the other woman sitting in the row ahead of us, who nodded eagerly.

They were both missing from the afternoon session. The speaker was the biggest bore in the world. The men had all conceded to shirt-sleeves. Climate control failed halfway through the seminar and it broke up early, releasing us from the stuffiness of the meeting room into the thick air of the city. I stopped in the lobby bathroom and took off my pantyhose, rolled them into an untidy ball and stuffed them in my purse before getting a cab back to my own hotel.

One of the men from my firm phoned my room and invited me to join him and the guys for drinks and dinner. We met in a crowded little place called Messina's, four male executives and me. It wasn't until I excused myself and went to the closet-sized bathroom that I realized I'd put my light summer slacks on over nothing. A careless mistake, akin to starting off to the supermarket on Saturday morning in my bedroom slippers. Mommy's got a lot on her mind. Martha, the No-Pants Executive. Guess what, dear, I went out to dinner in New Orleans with four men and forgot to wear panties. Well, women do reach their sexual peak at thirty-five, don't they, honey?

The heat was making me crazy. No air-conditioning here, either, just fans, pushing the damp air around.

I rushed through the dinner of red beans and rice and hot sausage; someone ordered a round of beers and I gulped mine down to cool the sausage. No one spoke much. Martha's here, better keep it low-key, guys. I decided to do them a favor and disappear after the meal. There wouldn't be much chance of running into me at any of the nude bars, nothing to be embarrassed about. Thanks for tolerating my presence, fellas.

But they looked a little puzzled when I begged off anything further. The voice blew over to me as I reached the door, carried on a wave of humidity pushed by one of the fans: "Maybe she's got a headache tonight." General laughter.

Maybe all four of you together would be a disappointment, boys. Maybe none of you know what a woman is.

They didn't look especially wild, either.

I had a drink by the pool instead of going right up to the hotel room. Carl would be coping with supper and homework and whatnot. Better to call later, after they were all settled down.

I finished the drink and ordered another. It came in a plastic cup, with apologies from the waiter. "Temporarily short on crystal tonight, ma'am. Caterin' a private dinner here. Hope you don't mind a go-cup this time."

"A what?"

The man's smile was bright. "Go-cup. You take it and walk around with it."

"That's allowed?"

"All over the Quarter, ma'am." He moved on to another table.

So I walked through the lobby with it and out into the street, and no one stopped me.

Just down at the corner, barely half a block away, the streets were filling up again. Many of the streets seemed to be pedestrians only. I waded in, holding the go-cup. Just to look around. I couldn't really come here and not look around.

"It's supposed to be a whorehouse where the girls swung naked on velvet swings."

I turned away from the high window where the mannequin legs had been swinging in and out to look at the man who had spoken to me. He was a head taller than I was, long-haired, attractive in a rough way.

"Swung?" I said. "You mean they don't any more?"

He smiled and took my elbow, positioning me in front of an open doorway, pointed in. I looked; a woman was lying naked on her stomach under a mirror suspended overhead. Perspiration gleamed on her skin.

"Buffet?" I said. "All you can eat, a hundred dollars?"

The man threw back his head and laughed heartily. "New in the Quarter, aintcha?" Same honey in the voice. They caress you with their voices here, I thought, holding the crumpled go-cup tightly. It was a different one; I'd had another drink since I'd come out and it hadn't seemed like a bad idea at all, another drink, the walking around, all of it. Not by myself, anyway.

Something brushed my hip. "You'll let me buy you another, wontcha?" Dark hair, dark eyes; young. I remembered that for a long time.

Wild creatures in lurid long dresses catcalled screechily from a second floor balcony as we passed below on the street. My eyes were heavy with heat and alcohol but I kept walking. It was easy with him beside me, his arm around me and his hand resting on my hip.

Somewhere along the way, the streets grew much darker and the crowds disappeared. A few shadows in the larger darkness; I saw them leaning against street signs; we passed one close enough to smell a mixture of perfume and sweat and alcohol and something else.

"Didn't nobody never tell you to come out alone at night in this part of the Quarter?" The question was amused, not reproving. They caress you with their voices down here, with their voices and the darkness and the heat, which gets higher as it gets darker. And when it gets hot enough, they melt and flow together and run all over you, more fluid than water.

What are you doing?

I'm walking into a dark hallway; I don't know my footing, I'm glad there's someone with me.

What are you doing?

I'm walking into a dark room to get out of the heat, but it's no cooler here and I don't really care after all.

What are you doing?

I'm overdressed for the season here; this isn't Schenectady in the spring, it's New Orleans, it's the French Quarter.

What are you doing?

I'm hitting my sexual peak at thirty-five.

"What are you doing?"

Soft laughter. "Oh, honey, don't you know?"

The Quarter was empty at dawn, maybe because it was raining. I found my way back to the Bourbon Orleans in the downpour anyway. It shut off as suddenly as a suburban lawn sprinkler just as I reached the front door of the hotel.

I fell into bed and slept the day away, no wake-up calls, and when I opened my eyes, the sun was going down and I remembered how to find him.

You'd think there would have been a better reason: my husband ignored me or my kids were monsters or my job was a dead-end or some variation on the mid-life crisis. It wasn't any of those things. Well, the seminars *were* boring but nobody gets that bored. Or maybe they did and I'd just never heard about it.

It was the heat.

The heat gets inside you. Then you get a fever from the heat, and from fever you progress to delirium and from delirium into another state of being. Nothing is real in delirium. No, scratch that: everything is real in a different way. In delirium, everything floats, including time. Lighter than air, you slip away. Day breaks apart from night, leaves you with scraps of daylight. It's all right — when it gets that hot, it's too hot to see, too hot to bother looking. I remembered dark hair, dark eyes, but it was all dark now and in the dark, it was even hotter than in the daylight.

It was the heat. It never let up. It was the heat and the smell. I'll never be able to describe that smell except to say that if it were a sound, it would have been round and mellow and sweet, just the way it tasted. As if he had no salt in his body at all. As if he had been distilled from the heat itself, and salt had just been left behind in the process.

It was the heat.

And then it started to get cool.

It started to cool down to the eighties during the last two days of the conference and I couldn't find him. I made a half-hearted showing at one of the seminars after a two-day absence. They stared, all the men and the women, especially the one who had asked me to go shopping.

"I thought you'd been kidnapped by white slavers," she said to me during the break. "What happened? You don't look like you feel so hot."

"I feel very hot," I said, helping myself to the watery lemonade punch the hotel had laid out on a table. With beignets. The sight of them turned my stomach and so did the punch. I put it down again. "I've been running a fever."

She touched my face, frowning slightly. "You don't feel feverish. In fact, you feel pretty cool. Clammy, even."

"It's the air-conditioning," I said, drawing back. Her fingers were cold, too cold to tolerate. "The heat and the air-conditioning. It's fucked me up."

Her eyes widened.

"*Messed* me up, excuse me. I've been hanging around my kids too long."

"Perhaps you should see a doctor. Or go home."

"I've just got to get out of this air-conditioning," I said, edging toward the door. She followed me, trying to object. "I'll be fine as soon as I get out of this air-conditioning and back into the heat."

"No, *wait*," she called insistently. "You may be suffering from heat-stroke. I think that's it—the clammy skin, the way you look—"

"It's not heatstroke, I'm freezing in this goddam refrigerator. Just leave me the fuck alone and I'll be *fine!*"

I fled, peeling off my jacket, tearing open the top of my blouse. I couldn't go back, not to that awful air-conditioning. I would stay out where it was warm.

189

I lay in bed with the windows wide open and the covers pulled all the way up. One of the men from my company phoned; his voice sounded too casual when he pretended I had reassured him. Carl's call only twenty minutes later was not a surprise. I'm fine, dear. You don't sound fine. I am, though. Everyone is worried about you. Needlessly. I think I should come down there. No, stay where you are, I'll be fine. No, I think I should come and get you. And I'm telling you to stay where you are. That does it, you sound weird, I'm getting the next flight out and your mother can stay with the boys. You stay where you are, goddamit, or I might not come home, is that clear?

Long silence.

Is someone there with you?

More silence.

I said, is someone there with you?

It's just the heat. I'll be fine, as soon as I warm up.

Sometime after that, I was sitting at a table in a very dark place that was almost warm enough. The old woman sitting across from me occasionally drank delicately from a bottle of beer and fanned herself, even though it was only almost warm.

"It's such pleasure when it cool down like dis," she said in her slow honeyvoice. Even the old ladies had honeyvoices here. "The heat be a beast."

I smiled, thinking for a moment that she'd said *bitch,* not *beast.* "Yeah. It's a bitch all right but I don't like to be cold."

"No? Where you from?"

"Schenectady. Cold climate."

She grunted. "Well, the heat don't be a bitch, it be a beast. He be a beast."

"Who?"

"Him. The heat beast." She chuckled a little. "My grandma woulda called him a loa. You know what dat is?"

"No."

She eyed me before taking another sip of beer. "No. I don't know whether that good or bad for you, girl. Could be deadly either way, someone who don't like to be cold. What you doin' over here anyway? Tourist Quarter three blocks thataway."

"I'm looking for a friend. Haven't been able to find him since it's cooled down."

"Grandma knew they never named all de loa. She said new ones would come when they found things be willin' for 'em. Or when they named by someone. Got nothin' to do with the old religion any more. Bigger than the old religion. It's all de world now." The old woman thrust her face forward and squinted at me. "What friend *you* got over here? No outa-town white girl got a friend over here."

"I do. And I'm not from out of town any more."

"Get out." But it wasn't hostile, just amusement and condescension and a little disgust. "Go buy you some tourist juju and tell everybody you met a mamba in N'awlins. Be some candyass somewhere sell you a nice, fake love charm."

"I'm not here for that," I said, getting up. "I came for the heat."

"Well, girl, it's cooled down." She finished her beer.

Sometime after that, in another place, I watched a man and a woman dancing together. There were only a few other people on the floor in front of the band. I couldn't really make sense of the music, whether it was jazz or rock or whatever. It was just the man and the woman I was paying attention to. Something in their movements was familiar. I was thinking he would be called by the heat in them, but it was so damned cold in there, not even ninety degrees. The street was colder. I pulled the jacket tighter around myself and cupped my hands around the coffee mug. That famous Louisiana chicory coffee. Why couldn't I get warm?

It grew colder later. There wasn't a warm place in the Quarter, but people's skins seemed to be burning. I could see the heat shimmers rising from their bodies. Maybe I was the only one without a fever now.

Carl was lying on the bed in my hotel room. He sat up as soon as I opened the door. The heat poured from him in waves and my first thought was to throw myself on him and take it, take it all, and leave him to freeze to death.

"Wait!" he shouted but I was already pounding down the hall to the stairs.

Early in the morning, it was an easy thing to run through the Quarter. The sun was already beating down but the light was thin, with little warmth. I couldn't hear Carl chasing me, but I kept running, to the other side of the Quarter, where I had first gone into the shadows. Glimpse of an old woman's face at a window; I remembered her, she remembered me. Her head nodded, two fingers beckoned. Behind her, a younger face watched in the shadows. The wrong face.

I came to a stop in the middle of an empty street and waited. I was getting colder; against my face, my fingers were like living icicles. It had to be only 88 or 89 degrees, but even if it got to ninety-five or above today, I wouldn't be able to get warm.

He had it. He had taken it. Maybe I could get it back.

The air above the buildings shimmied, as if to taunt. Warmth, here, and here, and over here, what's the matter with you, frigid or something?

Down at the corner, a police car appeared. Heat waves rippled up from it, and I ran.

"Hey."

The man stood over me where I sat shivering at a corner table in the place that bragged it had traded slaves over a hundred years ago. He was the color of rich earth, slightly built with carefully waved black hair. Young face; the wrong face, again.

"You look like you in the market for a sweater."

"Go away." I lifted the coffee cup with shuddering hands. "A thousand sweaters couldn't keep me warm now."

"No, honey." They caressed you with their voices down here. He took the seat across from me. "Not that kind of sweater. Sweater I mean's a person, special kinda person. Who'd you meet in the Quarter? Good-lookin' stud, right? Nice, wild boy, maybe not white but white enough for you?"

"Go away. I'm not like that."

"You know what you like now, though. Cold. Very cold woman. Cold woman's no good. Cold woman'll take all the heat out of a man, leave him frozen dead."

I didn't answer.

"So you need a sweater. Maybe I know where you can find one."

"Maybe you know where I can find *him*."

The man laughed. "That's what I'm sayin', cold woman." He took off his light, white suitcoat and tossed it at me. "Wrap up in that and come on."

The fire in the hearth blazed, flames licking out at the darkness. Someone kept feeding it, keeping it burning for hours. I wasn't sure who, or if it was only one person, or how long I sat in front of the fire, trying to get warm.

Sometime long after the man had brought me there, the old woman said, "Burnin' all day now. Whole Quarter oughta feel the heat by now. Whole *city*."

"*He'll* feel it, sure enough." The man's voice. "He'll feel it, come lookin' for what's burnin'." A soft laugh. "Won't he be surprised to see it's his cold woman."

"Look how the fire wants her."

The flames danced. I could sit in the middle of them and maybe then I'd be warm.

"Where did he go?" The person who asked might have been me.

"Went to take a rest. Man sleeps after a bender, don't you know. He oughta be ready for more by now."

I reached out for the fire. A long tongue of flame licked around my arm; the heat felt so good.

"Look how the fire wants her."

Soft laugh. "If it wants her, then it should have her. Go ahead, honey. Get in the fire."

On hands and knees, I climbed up into the hearth, moving slowly, so as not to scatter the embers. Clothes burned away harmlessly.

To sit in fire is to sit among a glory of warm, silk ribbons touching everywhere at once. I could see the room now, the heavy drapes covering the windows, the dark faces, one old, one young, gleaming with sweat, watching me.

"You feel 'im?" someone asked. "Is he comin'?"

"He's comin', don't worry about that." The man who had brought me smiled at me. I felt a tiny bit of perspiration gather at the back of my neck. Warmer; getting warmer now.

I began to see him; he was forming in the darkness, coming together, pulled in by the heat. Dark-eyed, dark-haired, young, the way he had been. He was there before the hearth and the look on that young face as he peered into the flames was hunger.

The fire leaped for him; I leaped for him and we saw what it was we really had. No young man; no man.

The heat be a beast.

Beast. Not really a loa, something else; I knew that, somehow. Sometimes it looks like a man and sometimes it looks like hot honey in the darkness.

What are you doing?

I'm taking darkness by the eyes, by the mouth, by the throat.

What are you doing?

I'm burning alive.

What are you doing?

I'm burning the heat beast and I have it just where I want it. All the heat anyone ever felt, fire and body heat, fever, delirium. Delirium has eyes; I push them in with my thumbs. Delirium has a mouth; I fill it with my fist. Delirium has a throat; I tear it out. Sparks fly like an explosion of tiny stars and the beast spreads its limbs in surrender, exposing its white-hot core. I bend my head to it and the taste is sweet, no salt in his body at all.

What are you doing?

Oh, honey, don't you know?

I took it back.

In the hotel room, I stripped off the shabby dress the old woman had given me and threw it in the trashcan. I was packing when Carl came back.

He wanted to talk; I didn't. Later he called the police and told them everything was all right, he'd found me and I was coming home with him. I was sure they didn't care. Things like that must have happened in the Quarter all the time.

In the ladies' room at the airport, the attendant sidled up to me as I was bent over the sink splashing cold water on my face and asked if I were all right.

"It's just the heat," I said.

"Then best you go home to a cold climate," she said. "You do better in a cold climate from now on."

I raised my head to look at her reflection in the spotted mirror. I wanted to ask her if she had a brother who also waved his hair.

193

I wanted to ask her why he would bother with a cold woman, why he would care.

She put both hands high on her chest, protectively. "The beast sleeps in cold. *You* tend him now. Maybe you keep him asleep for good."

"And if I don't?"

She pursed her lips. "Then you gotta problem."

In summer, I keep the air-conditioning turned up high at my office, at home. In the winter, the kids complain the house is too cold and Carl grumbles a little, even though we save so much in heating bills. I tuck the boys in with extra blankets every night and kiss their foreheads, and later in our bed, Carl curls up close, murmuring how my skin is always so warm.

It's just the heat.

THE POWER AND THE PASSION

Last call.

If I were going to put a warning on just one story in this collection, this is it. So, you have been warned.

It came to me one night when I was watching *The Lost Boys* on cable that people certainly do get cavalier when they become vampire killers, even when they're just ordinary people forced into the role by dire necessity. Think about it—basic, average citizens who have never even slaughtered a chicken for dinner suddenly become righteous killers ready to impale a living thing—excuse me, an undead thing—on a stake. Come *on*—without throwing up afterwards? I know they're vampires, but they usually look enough like people to be discomfiting to dispatch, I would think. I don't know, I've never killed anything outside of uppity cockroaches. But police officers often suffer terrible stress when forced to shoot someone in the line of duty, and I've never met a combat veteran of any war who wasn't affected, who didn't *care*. While many of us could probably be induced to kill under certain circumstances, I think it would take its toll on us. I don't think most of us are killers.

But you'd need a killer for vampires, and the best kind would be not a zealot, who could burn out inopportunely, but a textbook sociopath. However, there's a big problem—how would you keep a sociopath from joining the other side?

Actually, this is a story about pornography. Do you know what pornography is? Are you sure about that?

THE POWER AND THE PASSION

*T*he voice on the phone says, "We need to talk to you, Mr. Soames," so I know to pick the place up. Company coming. I don't like for Company to come into no pigsty, but one of the reasons the place is such a mess all the time is, it's so small, I got nowhere to keep shit except around, you know. But I shove both the dirty laundry and the dirty dishes in the oven—my mattress is right on the floor so I can't shove stuff under the bed, and what won't fit in the oven I put in the tub and just before I pull the curtain, I think, well, shit, I shoulda just put it all in the tub and filled it and got it all washed at once. Or, well, just the dishes, because I can take the clothes over to the laundromat easier than washing them in the tub.

So, hell, I just pull the shower curtain, stack the newspapers and the magazines—newspapers on top of the magazines, because most people don't take too well to my taste in magazines, and they wouldn't like a lot of the newspapers much either, but I got the Sunday paper to stick on top and hide it all, so it's okay. Company'll damned well know what's under them Sunday funnies because they know *me*, but as long as they don't have to have it staring them in the face, it's like they can pretend it don't exist.

I'm still puttering and fussing around when the knock on the door comes and I'm crossing the room (the only room unless you count the bathroom, which I do when I'm in it) when it comes to me I ain't done dick about myself. I'm still in my undershirt and shorts, for chrissakes.

"Hold on," I call out, "I ain't decent, quite," and I drag a pair of pants outa the closet. But all my shirts are either in the oven or the tub and Company'll get fanny-antsy standing in the hall—this is not the watchamacallit, the place where Lennon bought it, the Dakota, yeah. Anyway, I answer the door in my one hundred percent cotton undershirt, but at least I got my fly zipped.

Company's a little different this time. The two guys as usual, but today they got a woman with them. Not a broad, not a bitch, not a bimbo. She's standing between and a little behind them, looking at me the way women always look at me when I happen to cross their path—chin lifted up a little, one hand holding her coat together at the neck in a fist, eyes real cold, like, "Touch me and die horribly, I wish," standing straight-fuckin-up, like they're Superman, and the fear coming off them like heat waves from an open furnace.

They all come in and stand around and I wish I'd straightened the sheets out on the mattress so it wouldn't look so messy, but then they'd see the sheets ain't clean, so six-of-one, you know. And I got nothing for anyone to sit on, except that mattress, so they just keep standing around.

The one guy, Steener, says, "Are you feeling all right, Mr. Soames," looking around like there's puke and snot all over the floor. Steener don't bother me. He's a pretty man who probably was a pretty boy and a pretty baby before that, and thinks the world oughta be a pretty place. Or he wants to prove pretty guys are really tougher and better and more man than guys like me, because he's afraid it's vice versa, you know. Maybe even both, depending on how he got up this morning.

The other guy, Villanueva, I could almost respect him. He didn't put on no face to look at me, and he didn't have no power fantasies about who he was to me or vice versa. I think Villanueva probably knows me better than anyone in the world. But then, he was the one took my statement when they caught up with me. He was a cop then. If he'd still been a cop, I'd probably respect him.

So I look right at the woman and I say, "So, what's this, you brought me a date?" I know this will get them because they know what I do to dates.

"You speak when spoken to, Mr. Soames," Steener says, kinda barking like a dog that wishes it were bigger.

"You spoke to me," I point out.

Villanueva takes a few steps in the direction of the bathroom—he knows what I got in there and how I don't want Company to see it, so this is supposed to distract me, and it does a little. The woman steps back, clutching her light coat tighter around her throat, not sure who to hide behind. Villanueva's the better bet, but she doesn't want to get any further into my stinky little apartment, so she edges toward Steener.

And it comes to me in a two-second flash-movie just how to do it. Steener'd be easy to take out. He's a rusher, doesn't know dick about fighting. He'd just go for me and I'd just whip my hand up between his arms and crunch goes the windpipe. Villanueva'd be trouble, but I'd probably end up doing him, too. Villanueva's smart enough to know that. First, though, I'd bop the woman, just bop her to keep her right there—punch in the stomach does it for most people, man or woman—and then I'd do Villanueva, break his neck.

Then the woman. I'd do it all, pound one end, pound the other, switching off before either one of us got too used to one thing or the other. Most people, man or woman, blank out about then. Can't face it, you know, so after that, it's free-for-fuckin-all. You can do just any old thing you want to a person in shock, they just don't believe it's happening by then. This one I would rip up sloppy, I would send her to hell and then kill her. I can see how it would look, the way her body would be moving, how her flesh would jounce flabby—

But I won't. I can't look at a woman without the flash-movie kicking in, but it's only a movie, you know. This is Company, they got something else for me.

"Do you feel like working?" Villanueva asks. He's caught it just now, what I was thinking about, he knows, because I told him how it was when I gave him my statement after I got caught.

"Sure," I say, "what else have I got to do?"

He nods to Steener, who passes me a little slip of paper. The name and address. "It's nothing you haven't done before," he says. "There are two of them. You do as you like, but you *must* follow the procedure as it has been described to you—"

I give a great big nod. "I know how to do it. I've studied on it, got it all right up here." I tap my head. "Second nature to me now."

"I don't want to hear the word 'nature' out of *you*," Steener sneers. "You've got nothing to do with nature."

"That's right," I agree. I'm mildmannered because it's just come to me what is Steener's problem here. It is that he is like me. He enjoys doing to me what he does the way I enjoy doing what I do, and the fact that he's wearing a white hat and I'm not is just a watchamacallit, a technicality. Deep down at heart, it's the same fuckin-feeling and he's going between loving it and refusing to admit he's like me, boing-boing, boing-boing. And if he ever gets stuck on the loving-it side, well, son-of-a-bitch will there be trouble.

I look over at Villanueva and point at the woman, raising my eyebrows. I don't know exactly what words to use for a question about her and anything I say is gonna upset everybody.

"This person is with us as an observer," Villanueva says quietly, which means I can just mind my own fuckin business and don't ask questions unless it's about the job. I look back at the woman and she looks me right in the face. The hand clenched high up on her coat relaxes just a little and I see the purple-black bruises on the side of her neck before she clutches up again real fast. She's still holding herself the same way, but it's like she spoke to me. The lines of communication, like the shrinks say, are open, which is not the safest thing to do with me. She's gotta be a nurse or a teacher or a social worker, I think, because those are the ones that can't help opening up to someone. It's what they're trained to do, reach out. Or hell, maybe she's just somebody's mother. She don't look too motherly, but that don't mean dick these days.

"When?" I say to Steener.

"As soon as you can pack your stuff and get to the airport. There's a cab downstairs and your ticket is waiting at the airline counter, in your name."

"You mean the Soames name," I say, because Soames is not my name for real.

"Just get ready, get going, get it done, and get back here," Steener says. "No sidetrips, or it's finished. Don't even *attempt* a sidetrip or it's finished." He starts to turn toward the door and then stops. "And you know that if you're caught in or after the act—"

"Yeah, yeah, I'm on my own and you don't know dick about squat, and nobody ever hearda me, case closed." I keep myself from smiling; he watched too much *Mission Impossible* when he was a kid. Like everyone else in his outfit. I think it's where they got the idea, kind of, some of it anyway.

Villanueva tosses me a fat roll of bills in a rubber band just as he's following Steener and the woman out the door. "Expenses," he says. "You have a rental car on the other end, which you'll have to use cash for. Buy whatever else you need, don't get mugged and robbed, you know the drill."

"Drill?" I say, acting perked-up, like I'm thinking, *Wow, what a good idea.*

Villanueva refuses to turn green for me, but he shuts the door behind him a little too hard.

I don't waste no time; I go to the closet and pull out my traveling bag. Everything's in it, but I always take a little inventory anyway, just to be on the safe side. Hell of a thing to come up emptyhanded at the wrong moment, you know. Really, though, I just like to handle the stuff: hacksaw, mallet, boning blade, iodized salt, lighter fluid, matches, spray bottle of holy water, four pieces of wood pointed sharp on one end, half a dozen rosaries, all blessed, and two full place settings of silverware, not stainless, mind you, but real silver. And the shirts I don't never put in the tub. What do they make of this at airport security? Not a fuckin thing. Ain't no gun. Guns don't work for this. Anyway, this bag's always checked.

The flight is fine. It's always fine because they always put me in first class and nobody next to me if possible. On the night flights, it's generally possible and tonight, I have the whole first class section to myself, hot and cold running stews, who are (I can tell) forcing themselves to be nice to me. I don't know what it is, and I don't mind it, but it makes me wonder all the same: is it a smell, or just the way my eyes look? Villanueva told me once, it was just something about me gave everyone the creeps. I lean back, watch the flash-movies, don't bother nobody, and everybody's happy to see me go when the plane finally lands.

I get my car, nice midsize job with a phone, and head right into the city. I know this city real good, I been here before for them, but it ain't the only one they send me to when they need to TCB.

Do an easy 55 into the city and go to the address on the paper. Midtown, two blocks east of dead center, medium-sized Victorian. I can see the area's starting to get a watchamacallit, like a facelift, the rich ones coming in and fixing up the houses because the magazines and the TV told them it's time to love old houses and fix them up.

I think about the other houses all up and down the street of the one I got to go to, what's in them, what I could do. I sure feel like it, and it would be a lot less trouble, but I made me a deal of my own free will and I will stick to it as long as they do, Steener and Villanueva and the people behind them. But if they bust it up somehow, if they fuck me, that will be real different, and they will be real sorry.

I call the house; nobody home. That's about right. I got to wait, which don't bother me none, because there's the flash-movies to watch. I can think on what I want to do after I get through what I have to do, and those things are not so different from each other. What Steener calls the procedure I just call a new way to play. Only not so new, because I thought of some of those things all on my own when I was watchamacallit, freelance so to say, and done some of them, kind of, which I guess is what made them take me on for this stuff, instead of letting me take a quick shot in a quiet room and no funeral after.

So, it gets to be four in the morning and here we come. Somehow, I know as soon as I see the figure coming up the sidewalk across the street that this is the one in the house. I can always tell them, and I don't know what it is, except maybe it takes a human monster to know an inhuman monster. And I don't feel nothing except a little nervous about getting into the house, which is always easier than you'd think it would be, but I get nervous on it anyway.

Figure comes into the light and I see it's a man, and I see it's not alone, and then I get pissed, because that fucking Steener, that fucking Villanueva, they didn't say nothing about no kid. And then I settle some, because I can tell the kid is one, too. Ten, maybe twelve from the way he walks. I take the razor and I give myself a little one just inside my hairline, squeeze the blood out to get it running down my face, and then I get out of the car just as they put their feet on the first step up to the house.

"Please, you gotta help me," I call, not too loud, just so they can hear, "they robbed me, they took everything but my clothes, all my ID, my credit cards, my cash—"

They stop and look at me running across the street at them and the first thing they see is the blood, of course. This would scare anybody but them (or me, naturally). I trip myself on the curb and collapse practically at their feet. "Can I use your phone? Please? I'm scared to stay out here, my car won't start, they might be still around—"

The man leans down and pulls me up under my arm. "Of course. Come in, we'll call the police. I'm a doctor."

I have to bite my lip to keep from laughing at that one. He's an operator maybe but no fucking doctor. Then I taste blood, so I let it run out of my mouth and the two of them, the man and the kid get so hot they can't get me in the house fast enough.

Nice house. All the Victorian shit restored, even the fuzzy stuff on the wallpaper, watchamacallit, flocked wallpaper. I get a glimpse of the living room before the guy's rushing me upstairs, saying he's got his medical bag up there. I just bet he does, and I got mine right in my hand, which they do not bother wondering about what with all this blood and this guy with no ID and out at four in the morning, must be a criminal anyway. I used to ask Villanueva, don't they ever get full, like they can't drink another drop, but Villaneuva told me no, they always had room for one more, it was time they were pressed for. Dawn. I'd be through long before then, but even if I wasn't, dawn would take care of the rest of it for me.

They're getting so excited it's getting me even more excited. I look at the kid and man, if I'd been anyone else, I woulda started screaming and trying to get away, because he's all gone. I mean, the kid part is all gone and just this fucking hungry thing from hell. So I stop feeling funny about there being a kid, because like I said, there ain't no kid, just a short one along with the tall one.

And shit if he don't twig, right there on the stairs. I musta looked like I recognized him.

"We're burned! We're burned!" he yells and tries to elbow me in the face. I dip and he goes right the fuck over my head and down, ka-boom, ka-boom. Guess what, they can't fly. It don't do him, but they can feel pain, and if you break their legs, they can't walk for awhile until they can get extra blood to heal them up. The kid's fucking neck is broke, you can see it plain as anything.

But I don't get no chance to study on it because the big one growls like a fucking attack dog and grabs me up from behind around the waist. They really are stronger than normal and you better believe it hurt like a motherfucker. He squeezes and there go two ribs and the soft drinks I had on the plane, like a fucking fountain.

"You'll go slow for that," he says, "you'll go for days, and you'll beg to die."

Obviously, he don't know me. I'm hurting all right, but it takes a lot more than a couple of ribs to put me down and I never had to beg for nothing, but these guys get all their dialog off the late show anyway and they ain't thinking of nothing except sticking it to you and drinking you dry. Fucking undead got a, a watchamacallit, a narrow perspective and they think everyone's scared of them.

That's why they send me, because I don't see no undead and I don't see no human being, I just see something to play with. I gotta narrow perspective, too, I guess.

But then everything is not so good because he tears the bag outa my hand and flings it away up in the hallway. Then he carries me the rest of the way upstairs and down the opposite end and tosses me into a dark room and slams the door and locks it.

I hold still until I can figure out how to move and cause myself the least pain, and I start taking off my shirts. I'm wearing a corduroy shirt with a pure linen lining sewn into the front and two heavy one-hundred-percent cotton t-shirts underneath. I have to tear one of the t-shirts off, biting through the neck, and I bite through the neck of the other one but leave it on (thinking about the guy biting through necks while I do it), and put the corduroy shirt back on, keeping it open. Ready to go.

The guy has gone downstairs. I hear the kid scream and then muffle it, and I hear footsteps coming back up the stairs. There's a pause, and then I see his feet at the bottom of the door in the light, and he unlocks the door and opens it.

"Whoever you think you are," he says, "you're about to find out what you really are."

I give a little whimper, which makes him sure enough to grab me by one leg and start dragging me out into the hallway, where the kid is lying on his back. When we're out in the light, he stops and stands over me, one leg on each side, and looks down at my crotch. I know what he's thinking, because I'm looking up at his and thinking something not too different.

He squats on my thighs, and I rip my shirts open.

It's like an invisible giant hand hit him in the face; he goes backwards with a scream, still bent at the knees, on top of my legs. I heave him off quick. He's so fucked I have time to get to him, roll him over on his back and give him a nice full frontal while I sit on his stomach.

203

It is a truly def tattoo. This is not like bragging, because I didn't do it, though I did name it: The Power and The Passion. A madwoman with a mean needle in Coney did it, one-handed with her hair standing on end, counting her rosary beads with the other hand, and when I saw it finished, with the name I had given it on a banner above it, I knew she was the best tattoo artist in the whole world and so I did not do her, I did *not*. It was some very ignorant asshole who musta come in after I did that split her open and nailed her to the wall with a stud gun, but I caught the beef on it, and the tattoo that saved her from me saved me from the quick shot and gave me to Steener's people, courtesy of Villanueva who is, I should mention, also Catholic.

So it's a tattoo that means a lot to me in many ways, you see, but mostly I love it because it is so perfect. It runs from just below where my shirt collars are to my navel, and full across my chest, and if you saw it, you would swear it had been done by someone who had been there to see what happened.

The cross is not just two boards, but a tree trunk and a crossbar, and the spikes are driven into the forearms where the two bones make a natural holder for that kind of thing—you couldn't hang on a cross from spikes driven through your palms, they'd rip through. The crown of thorns has driven into the flesh to the bone, and the blood drips from the matted beard *distinctly*—the madwoman was careful and skilled so that the different shades of red didn't muddy up. Nothing muddied up; you can see the face clear as you can see where the whips came down, as clear as the wound in his side, (which is not some pussy slit but the best watchamacallit, rendering of a stab wound I have seen outside of real life), as clear as you can see how the arms have pulled out of the sockets, and how the legs are broken.

You just can't find no better picture of slow murder. I know; I seen photos of all kinds, I seen some righteous private art, and I seen the inside of plenty of churches, and ain't nobody done justice to nothing anybody ever done to someone, including the Crucifixion. Especially the Crucifixion, I guess.

Because, you see, you cannot take a vamp out with a cross, that don't mean dick to them, a fucking plus-sign, that's all. It's the Crucifixion that gets them, you gotta have a good crucifix, or some other representation of the Crucifixion, and it has to be blessed in some way, to inflict the agony of the real thing on them. Mine was blessed—that madwoman mumbling her rosary all the way through the work, don't it just figure that she was a runaway nun? I wouldn't a thought it would matter, but I guess when you take them vows, you can't give them back. Sorta like a tattoo.

Well, that's what that madwoman believed, anyway, and I believe it, too, because I like believing that picture happened, and the vamp I'm sitting on, it don't mean shit if he believes or not, because I got him and he don't understand how I could even get close to him. So while I go get my bag (giving a good flash to the kid, who goes into shock), I explain about pure fibers found in nature like the linen they say they wrapped that man on the cross in (I think that's horseshit myself, but it's all in it being natural and not watchamacallit, synthetic, so that don't matter), and how it keeps the power from getting out till I need it to.

And then it's showtime.

I have a little fun with the silver for a while, just laying it against his skin here and there, and it crosses my mind not for the first time how a doctor could do some interesting research on burns, before I start getting serious. Like a hot knife through butter, you can put it that way and be dead on. Or undead on, ha, ha.

You know what they got for insides? Me neither, but it's as bad for them as anyone. And I wouldn't call *that* a heart, but if you drive a pure wood stake through it, it's lights out.

It lasts forever for him, but not half long enough for me. Come dawn, it's pretty much over. Them watchamacallits, UV rays, they're all over the place. Skin cancer on fast forward, you can put it that way. I leave myself half an hour for the kid, who is not really a kid because if he was, he'd be the first kid I ever killed, and I ain't no fucking kid killer, because I seen what *they* get in prison and I said, whoa, not *my* ass.

I stake both hearts at the same time, a stake in each hand, sending them to hell together. Call me sentimental. Set their two heads to burning in the cellar and hang in just long enough to make sure we got a good fire going before I'm outa there. House all closed up the way it is, it'll be awhile before it's time to call the fire department.

I'm halfway to the airport when I realize my ribs ain't bothered me for a long time. Healed up, just like that.

Hallelujah, gimme that old-time religion.

"As usual," Steener says, snotty as all get-out, "the bulk of the fee has been divided up among your victims' families, with a percentage to the mission downtown. Your share this time is three hundred." Nasty grin. "The check's in the mail."

"Yeah," I say, "you're from the government and you're here to help me. Well, don't worry, Steener, I won't come in your *mouth*."

He actually cocks a fist and Villanueva steps in front of him. The woman with them gives Steener a really sharp look, like she's gonna come to my defense, which don't make sense. Villanueva starts to rag my ass about pushing Steener's hot button but I'm feeling important enough to wave a hand at him.

"Fuck that," I say, "it's time to tell me who *she* is."

Villanueva looks to the woman like he's asking her permission, but she steps forward and lets go of her coat, and I see the marks on her neck are all gone. "I'm the mother. And the wife. They tried to—" she bites her lips together and makes a stiff little motion at her throat. "I got away. I tried to go to church, but I was . . . tainted." She takes a breath. "The priest told me about—" she dips her head at Villanueva and Steener, who still wants a piece of me. "You really . . . put them away?"

The way she says it, it's like she's talking about a couple of rabid dogs. "Yeah," I tell her, smiling. "They're all gone."

"I want to see the picture," she says, and for a moment, I can't figure out what she's talking about. And then I get it.

"Sure," I say, and start to raise my undershirt.

Villanueva starts up. "I don't think you *really* want—"

"Yeah, she does," I say. "It's the only way she can tell she's all right now."

"The marks disappeared," Villanueva snaps. "She's fine. You're fine," he adds to her, almost polite.

She feels the side of her neck. "No, he's right. It *is* the only way I'll know for sure."

I'm shaking my head as I raise the shirt slowly. "You guys didn't think to sprinkle any holy water on her or nothing?"

"I wouldn't take the chance," she says, "it might have —"

But that's as far as she gets, because she's looking at my chest now and her face — oh, man, I start thinking I'm in love, because that's the look, that's the look you oughta have when you see The Power and The Passion. I know, because it's the look on my own face when I stand before the mirror and stare, and stare, and stare. It's so fucking *there*.

Villanueva and Steener are looking off in the opposite direction. I give it a full two-minute count before I lower my shirt. The look on her face goes away and she's just another character for a flash-movie again. Easy come, easy go. But now I know why she was so scared when she was here before. Guess they didn't think to tell her about pure natural fibers.

"You're perfect," she says and turns to Steener and Villanueva. "He's perfect, isn't he? They can't tempt him into joining them, because he can't. He couldn't if he wanted to."

"Fuckin A," I tell her.

Villanueva says, "Shut up," to me and looks at her like he's kinda sick. "You don't know what you're talking to. You don't know what's standing in this room with us. I couldn't bring myself to tell you, and I was a cop for sixteen years —"

"You told me what would have to be done with my husband and son," she says, looking him straight in the eye and I start thinking maybe I'm in love after all. "You spelled that out easily enough. The agony of the Crucifixion, the burning and the cutting open of the bodies with silver knives, the stakes through the hearts, the beheadings, the burning. That didn't bother you, telling me what was going to happen to my family —"

"That's because they're the white hats," I say to her, and I can't help smiling, smiling, smiling. "If they had to do it, they'd do it because they're on the side of Good and Right."

Suddenly Steener and Villanueva are falling all over each other to hustle her out and she don't resist, but she don't cooperate, either. The last thing I see before the door closes is her face looking at me, and what I see in that face is not understanding, because she couldn't